A Father's Burden

By: Kevin Aller

Kevin Aller

Copyright © 2011: BEMO
All rights reserved.
First print 5/12
This is a book of fiction. Any references or similarities to actual events, real people, or real locations are intended to give the novel a sense of reality. Any similarity to other names, characters, places and incidents are entirely coincidental.

All right reserved. No part of this book may be reproduced in any form, or by any means without prior consent of the author and publisher as a collective, except brief quotes used in reviews.

ISBN- 9798710627341

Cover Design: Crystell Publications
(405) 414-3991

Printed in the USA

A Father's Burden

ACKNOWLEDGMENTS

To my Mother Yvette Aller, Pop Dukes (R.I.P.) Kevin Beathea, Big Bemo & my second Pop's Gustavio Olivieri, without you all the King wouldn't be here. To my sister Yolanda "Boom", Remya. MY brotha's Adrian "lil E", Kevi Moe (R.I.P.) Anthony Rundtree (R.I.P.) Debo. To all my kids Quantiah, Quanesha Lil Bemo, Ronald Mccloud, Raven Douglas & My maybe's. All my Nieces and Nephews. Big Flex Publishing for helping me make this book happen, thank you. MY Big Homie Kevin Chiles & Tiffany Chiles Don Diva Magazine and the whole Don Diva Family. Thank you for all your help. To Michelle Queen – I see you!!

I know over a million soldiers, so if I forget you, best believe all of you will be in the next book! Sex, Money, Murder... Keep writing my Sex, Money, Murder family. Barney Blow, Mac 11, J-Boog's CB Amir (AKA) Hot Boy. Omega Red (N.J.) Killer T, The God, Lil Nut Case, Star Money, X, Cash from Clay, Ray Kwan, Smack Fat Daddy, Big Hev from Webster, Big Boo, Booblocks Tyson, Mos from Clay, Dap, Melley, The whole Clay Ave. La Brim, Tye Guns, Friut Kwan Bailey, E-Bay, World, T-Black, Ko'n, Boy George, Shamik, Manny, G-27, Rat Hunters The whole U.B.N. N.Y.B. BLova and D.Q. Chops, The Miller gang, The Brims, Stones, Mac Bailer, Paw's (S.M.M.) Lacey, I mean (B.K.) Castle Hill, Soundview, Webster Clay, Shyty Ave, Sheridan, The Whole Bronx, My Harlem Block 139 Lennox Ave, 140 All Day (R.I.P.) T-Money BX & Harlem (R.I.P.) Big L (R.I.P.) Big Lee (R.I.P.) Cornell (R.I.P.) Kerry (R.I.P.) Rich Porter the one & only. His LiL Bro too!! Omar. Ike my bro. Lol Reggie White(rip) Gatter aka my D. (rip). (rip) Ike my bro (rip) Reggie, White Red Diamond, my Cha Town Boo Ziggy Wood, Kevi, T, I.Z. Finster, many more. Oh, to my Harlem Wife Lady, Bemo Aliyah 140 4'Lite, love ya. Evelyn (AKA)Boobie MY Queen's Crew, A story Projects, Queen Bridge, Homie Cash Y.G. & his Sista, Gotti, E, Main, many more. My Brooklyn Mob Turf, His Brotha Marcey, Marley G, Pappoose, U family now Kurgger JunBug (AKA) 155 The Stoney, My Brotha Your Sister, Hussle Hard Main 0, Mousey. All my Homies Up State New York Doing Life or better. JZZ, Elie Brim, Dizzy, All the Highs, Low's, All the Lady or Sex Money Murder, Remy Ma, Tyke, Chris, Dell (N.J.) Love U Sis Shakia (N.J.) Kirsten, Zyproach Makiba Kwana, Tiffany, Jackey, Stormi, (BK) Red, Dollar, Key Key, Big Moe, NaNa, Lena Lisa Secert, The Common Girls, Miss Ya, Jen, Beckey Boo, Dawn, Keally Davis Kelly Burns, Lizz, All her Sista's, The whole Kingston NY. N.C. Pit, Clev, N.Y. S.C. Tex All the Spot's we hit up & all the girls and kids we left behind The rest of the R.I.P. list, Big Nose Troy (Queens) Black Just Sten Baby Jay, Main, Pop Lody Pop, Sean Polight, Will Carenten

Kevin Aller

D Lush, His Brotha, Kaydow, Rich Porter, T-money Both of them, Hen Dog, Mell Murder, Boonka, The Williams Brotha, Frisk, E-man Dave the twin. To all my dead homies, I got you in the Sex, Money, Murder, we got movies and all record labels, clothing lines We got it all, what up? Camron, Mase Murder, Lord Tariq, Peter Guns Cory Guns, Mysone, Chi Ali, Pistol Petey, Red Cafa, Vado J-Mills, Big Tone, Minnesota Edy Cheba, Money Boss Yapoe, Flip, Cocaine City, Hell Rell, Keisha Cole, Karma Lee family too for doing the right thing when most people turn their back. For my LiL Sista Remy, Sean Pec eyes, get at me. 50 Cent, you too. I'm writing Wise Rucker Crew, and one to all my Basketball Crew, I used to dog

Kenny Satterfield, Cory Fisher, Kareem Reid, Black WiPDow, Skip Yamoe, Yoda, Markie, Sam Cassale, Sham God, Richy Parker, Brain Rease, Dammit, it's so many. I got you. To all my Rappers, Models, Actors, I'll holla later. Last but not least to God, My Lord & Savior. Sit back & enjoy the first step & the next one is Sex, Money, Murder, the real story. No more bits & pieces, no more waiting. To a few last Good People (R.I.P.) to Cira Glyenn Pebbels, Boo, Cat what up BK. All day your twin boys Kay and Seg & Big Kwan Tell your Aunt She should have knocked Lali All out, She still my girl. Dada from uptown, very good man Puffy just don't know u a real dude. 200% Smiley all my uptown dudes, Valley 214 St. The last of my (R.I.P.) list Frickkle Face

Chirs, Caddy Dave, Orlando, to all my aunts' Spanish side and black. My fake ass cuz Johhny LiL U still owe me 78 grand, My cuz Ski, Larry, His kids. To my Baltimore Crew, Enina U the one Sorry I left you. You just don't know the Superstar I turn into; you are in the Sex, Money, Murder book. Billy Willy his twin cuz Missty & Chirsy miss you. The gamblen spot Fraud Ass Blue, Kurt Jug, Windell, Rahyeh, Frank Nitty, Shorty Nat, good man. Kevi I, Jeff Sparks, Jeff to the left, Jeff, Missy (R.I.P.) Mell Qaizzy, Detroit Lou, Green Eye Sean, Jason Michelle, Triple C, Mighty Whity. Shout outs to Lamenah, Lauryen, Tasha, Nikki Minji, Nadia, Kia, Max, Michelle, the hommies from 187 web sade, Lisa, Saliyma.

Okay Let's Get It Shaken to my daughters, Quanesha and Quiantiah. My grand-daughter Zoey and Journey. My grandson, Daniel, my son, Kingston and Roney Mccloud. To my sister-in-law, Chirs Ellison, my niece, Prioshia, Ivan Adrian Jr. and all the rest of my sista's from another mother. My baby, Josset, I see u girl. Get ready to shine. I also got to shout out my only Harlem wife, Aaalliya Dry Dale. To my only street wife ever, Rema Roza. Thank u 4 all ur help. You know how I luv. Lol, you're a special girl. Pistol Pete, we're here, miss ya lip P. What up, boy. Stay strong and smart, ur pops luv u. We're doing the gotti law. This is what it cost to be a super star to the game of snakes. Big shout out to the don of Harlem, Kevin Chilies and

A Father's Burden

his wife Tiffany Chilies, P. Charty, his son & the rest of his family. To my day 1 hommies, thank u for all ur help & everything u doing. May Allah guide u & bless u!! We came a long way. Zigg & Wood, remember rich porty was going to bless u 4 our block. What's up Steavn Ward, cuz I miss ya. Keep shinning bro. Shanelle Sharpe, what's up? Mama, look out for this the next big star. Y'all watch out, she's here. Funky Flex, what's up? U came along way, at least u back to the roots. We started this shit, and u always holding my lil hommies down. Hocus 45 Dolla, what's up. Shit, the whole Harris family, ur getting deep. lol The obstacle to turn into the big hommie u are blazer luv to all the blazers up state jungle poke pow. Hot Boy K Moe, N. J. down south, all over, we still here stronger. 21 Savage, what's up? Little Savage, Rocko and all the blazers in ATL, Nancy N Chareie, Kim, hats off to La Brim Eli Brim, Fatboy, aka. Flip Derby Brim, aka. Pablo Deniro from Manning SC. Nitty Brim Killa Reek, free the count. Shout out to BCB!! the FTB'S 36st & in south Barolina, havoc papa shout out to the blazers in m-town!! Mo Beatz pbr!! Young Melly. the don killa, SB. Relax to some disco boss. Hev, what's up to the mac balla family. What's up to the apes, dick wolf ty gun's, Stony, Kevi, Forst, Beno from Queens, Slick Pulla and the whole UBN. I won't miss a soul in the bible, Sex, Money, Murder book, facts omega red nut case mac 11, Hack Baby Uzzy Kas Yayo my RBG niggas Wise Brimnal Gu holding up shine, Killa E from nj (Bip) S.I. Shortz my Murda Block Komrade Mass Queen Street Gang gett'em up bandanna Red Divinci Bity Bills Lad Red, Camden New Jersy Heffe Jess Money Meak J5 Sb 25 from Burlington Murder Ave. Cmd Myu Oike boy Memphman Pop off so Calico Trenton fool's Capo Murder Melo Quizzy Calyn 1 Boogie Massey Frank White Lolo Blaze Gottio Tee Tee Rock Abye Roxy come from under the rock still waiting on ur help with the book. Tyson the big blazer. Luv ya sound view girls Shanqua, Tanya, Mckenzie, Jaismen, Kawana so many ur be in the smm book thoi castle hill girls nana Tiny Temple Tiff her twin Yolanda dam I've been gone to all ur Webster girls Chazz Zee, Black Tina Chala Angee Mimi, Lil Kim, Makey ba Moo-Moo Kawana the old heads young heads Evelyn Boobie Yoy. What up miss ya 1400 1300 1200 every side Washington Ave. shout out to the whole cross town I be here forever lol Clay Ave. Collage Findley Shyster Ave. Shirden Carol Place 170 collage the list is huge u know who u are u fuck with Bemo, Tiny Biz aka Jay Loc 83 St. Big Biz to the rest of the Locz u know we fuck with each other B & C! ur some real g's for real S.dot Mach Murder, Star C.B. always luv ya baby bro. Never 4get that even tho u on some shit Boo Boo Smack Lil E, luv ya but u 200% some shi. Tuso, what up baby boy, miss ya Scar Stretch. Ziggy what up Woods Sham. God Howie Mike Bruno Tiny Bum my son what up, Guy Fisher, Cuff Kon g 27 - Money Mike, Boy George, Storm Camron Mase Vadoo my Harlem block 139 140 Ave. all day Jaylen & Jaliya, Rosa aka Tita the low ryder, Brim Treside Pureblood 1 shine Joe Lite Nino Brim Smooth, Brim Jon Jay Rizzo Brim Omega, Lil Omega

Kevin Aller

the whole N.J. what up shine hard this is the Bip Section fallen solider Big Bear, Vinom, Kawiiy, damu N.J. Big Bemo Chickin Wing aka G One Arm N.J. Geeya Anne castle hill sista Mel Guizzey, Big Notty smm nce man Frisk Dave twin Kayron Carlton Hynes Bo Homerside, Rich Porter his Nephew Carnell Kerry Reg White Boy Boy Big 1 Big Lee, miss ya Gerrod Caddy, Dave Boonka Amir the Williams Murdock BoBo Orlando, Jay Ski Will Carenton Ladew Dondee Dave Tyson, Chuck Angee Ike, my bro luv ya always. To the head queen, Dorty Aller, Luis Aller Boober Locks, miss ya Scrap the Blazer from queens parten my soul I 4 got ur handle, Brazeey Jashed Muntagir aka Shed Jayo TS, YB, Castle Hill T-Mass, Soundview NuNu!! Money Brim T, Money Mac, Capo Reek Selve 45 way of life Trinton head shout real lady Don Juan Boogs XO Nic Ruga Dinero Ghost Blazer Boobie his wife what up NJ Premo Oskino CJ Mill 59 Blazer Skar Brim G Real Strange, Zoe Q Murda Murder NJ Capo. What up Ox Paterson, the NJ down south 5 Bourghos Brazy face J Swoft J Chunk good eye juice, Porsha Jonson Mawanua Tasha Delores Lee Bow Big Kap aka Big Dab Top 5 Dead or alive in the feds hard to guard!! live from queens Big Tim La, Phil what up! Black from web, miss ya. Big Brian, what up under their ground. Al Banknee, Mob Alex what up Bg Baby, J Whighty Strong Jim Ice BGF what up baby bro stay strong always, umm's there's so many solider girls I miss ya all. U'll never be forgotten u'll be in the the bronx bible for sure the music here the movie & no 1 got the real Sex Money Murder story, but 2 people Pistol Pete and Bemo. I won't keep u waiting. It's here what up to the rapper's actors even the frauds ur still faken lol god bless enjoy the book dropping 3 more the movie here the one in only Bemo sex money finest!!! Castle Hill we here baby the un forgotten peace!!!

Michael Fonseca. A.KA. chico mike = from Miami

Vonnor Twick Lance A.K.A. Gotti = from Naple Florida

Dela Starks A.K.A. Dela=from Lakeland, Florida

Kenneth Williams AKA Coke Beezy = from Tampa Florida

Raheem Bacon AKA 350 Heem = from Lakeland, Florida

Marquan Brision AKA 350 Quan= from Lakeland, Florida

King Pimp- Shout Out to Brooklyn! Spass, 1090, Cornbread

Chapter One

It was July 31, 1975, around 9:45 P.M. While in the Bronx, at Jacobi Hospital. Screams could be heard, "Ahhh!" She screamed, as she was on her back, sweating bullets.
Push, push, push, she heard, as the doctor spoke, "Yes, there you go. I see the head. Push! Push!" She takes a deep breath, and she pushes.
After her baby boy popped out, his mother laid back in complete pain and joy. As the doctor cleans the baby off, he takes his first breath of air, and the baby boy starts to cry. Finally, the doctor brings the newborn baby to his mother.

Now, as this boy was born, the mother was just a baby herself. She was sixteen years old, and her name was Yvette. The child's father name was Adrian, but they called him A. Now A was only nineteen years old. He had dreams of becoming a basketball star, but as always, A was caught up in the streets. Now A made his first million dollars at the age of 18, but he wasn't there to see his son born. The past two nights when he'd taken his girl to the hospital, it was false labor. So that third night, he did not go, and ironically, that was the day his son was born. The mother of his child was Yvette, so when she gave birth, her mother was right by her child's side.

A Father's Burden

The first thing that morning, A was by Yvette's side. Yvette was happy to see A, but at the same time, she was mad at him because he wasn't there during the birth of their son. While A held his firstborn in his hands, he was so happy to see a replica of himself, once little A looked up at his father's eyes. Now, as the day turned into night, Yvette's mother walked into the room. Yvette's mom loved A because he was a smart kid, but she also knew that A was getting too close to the streets.

So Yvette's mom said, "Now you got the biggest task in your life, Adrian. You have a son. It's going to cost a lot of money to take care of him, and it is a big responsibility, so what are you going to do?"

A looked at Yvette's mother with a smirk on his face, because A knew that she was an old-fashioned mother. Yvette's mom had been working all her life. She took care of five kids with her husband, who had been with her from a young age.

Yvette spoke up, "Ma, please, not now."

Yvette's mother responded, "When you think it's time?"

As A got an attitude and passed little A back to Yvette, he stated, "My son won't need for nothing. I got enough money to own the world."

But Yvette's mother didn't want to hear that, she said, "A, I love you like a son, but no drug money is allowed in my house. I will not accept it, me and my daughter surely will not have anything to do with it."

The room was quiet. Every word Yvette's mother said went right to A's head. A kissed Yvette and said, "Yo, I'm out. Call me when it's time for you to go home," and he walked out and said *bye* to Yvette's mother.

You could see in A's face that he was very furious. But he had the utmost respect for Yvette's mother. He would never raise his voice or disrespect her or Yvette. That's why he just left the room. Just seconds later, Little A started crying. It was like he felt his father's pain and knew something was wrong.

Yvette immediately catered to her son while talking to her mother.

"Mom, why you have to start this now?"

"Baby, I want the best for you. You made the choice to have that boy, and as long as Adrian is in the streets, it's going to be nothing but bad luck," Yvette's mother said, holding her daughter's hand, and looking into her eyes. "Baby, that street life is cursed," she insisted, as she looked at her grandbaby. "Umm.. He looks just like his father."

"Yes, he does," Yvette said.

As the night came to an end, visiting hours were almost over. As for Little A, he was a big baby. When he was born, he weighed 7 pounds 11 ounces. Yvette's mother left, and Yvette fed and rocked her newborn son to sleep. Around 12:00 A.M, the phone rang. Yvette had just fallen asleep but was easily awakened.

"Hello," a sweet voice said.

"Hey baby, what's up?"

"Hey baby. Where are you?" Yvette said.

"Ma. I'm with the boys. We're out drinking, celebrating my son's birth," A said.

"Baby, you know how my mother is…," A cut her off, right before she finished.

"Baby I know, I just let her blow off some steam. But really, I didn't call to talk about that. I called to check on you."

Yvette knew A was a very smooth guy who had a clever way with words, and that's how he always made Yvette laugh. They were so close that they were best friends. She was a smart girl too, and so was he. The way they clicked was perfect. After talking for an hour, A had to make a run.

"Baby, I got to go take care of something."

"What?"

A said, "Baby, if it doesn't make dollars, then it doesn't make sense."

A Father's Burden

So she said, "A, when are you coming up here to see your son?"

"Is your mom's going to be there?" He asked.

"Yeah, but I'll tell her not to come, so you can."

"No, don't do that. Just call me when she leaves, and I'll come then. Okay.

"Yeah."

"Okay, baby. I love you. See you tomorrow."

"I love you too, be careful," Yvette said.

"Baby, I'm alright, just make sure you take care of my little man." They both laughed at his comment.

A few days passed; and it was time for Yvette and Little A to go home. A arrived, and surprised her by with a brand-new Benz. Now he wasn't the flashy type. All he did was hug the block, selling heroin. And at this time, A was getting heroin from Nicky Barnes, the biggest heroin dealer in N.Y.

As Yvette, A, and Little A exited out the front entrance of the hospital, Yvette looked around.

"Baby, did you come in a cab?"

"No," he replied, causing Yvette to look at him funny. She knew he had money, so that wasn't the problem. Finally, they walked towards the parking lot and came up on a white Benz. Yvette's eyes opened wide.

"A! Where did you get this?"

"Baby this is mine. I got it for you to drive when you go to doctor's appointments."

"I love the car, but baby I can't drive. Plus, my mom isn't going to allow me to have it?"

"Shit, don't let her see it then."

"No, I'm good," Yvette concluded,

You see, Yvette loved A for who he was and not his money or his street fame. A didn't have to have a dime; she loved him for him. In fact, he had to always force her to take money. But he loved her because she couldn't be bought. So, their relationship was built on trust, love, and loyalty. In his mind, they were one. A opened the door for Yvette, then put little A in the new car seat he'd just bought.

They sat up in this new, big white Benz, like little kids who'd won a shopping spree. Not to mention that A and Yvette were short. As they both cuddled in the leather seats, he turned on the cassette player, bumpin' the Ohio Players. As Yvette moved her head, the clear tone of the music was captivating. Smiling at her expression, A leaned over and kisses Yvette on her lips, "Baby, are you hungry?"

"Yeah, I want some seafood," she replied.

The biggest seafood spot in the Bronx was called, City Island. So, he headed there. As Yvette rode in amazement, wild thoughts ran through her mind. She was thinking about the last time A, her, and her mother were together in the hospital. All she could remember was her mother saying, *"Street life is a curse. It's nothing but trouble."* As they rolled down the freeway, A noticed she was in deep thought and engaged her in conversation.

"Baby, what's wrong?"

Yvette looked him in the eyes, and then looked back at the baby. She saw the past, looking into Big A's face, upon catching herself, she replied, "Nothing baby."

"Come on, something's wrong."

"A, are you going back to school? Are you going to stop hustling?"

"Come on baby, don't start that Betty X shit. I can't leave all of this."

From that statement alone, Yvette knew A was not leaving the streets, and her mother wasn't going to allow them to be together. When they finally got to City Island, they stood outside of the car, eating clams, shrimp and fries. While talking, A realized spending quality time with his baby made her happy.

"I got another surprise for you," he said.

Yvette perked up, "What is it?"

"Wait, you'll see."

A Father's Burden

"Okay. A make sure you stop at the store to buy the baby some milk."

After stopping to get the milk, they headed towards Manhattan. During their trip, Yvette questioned him all the way there.

"A, where are we going?"

"Baby, just relax," he replied.

"Okay," she said, watching as they got off the highway, onto 96th Street. Yvette looked shocked, wondering exactly where they were going.

When they stopped at the light, A looked over at Yvette, "Close your eyes, Yvette." He reached over and wrapped a scarf around her eyes. Baby A just slept quietly as A drove a few more blocks to 87th Street. As he pulled into an inside garage, then helped Yvette out of the car. He grabbed the baby's seat, with little A in it, and walked to their destination. Holding Yvette's hand in one, and the baby seat in the other, Yvette tries to speak. Seconds before she could get too much out, he told her to be quiet, "We'll be there in a few seconds."

As the elevator comes to a stop, the door opens, and they walk in. All of the lights were off when A shut the door behind them.

"Baby, are you ready?"

"Yeah! Please take this blindfold off my eyes," Yvette stated.

A did as his baby asked, then turned on the lights. Yvette almost fainted, the condo was huge, and the view overlooked the Westside highway. You could see Jersey City. What's so shocking was that Yvette lived in the projects and so did A. The entire time he's been hustling, A hadn't been spending his money. All he did was stack his money for a rainy day. Yvette hugged him so tight, she had tears in her eyes.

"Baby, how you get this?" She asked.

"I bought it for you and my son." Yvette was, so ecstatic, that she told him they needed to get a bottle of Dom Perignon.

"Yeah, we have to make a toast to us!"

But little did A know; Yvette feared the upcoming changes that were about to take place in their lives. A went to the closet and pulled out a duffel bag and said, "In the morning, go pick out the furniture and buy the baby's crib and all the stuff you want in this new apartment."

Though Yvette was still a child, she was smart as hell. So as A dumped the money on the floor, Yvette questioned, "How much is this?"

"$100,000. But don't worry about all that. Here, take this money and go buy the most expensive furniture and clothes you want. Basically, whatever your heart desires."

A was in love with his girl, he looked into Yvette's eyes, and started to get horny. Although she was 16, she had the body of a twenty-year-old. He rubbed on Yvette and began kissing her. As he delicately rubbed her on her shoulders, his hand found their way to her ass.

"Sexy Chocolate," is what A called her whenever he got hot.

"Sexy Chocolate my ass. Baby, I got stitches all up in my pussy. Boy, we can't fuck for at least six weeks."

"Damn! I forgot," he expressed, calming down.

Realizing it was not a go, they just laid on the floor, talking and hugging - while admiring their baby. In time, they fell asleep. First thing the next morning, Yvette fed their baby, while her man overslept. Once she woke him up, A got dressed and they went shopping to buy the baby a crib, and all of the necessities needed to furnish their home. Shortly after returning home, their items were delivered.

"Ms., you live in this big apartment by yourself?" The delivery man asked, putting the rugs on the floor.

"No!" she replied, picking up her phone to call her cousin Jan, who was her old road dawg. She wanted her to keep her company. *Damn, these two kids in an apartment worth $100,000 are truly on top of their thang*, she thought to himself, looking around

A Father's Burden

her apartment. She knew when A came home, he was gonna be happy with the way it looked, and she was right.

When A came home, he entered with a bottle of champagne and some bomb ass weed for them to smoke a joint. A few days later, Yvette was still transitioning into their new condo. She liked it, but she still didn't feel comfortable. In fact, she was scared to stay there alone. Jan would always say, *'You are living like a queen'*, but she would have rather stayed in the projects. See somehow, she felt more comfortable there. Yvette missed her mother, and due to their very close relationship, she called her mother every day. However, for some reason, Yvette's mother had not called her in the past few days. Yvette's mom wasn't worried about Yvette, because she thought Yvette was staying at A's mother's house and had no idea that her daughter was living in a condo that she couldn't never afford.

***

As time progressed, days turned into a year later. Finally, Little A was about to celebrate his first birthday and it was being hosted at Yvette's condo. Yvette's mother learned of her daughter's living arrangements and was finally able to catch up with A.

"Boy, I didn't raise my daughter in the streets, and I don't want you to take care of her and my grandson with street money. Your son is getting older and he's gonna need you in his life."

"Look, Ms. Bernadette no disrespect, but I'll never work for some $7 dollars an hour. I make $7,000 an hour."

"Baby, that devil is on you tough. I'mma pray for you. I just thank the Lord that you are here for your son's first birthday, but tomorrow is not promised, so you better pray for a covering," she insisted, walking off.

As Yvette entered the kitchen where her mother and A were talking, Yvette walked in only to see A walking out the door. She spoke to him, but he kept walking, so she ran into the hallway after him.

"Where are you going?"

"Yo, I'm out. I'm tired of your mother. I hate her preaching to me. Vette, I'mma do what I do, so she needs to chill."

"A, she loves you. She doesn't mean any harm; she just wants the best for you."

"Well, she needs to stop with the lectures and let me live.

Chapter Two

It was money time. A and his dawg Dundee had to pick up their stash. Some time ago, they had more than $250,000, but the stash had steadily grown since. A wasn't sure of the exact amount, but he knew it was at least $1 million dollars. And there were 100 keys each.

"Dawg, where you get all that shit?" A asked. Dundee had a spare room in a house, but they were never there. Dundee pulled out the key and gave it to A.

"Dawg, me and you are the only ones who have this key..., A, every time I called that bitch's house, she didn't answer..."

For some reason, Dundee knew she gave him up. *Wow!* A thought. He remembered how many unmarked cars passed by, but he thought he was just bugging out. So yeah, as we all knew, they found a girl three days later with her head cut off, and that's why Dundee hadn't been back on the block. Dundee knew he had to go but had to bless his man.

"'A' keep the drugs and here's another million just in case you had to bail out."

Once they were headed back to the block to drop off work, A got into the car with Dundee. Completely unaware if this would be the last time, they would see each other or not, Dundee parked on the side of the block. Out of nowhere, A got this funny feeling in his stomach, so he jumped on the phone.

"Hello."
"Sup Baby."
"A! Hey! Baby, it feels like forever since the last time I saw you."
"Baby, I'm coming to see you today, kiss my son for me......" he said, before suddenly hearing gunshots that sounded like someone fired off about 700 rounds.
"A what's wrong?!" Yvette screamed. The shock from the shots caused him to drop the phone.
"It was two cars," People started reporting, as A leaned down to pick up the phone.
"A, what's going on?"
"Vette, I'll call you back."
"What! No... hold on?" Yvette frantically screamed, but it was too late, he'd already hung up.

A took off running toward Dundee's car, and once he got close to it, you almost couldn't recognize it or Dundee for that matter. He had so many holes in him, he looked like a polka dot shirt. A dropped straight to his knees and cried. Sure enough, he'd lost the other half of his life. As A cried, this incident fucked him up so bad that by the time he got to his crib downtown, he went to the van.

"Man, all this shit took my man's life," he fussed, taking everything up to his apartment. He opened the door and got cooked up. A stayed in the house for two straight weeks getting high. Finally, Yvette showed up to check on him, but not with Lil A. When she walked into the apartment, clothes were all over the place, and A was sitting at the bar still getting high.
"Boy, what are you trying to do, kill yourself?"
"Where's my son?" He mumbled.

A Father's Burden

"I didn't bring him. Was I supposed to bring him to see his daddy like this?" She fussed, walking to the bathroom to run him some water.

He hadn't washed up for days, and it hurt Yvette to see him look like he was looking. She loved this boy so much, that she would have walked to the moon and back for him. Once the water was ready, she undressed him, and looked at her son's father's face and hurt for him. *Damn, he's in such bad shape that I've gotta wash him up like I do for our son,* she thought.

At that moment, A seemed like a young child who needed someone to care for him. And that's exactly what Yvette was going to do. She washed him from head to toe, dried him off, and put him to bed. As she started to clean up the house, she saw bags of money and drugs. While she cooked A some dinner, she just felt as if something was wrong. When she woke him up, she fed him. After he ate, he fell back to sleep.

Yvette cleaned up the kitchen and left him alone. While he relaxed, she took a moment to roll and smoke a joint. She looked out the window towards the Westside Highway, she remembered when she and A first met. After getting high herself, Yvette jumped into the shower, cleaned herself, and then laid in the bed next to him, wearing only a long shirt. After lying there for a while, she fell asleep. In the middle of the night, A woke up, and the first thing he did was take a drink. He had a horrible headache from getting so high.

While trying to relax, A began to hallucinate. He began to think of his dawg, Dundee. It was as if his homie was right there in the room with him. He remembered the last time he saw Dundee. Before he saw him, he had not seen Dundee for a week and a half. He felt something was wrong because they always made it a point to see each other. He couldn't help but reflect on an old conversation.

"Yo A what's up baby?" Asked Dundee

"Nothing," A replied.

"Meet me at your place," Dundee directed. Dundee was heavy in the streets, so he always kept a gun on him. But now, he had two. As he got into the elevator, he pulled out at least 62 grams of coke. A always kept a bottle of champagne in the house, so when he got there, they began to get high.

"What's up, Ma," A said to his mother.

"Hi, ma…" Dundee said.

"Dundee, where you been? I haven't seen you in two weeks." Ms. Doris said.

"Ma, I've just been laying low for a minute."

Now Ms. Doris was raised in the streets, but she never told her boy shit because she knew A was too smart. But she told him that he would lose Yvette to those streets because he had picked the wrong one. So that thought ran through Ms. Doris' head.

As they walked to A's room, Ms. Doris asked if they were hungry.

They both said no.

Then out of nowhere, as if she had sensed something was wrong, Ms. Doris advised, "Dundee just stay off the block. Go back to where you were for a little while. And I know you got your gun on you. Just keep it ready."

How could Ms. Doris has known that Dundee might be in trouble and that something could happen to him? A knew that his mother cared about Dundee as if he was her son. She never really said anything to them because she thought they were smart enough to know how to take care of themselves. This time, however, he felt his mother might have had a sixth sense. A looked to the floor. Dundee looked up. A knew she had a point. But he didn't know what had happened and why Dundee had been laying low. They went into the room, closed

A Father's Burden

the door, and sat down. A pulled out the bottle of champagne. They started sniffing, drinking, and talking.

Dundee said, "Yo, A, I've been laying low because I robbed somebody from Queens, and he is as powerful as Nicky."

A replied, "Man, why you rob him."

With a nervous look on his face, Dundee began telling what happened.

He said he was out in Queens, fucking this girl, and he looked out the back window of the girl's house. He saw this van with three dudes. He saw them going into a house with 15 duffel bags. Right away Dundee knew it was the jackpot, so he asked the girl who lived there.

The girl ran down the spill on this dude. It was Fat Cat's father, and she said it was a stash house. So off impulse, that night Dundee was up in there. The old man was there. There was so much coke, dope, and money it was a shame. So Dundee knew he had to kill him. The old man looked up and saw Dundee.

The old man said, "I can see you're not from here so just take what you want and leave."

So why didn't Dundee just do that? He said, "Shut up!"

The old man said, "Youngster, I'm going to tell you where everything is at. Just get it and go. Young man just don't hurt me. This shit doesn't mean nothing to me. I could make it all back, but my life I can't make or bring back."

Dundee said, "Okay", thinking to himself, this old man is stupid. So as he opened up the secret closet, his eyes lit up. Shortly afterward, Dundee put four shots in the old man's head. Loading up his car, Dundee knew he couldn't really trust the girl he was fucking. But she really didn't know him that well, just what block he was from. Now he was getting money and she was just a money hungry ho. Fueling and sniffing coke, he gave her some coke and money so she could move. He gave her one key of coke.

But it didn't go like that. She never told Dundee that Fat Cat had bought that house for her.

He later saw that he had made a bad choice. And really from that day, his life changed. Soon afterward he would have to pay for that bad choice with the ultimate of sacrifices, his life. A began to cry. He now wished he could have done something to keep his dawg Dundee safe. A's mother had cautioned Dundee to continue laying low, but even that advice could not save him. A began to drink some more. He sniffed a little more coke, and some tears began to make their way down the sides of his face. He loved Dundee like a brother and his death was hard to take.

***

Thoughts were flying through A's head, as he mourned Dundee. He had taken his dawg's death very seriously. And it was as if he had dropped off the scene himself. He had been in his crib, drinking, sniffing, and remembering the good times with Dundee. It wasn't easy for him. He had gotten so low that he hadn't bathed or even cared about anything.

Meanwhile, Yvette had quite a bit on her mind. She was worried about A, but she knew things could not continue. She loved him, but she did not like the lifestyle that he was living. And now that she had a son, she did not want him to follow his father's path. She knew that A would do anything for her, but she didn't want anything to do with the street life that he was leading. She loved the apartment, the furniture, and the thought of knowing that she did not have to want for anything, but she did not like the way it was coming to her.

A Father's Burden

So, a few minutes later, Jan walked into the room to talk to her road dawg, Yvette. Jan asked, "Yvette what's wrong, why you crying? What's going on? Cuz, I'm on your side to the end. But you're crazy girl, I don't know one girl who would walk away from everything she could have in this world like that."

Jan had a different look on things. She liked nice things and she thought Yvette had many nice things that she herself would enjoy. But she knew Yvette had different thoughts. Yvette knew that she and A might have to split. She loved him very much, but she didn't want to see anything bad happen to him. She certainly did not want him to end up like Dundee had. That would be so tragic for Little A. Jan suggested that Yvette change her mind about A and the things he wanted to provide for her.

"Yvette, I wouldn't leave. I'd be right by A's side."
As they gave each other a hug, Jan said, "There goes that smile." They both started laughing. "Now let's go back out there and enjoy your son's first birthday." And that's what they did.

Jan knew as one king left, another king rises. As Lil A was running with the other kids, she thought of how much he resembled his father. *He's going to be just like his father, but probably more vicious,* she thought.

A couple of weeks passed. A hadn't called Yevette. He had been in a bad funk and was still drinking and sniffing coke like a baby addict. He wasn't using it; he was abusing it. He had it to do and to waste, and that's what he did. His absence was taking a toll on Yvette. At night, she would cry thinking about her man.

Several months later, A tried to take money to Lil A, but Yvette would not accept it. They used to be happy, but now it was like all they did was beef with each other. A would come with thousands for his son, but Yvette never took it. Ms.

Bernadette wouldn't let her. She would always tell Yvette, "We will be alright."

Since Yvette is a young- child, she really didn't understand her mother, and Ms. Bernadette could see that. So, Yvette ended up running the streets, partying in Harlem, while Ms. Bernadette took care of Lil' A.
Then it happened. One day A saw her on the block.

A said, "Baby listen. I'm rich, I'm never working, so you don't have to work, and can make your mind up about what you want to do? Are you coming home with me or what? Or do you want to stay here in these dirty projects?"
She said, "A don't put me in this spot. I'm not turning my back on you or my family." She could tell that he was mad. He raised his voice. He had an angry tone, but she did not want to continue this discussion on the street. She said, A you just mad, I'll talk to you later."
He said, "I'm not mad, I'm for real! What are you going to do?" Yvette tries to hug him, but he pushed her arm down.
Yvette pleaded, "A don't do this."
A said, "I'm waiting for an answer… Well, whenever you need anything for my son, you know how to find me." As she began to walk away, Yvette stopped.
"I'm out! A, I don't need money, just you."

A heard those last words. He walks to the steps. The hallways were pissy. He remembered what Ms. Bernadette said. He knew Yvette was a good girl. He knew the money didn't impress her. But A had no intentions of turning away from the streets. What's funny was, there was one side of A that actually wanted to stop. But, the other side of him said, '*Nigga you're the man! That girl and her mother are crazy. You're a millionaire, what the fuck is wrong with her?*'

As he walked out the back of the building, Yvette was in her room looking out the window with Lil' A in her arms. As

A Father's Burden

A stopped and looked up, he saw two people staring down at him, but he kept walking. He reached his Benz, opened the door, got in and drove off to 53rd Street, as tears were falling down Yvette's face. Lil' A wiped them away with his little hands not really knowing why his mother was crying.

As she hugged Lil' A tighter, she knew he was a splitting image of his father. Sometime later, Yvette and A were together again and this time, they were not arguing. It was a more peaceful time for A. Yvette began fixing breakfast. Then she got dressed.

A asked, "What does this mean…," referring to the breakfast, "Are you coming back?"

Yvette said, "I never left, you know what I want and ask for, so until then I'm just going to let you do you. I'll always be there no matter what. Like now you need me here. I'm done so I got to get back home to take care of your other half."

A had a stupid look on his face. He knew that Yvette was growing, but still couldn't be bought.

She kissed him as he offered her some money. She still refused it.

She said, "I'll take the train. I love you." Then she walked out as A laid there and pulled out some more coke and started sniffing. As he thought to himself, 'how can everything so good go so wrong'? The thought played in his head like a sad love song.

***

As 2 years pass by, Lil' A was growing older. Now Lil' A was two years old and Big A is getting bolder. So he started driving by the school again, and started sliding with this girl named, Barbara. Now Barbara came from a big family with like five girls and five boys. All the girls -- Barbara, Fay, Kim, Tamisha, and Jill were hot. They could have started their own modeling company if they wanted. They all were different complexions.

A started fucking around with Barbara. As you know in the streets word traveled far quickly. So, one day in school Yvette rolled up on Barbara and asked her if she was fucking with her baby's father. Barbara said no, so Yvette was like, *okay*.

Yvette then told Barbara, "I better not catch you two together." The two girls then mean mugged each other and walked off.

So now it's summertime. School's out. Yvette rolls up on A and says, "Nigga, it's like that? You disrespect me like that? You got a nerve to be fucking with Barbara from my projects? But A denied it.

He said some old slick shit like, *do you want me to ask her to your face*, and knowing Yvette, she said yeah. But this was the difference between Barbara and Yvette, you see Barbara, wanted the money and fame, whereas Yvette could care less.

Preparing her for a moment such as this one, A had told her if she wanted to roll with him, she had better not ever say nothing to Yvette, because he would cut her off. So this is how A played Yvette.

Yvette and A pulled up on her in the projects, and A called Barbara to 'the car.

As Barbara walked up, she bent down and said, "What's up? Are you looking for my brother or something?"

A said, "You know my baby's mother, Yvette, right?"

"Yeah, from school and from up here in the projects," she said.

A said, "Yo, do I mess with you?"

"Hell no!" She replied.

"You see Yvette?"

Yvette stared at Barbara with a look that could kill. For some reason, Yvette knew and felt they both were lying. I guess you could call this a *woman's intuition*.

A Father's Burden

As Barbara said, "Is that it, because I got to go?"

A said, "Yeah, thank you."

As Yvette turned her head, A rolled up the window. But before he drove off, he beeped the horn. As Barbara turned back around, he said, "Yo, tell your brother I need to holla at him…"

"I will."

"And here, take this for yourself for the inconvenience." A handed her a wad of money.

Barbara grabbed the money so fast; Yvette just sucked her teeth and said, "Ho bitch!"

Barbara was scared to death of Yvette because even though Yvette was a good girl living in the projects puts you to the test, and the word was Yvette could get down, she didn't play at all. Yvette was a fighter. So Barbara just walked off.

"Why you call her that?" A said.

"A, I still don't believe you. That bitch is a liar and you are too. I just better not catch you with that ho because I'm going to fuck her up. Then me and you will be next."

Now A is all skinny and shit, and Yvette is a thick little wild thing. he knew she was for real. A drove off thinking to himself how he got over on Yvette. Barbara walked into the store just to count the money and it was $1,000 all in hundred-dollar bills.

Now meanwhile, A and Yvette were on their way to get something to eat. As the music played, A lit up a joint. He took some pulls and then passed it to his baby.

All Yvette could do was smoke and think, this nigga is lying to me. She would definitely cut him off if he was fucking with a bitch from her projects. So they finally wind up at Yvette's favorite spot, City Island. As they ate seafood and drank, they got back into the Benz. A headed to their condo because now they both were high and horny.

As they drove on the highway, A thought to himself that it was a close call how Yvette made them confront each other. But as he knew it would happen, it did. He had it planned out already. And that stunt right there drew Barbara close to him because he knew Barbara just wanted money, and he had a lot of that. So he knew how to manage both women.

Barbara was one of the cutest girls in the school and the projects. She was caramel complexioned, slim, with a big ass, and breasts out of this world. He felt good that he had copped that and liked that she seemed drawn to him. As much as he liked Yvette, he lusted for Barbara. Now they reached the crib. Yvette jumped right into the shower. As soon as he counted the money he had made for the day, he jumped into the shower with Yvette.

He missed his baby with her dark complexion and soft skin. She washed her baby up from head to toe. He laughed when she wiped his asshole down. Then he did the same to her. As they rinse themselves off taking off the soap, Yvette sits on the edge of the tub and A stands up.

She grabbed his dick and put it to her soft lips. As his head goes back, she played with his head in her mouth. Yvette's long black hair is all the way to the back as she deep throats A's big dick.

A grabbed Yvette by her head and pulled it to him so she could go faster. Seconds later as A is about to cum, he pulled out because he would never come in his baby mother's mouth because she had to kiss his son.

Then he pulled Yvette up and turned her around and slid his dick in. It felt so good to her, but she couldn't grab on to nothing, so she held the side of the tub. A started to move slowly, and then he sped it up. Now he's ramming it in as Yvette yells harder! Harder! A goes harder, she's yelling his name. His full name now, Adrian! Adrian…, as he pumps harder! The next thing you know Yvette pulled down the shower curtain, but they don't stop as A comes all in Yvette's hot and soaking wet pussy. They turned the water off as Yvette sat her thick ass on the sink. While A immediately focuses on her pink pussy, she wraps her legs around his waist, and he goes to work. Yes, and work he did! Yvette scratches A's back, but A doesn't stop, as they make their way to the bedroom still making love.

After Yvette finally falls asleep, A goes back to counting the money he made that day. A looked at his pager, seeing Barbara's number appear several times. Glancing over to be sure Yvette was still asleep, he called Barbara from his cell.

"A! Where are you? I want to suck your dick."

As A laughed, he said, "My house in New Jersey, I won't be back in the city until morning."

Barbara said, "Oh, you're probably with your crazy baby's mother."

A laughed and replied, "Come by the projects tomorrow, so I can take you shopping."

"Okay, but don't waste all of your energy with her. Save some for me," she told him.

"Don't worry, I will," A promised.

Barbara said, "Oh, I bought you something too."

He replied, "I gave you that for yourself. Yo, give that to one of your brothers. Boo, I don't take nothing from girls that don't buy it with their own money."

Barbara stood quietly and thought to herself about A being with Yvette and not coming back to the City to be with her. She felt like she had gotten played.

A hung up the phone. He walked into the room to watch his baby sleep. There was a nice breeze flowing through the condo. Yvette was still sound asleep, like the deep sleep of a baby.

A continued counting his money. He stopped to look out the window at a few cars on the Westside Highway, and the lights from Jersey City. His thoughts began to wander. His thoughts were everywhere, especially in regards to not wanting to break up with Yvette, how he wouldn't turn his back on the streets, how much he loves his son and how Dundee runs through his mind daily.

As he takes a one and one, (that's a sniff of blow), A started to abuse the coke much harder. Then the wild side came out. He started to think about how Barbara sucks a good dick and how he first met her. Barbara was with her sister, Fay, and they were standing at the bus stop. A was coming out the store, as some undercover jumps out. Come to find out, one of A's workers made a direct sale. Fay and Barbara knew who A was from his reputation. His name was ringing bells all through the projects, so the cops got A and a few other people on the wall. They put the cuffs on everybody except for A.

"Captain, what we do with this one?" The officer said.
"Is he dirty, does he have any weapons or drugs on him?" The captain asked.
"No, he just came out the store. But he does have a lot of money on him. $1,800 dollars to be exact."
"Boy, where you get that money from?" The captain asked.
"I'm waiting for my girl. We're going shopping for our baby," A replied, forcing the captain to smirk.
The officer said, "Captain, he's lying. I think we should take him in for warrants."
They finally put cuffs on A, and all this time Barbara was watching.
"Why you got my boyfriend handcuffed? He didn't do anything." Barbara asked as her sister Fay stood right beside her.
The captain looked at the officer, "You see he wasn't lying. Let him go."

A Father's Burden

As the officer did what he was told, A just looked at Barbara. One half of him was shocked; the other half was like, *Thank you, I owe you baby.* Still in the moment, Barbara grabbed A's hands and walked towards the projects.
"I finally get to take your hand. You were kinda scared."
A said, "You're right. They thought I only had $1,800 on me. But I had $10,000 in the soles of both my sneakers.
As the girl's eyes lit up, A smiled and said, "But thank you so much. I owe you. What are you doing? You got somewhere to go?"

A was very excited. This was a nice-looking woman. She seemed nice and it seemed that she really cared about him. This woman was quick thinking and seemed to have a good sense of how to get what she wanted. It took a confident person to make the move that she made in front of those cops. She had saved him with some of her wit.
As they walked through the projects together, they talked and seemed to be building a good bond. Barbara was running her mouth. Somehow, A knew she wanted to fuck. She was setting the scene for them to have a good time together.

Barbara said she was going to her mother's job downtown.
"We just came from our aunt's house; maybe we could drop my sister off and then chill."
Barbara thought to herself, boy if I get him, I'm straight.
"Come on, I will take you," A said.
They walked through the parking lot to A's Benz. The girls were so happy because this was the first time they had been in a Benz.
As they jumped in, A turned on the music. Grand Master Flash was bumpin'. The girls were all smiles.

"Y'all smoke weed?" A asked.
Both the girls said, "Yes!"
"Light this up," he instructed, and Barbara did as she was told. Then pulled off, and what was funny was that as they got

a few blocks away, they got caught at a red light. A police car pulled up beside them, and it was the captain. They were trying to look into the Benz, but the window tint was too dark. The girls started to panic, so A spoke up.

"Don't worry, or jump, or move all crazy. Just relax, they can't see in here."

As Barbara held the joint low in her hand, the captain was staring hard. But they made the right turn on red towards the precinct, and the girls deeply exhaled.

The light turned green, A laughed. "Who was scared now." He asked, forcing Barbara to smile. So this is how A remembered how Barbara saved him from getting locked up, and how she took care of him so well that day.

A dropped Fay off downtown as Barbara said, "Girl I'll see you at home later. I'm chillin' with A.

A stared quietly.

Fay said, "No you're not because I will have to go home by myself to the Bronx."

"You don't have no money Fay?" A asked as she shook her head, no. Handing her some money, he said, "Here go $50 so you can get something to eat and come back to the Bronx in a cab."

Fay said, "Thank you… see you when I get home," and then took the money. The two sisters looked at each other and A pulled off.

Then Barbara said, "Finally, I got you to myself. Now you can do me."

A said, "Girl you're not ready." But little did he know, she was ready. But was he ready for her? As A lit up another joint. He passed it to Barbara. "We're just going to drive around Harlem for a few hours…" Barbara just stared at A so hard. A asked, "What's wrong with you."

She responded, "I just want to do something to you so bad."

A asked, "What?"

She said, "I'm just a little bit nervous because I might not get to do it again. But I know for sure you would want more. But how would you look at me?"

A said, "Girl I'm grown. So if you want to hang out with a grown up you must do grown up things." As soon as he said that, she passed the joint back to him, took the gum from her mouth and said, "Hold this..."

A said, "Girl, what you want me to do with this?"

She said, "Just give me 150 seconds and I'll take it back."

A, said, "Okay, 150 seconds."

She grabbed A's crouch, unzipped his pants and pulled out his dick and went to work.

At first A was still trying to drive, but the way she had her mouth so wet and deep throated he had no choice but to pull off to the side of the road. She was sucking his dick so well. She was very good at giving head. She knew how to work her lips, her tongue, and her mouth. And those fingers were an extra pleasure. He tried to keep his concentration, but he almost hit another car. But as the driver of the old beat-up car saw A's expensive car, he stopped. A pulled over and double parked.

Barbara continued, and quickly went to work again. The funny thing about it was that she did such a good job in 150 seconds. And the biggest prize of all was A cumming in Barbara's mouth as she sucked and slurped every drop of it. Finally, she pulled his dick from her mouth, retrieved her gum and put it back in her mouth.

She said, "You see, I told you. You'll never find a girl like me. I really want you. I want to do you."

To prove her point, all the way home to the Bronx all she did was suck his dick.

A jumped out of his trance because he heard Yvette say, "Nigga, I hope you were thinking about what you've been doing to me and not that ho..." For some reason Yvette knew A had been up to something. As Yvette walked away, she sat down on the bed, picked up the phone, and called Jan. As she looked at A's beeper, she saw that someone had called him 129 times. She handed the beeper to A and said, "Oh, here's your beeper and someone called you 129 times. It's that bitch you probably been daydreaming about…!" She continued, "You need to be with her because you just up there staring out the window all crazy and shit thinking about that bitch."

A knew it was true. Yvette was there because she was going away for the summer, and she wanted to get her some before she left.

This trip would cost Yvette because over the summer A and Barbara got closer. I mean really close. All A did was spoil Barbara on top of fucking her with no condom.

Yvette went south with her family. Lil' A was growing so fast. One day Yvette called back to New York and contacted her cousin Jan.

Jan said, "Cuz, I didn't want to tell you this, but I saw Barbara jumping into A's car one night after the club. Girl, Barbara's dressing all fly and shit, now."

Yvette asked, "How you know it was A's car?"

Jan said, "It was. Everybody's been seeing Barbara in his car in the projects a lot."

Yvette was extremely upset. She loved A and didn't want anyone else messing with him, especially not that yellow-ass Barbara.

She said, "As soon as I get back; I'm going to beat that bitch's ass."

Jan asked, "Why?"

Then Yvette explained to Jan that she and Barbara had already bumped heads. She said, "Cuz, I'm going to call you later, okay."

Both girls said, "I love you."

Ring, ring! As soon as Yvette hung up from talking with Jan, she called A.

A picked up the phone. He said, "Hello, who is this…?"

A Father's Burden

"Hello! Who do you think this is? It's your little bitch." Right away, A knew that voice. "What's up, baby?" He asked.

"What's up my ass," Yvette answered back. "I hope you are having fun because as soon as I catch your little bitch, I'm going to beat her ass, and I'm not fucking you no more...!"

A snapped back, "Who the fuck you think you talking to? First of all, I'm not fucking with nobody. You're also letting your mother think for you, and we need to stop fucking with each other like that?" I hung up.

Yvette was so mad because she loved A. Despite what A told her, she knew he had been messing with Barbara. She wondered how she would deal with A when she got back to New York. Would their relationship take a big turn for the worst? Would he still love her? A lot of thoughts danced through her head. She was mad, real mad. A mentioned her mother, but she hadn't talked to her mother. She wondered if she should even tell her mother about her thoughts regarding A. She didn't want to start anything new with her mother. After hanging up the phone, A went back to sniffing coke and whatever else he was doing. Somehow, he wasn't worried about Yvette's threat to stop fucking him. He somehow knew she really didn't mean it. She'd want to be with him again.

Chapter Three

Now that summer was over it was time for school, Yvette was back at home and she never went back to her old condo again.

One night before school, Barbara spent the night with A, and she broke the news. She said, "A, you know I'm pregnant. I'm four months along."
A said, "So!"
She asked, "What you want me to do, keep it or not?"
A said, "Keep it."
Barbara said, "What about Yvette?"
A said, "I'm not fucking with her no more."
That was all Barbara needed to hear.
A said, "I got enough money to take care of both of the kids."

So now the word was out. Everybody knows A is messing with Barbara, but Yvette hasn't run into her yet. Barbara seemed to have changed so much. She was dressing better these days. Everything was always new. Somehow the new clothes and hairdo made her seem so much more attractive.

A Father's Burden

One day shortly after Barbara's big announcement, A was over to Yvette's mother's house. Yvette was not her usual self. She was not as friendly as she usually was. So, he just played with Lil' A for a few hours.

As A was leaving, he looked over at Yvette and in a matter of fact tone he said, "Oh, Lil' A might be having a brother or sister soon."

Knowing she wasn't pregnant, she got mad. She threw a cup of soda in A's face and said, "You don't have to say shit to me. Just come and check your son."

A just walked out.

Yvette couldn't wait for school the next day. She was hopping mad. She was going to make it her business to catch up with Barbara. She called her road dawg, Jan and told her the bad news. She then told her what she was going to do.

She was not going to wait for school to end. She and Jan ran up to Barbara's homeroom class, but Barbara was scared to come out.

Then Yvette said, "Bitch, you're going to come out, or I'm going to come in that classroom to beat your ass!"

Barbara said, "Yvette I don't want to fight you. I'm pregnant."

Those words just incensed Yvette. As if she wasn't already angry enough, those words just made her angrier. Bam! She hit Barbara with a closed fist. She began beating her with no mercy. She whipped Barbara's ass all the way out into the hallway. Yvette was doing it all hitting and kicking her. Then Barbara's two sisters came over. As soon as they came over to the fight, Jan was on one of them and Yvette got on the other one because Barbara was hurt. As the fight escalated, a few teachers finally came out and broke it up.

All four girls were taken to the principal's office and were suspended from school. By the end of the day the news throughout the projects was that day was the end of Yvette's and A's relationship.

As a result of losing someone who had really cared about him and had his back, A started to go backwards, and Yvette moved forward. A was well-respected on the streets. For many, he was the man. He had power and money. However, it was Yvette who kept him balanced. Without that balance, he quickly turned to drinking and regularly sniffing coke.

When Dundee was killed, it was Yvette, who came in to settle him and help him to transition from Dundee's death. She was a good, supportive mate for him. She cooked for him, cared for his needs, and made sure she offered lots of moral support. She loved him for who he was as a kind-hearted person. Even though she did not like his dealings in the street, she still dealt with and cared about him because she wanted to see him do well. Yvette never just liked him because of his money. In fact, she never took any of the money he offered her, and she didn't feel comfortable living in the condo.
Losing Yvette also meant he might possibly lose the support of Yvette's mother, Ms. Bernadette. She treated him like one of her own. Would that now change?

Lil' A was getting older. He's three years old now. A is messing with a girl named Lisa. They were in love. And they would get high all day. Lisa was different from Barbara and she really loved A, and not for his money. Lisa had another baby, a boy. She named him, Kevin with A's name Adrian as his middle name. Kevin and Lil' A looked just alike. Meanwhile, Yvette got married to a guy named Louis, and gave birth to a baby girl.

A Father's Burden

Now A's mother, Doris, was very sick. She went to the hospital and was on her death bed. Yvette took Lil' A to see her. Lil' A looked shocked, because Ms. Doris had lost all her hair and was very skinny. Mrs. Doris was very fond of Lil' A. She gave him some money to buy school supplies. "Baby don't turn out like your father. Stay away from the streets," she said in a raspy tone her last words to him.

In a soft voice, he said, "Grandma, I'm not going to be like him. I will do the right thing."

Ms. Doris just smiled and then turned her attention to Yvette as she said, "Baby you did the right thing by moving on. Adrian is out of control. He went from having everything to having nothing. He lost the best two things in his life, you, and now he's losing me."

The two ladies started to cry. That was the last day that Lil' A saw his grandmother because she died that same week. His father had fallen so low. While A had only done powdered coke and drank alcohol, somehow crack became the new drug of choice on the streets. After a while, he tried it too and found himself hooked. He had violated one of the key rules in the drug world. *'Don't get high on your own supply.'* He had fallen in love with getting high so much that he became a user.

When his mother was in the hospital, he was so strung out that he never went to see her. When she died, he finally fell all the way apart. He was hooked on crack so bad that his life continued to deteriorate. A was so hooked that even Lisa left him. She and Kevin moved to upstate New York, but the boys always stayed in contact. Lil' A still loved his father so much.

Lil' A fondly remembered Big A calling his name in the hallways of the project and how he'd run through the hallway to see him. As they talked in the hallway, Big A, referring to Kevin, would say, *A this is your little brother. You must always look out for him.* Lil' A would always say, *Okay daddy.* Then he would always comment on how they looked just alike as if they were twins.

***

Lil' A was becoming quite the nice young man. Yvette was a good mother. She wanted to teach him all the right things and help him to become a good person. Yvette would always tell her son, when you meet a girl, you treat her with respect. Always respect her. And if she has any kids you treat them like they're yours. That thought would always stay in Lil' A's mind.

Just like Grandma Dorothy used to always say, "Your mommy's little boy and daddy's little soldier." But A was too young to comprehend that. But the statement would come up again later when Lil' A was 10 and Kevin was 5 years old, and so was Lil' A's sister Nina. Lil' A would always ask for his father. He often remembered how Yvette took cabs to pick up his father. Now, at least one time a month, she was taking both boys out. Big A would always school Lil' A on his expectations. Likewise, he was interested in how he was doing in school, or if he was looking out for his mother?'

A would say, "That's right, you the man now. Did you talk to your brother?"
Lil' A would say, "Yes."
Big A would always say, "That's my boy!"

Big A was cracked out, but still a legend. Lil' A remembered his father could never sit still. He could never watch a whole movie. Big A would get up and take Lil' A with him as they went to the bathroom. Now Lil' A never

A Father's Burden

knew why his father couldn't sit still, but as soon as they got to the bathroom, they would go to the same stool. As big A would pull out his crack pipe and take a hit. Lil' A would sit there and look puzzled at his father.

All Big A would say was, "Baby boy, you never go back and tell your mother what I do. Whenever you hang out with me, you keep everything between us. The first time your mother repeats anything we do together, you will never hang out with me again. You hear me boy?"

"Lil' A would always say, "Yeah."

Big A knew what this was doing to his son. The entire situation was affecting Lil' A to the extent of him having fear in his eyes. So after 30 minutes in the bathroom, they returned to the movie. Yvette knew Big A was up to no good, so Lil' A just sat there because he would never turn on his father, no matter what. He loved him too much. I guess a father doesn't always know how much a child loves him.

This experience was adding fire to Lil' A's eyes. As the movie ends, they would go back home, and Big A would walk home from Yvette's mother's house after a day with his son. He had a great day with his son, but he couldn't wait to get back home to smoke crack. Now crack hit so hard that the finest girls got hooked and looked like zombies.

Barbara's sister, Fay, got hooked badly. Barbara wound up having a baby girl. Her name was Nicky, and she was the same age as Kevin. So, all these kids are around the same age, with Lil' A being the oldest. As crack wiped out a big portion of the neighborhood, a lot of kid's mother's and father's got hooked on crack really bad. But thank God Yvette, Barbara, and Lisa didn't, even though Big A did and had become a kingpin at a young age.

Let's just say that Big A fell victim to what we know as 'the game'.

***

So Lil' A is 15 years old now. He has a crush on this girl named, Verwana. Now Verwana had a bunch of sisters there were three of them. One was named, Keisha she was the oldest. Then came Verwana and then Ann. Keisha had a son, and her baby's father was a stick-up kid. He was hooked on crack and was always in and out of jail.

Lil' A used to try to push up on her. Keisha would always say, 'Lil' A, I got a son. If you think you could mess with me, you need money because I got to take care of my son.' Lil' A would always say, 'when I get some money I will come and get you.' Keisha would smile and walk away. You see Keisha was older than Lil' A and she would always mess with the older dudes. They were always selling drugs, so they had money. They used to always be at Keisha.

Now Keisha looked just like Janet Jackson. I mean she was bad. Verwana was dark skinned and she looked good too, with a shape like Venus Williams and Ann was skinny, she resembled Monica. Lil' A never got with Keisha, but as a child he always tried.

One day when Lil' A was spending a weekend at his mother's house on 187th and Clay Ave., he was in the hallway on the fourth floor with a couple of friends. They were doing what the average 15-year-olds did, and that was smoking weed. They heard sirens and cars burning rubber when suddenly a car flew by with cops on its tail. They heard a loud boom and seconds later a Hispanic dude was running down the block. You know kids have to be nosey, and so they stepped out to see what was happening. Lil' A saw the

A Father's Burden

Spanish man running toward them, bleeding, with a big duffel bag in his hand.

Lil' A spoke to the man, "Man, you alright...?"
The man said, "No! I have to hide."
The other boys stood shocked, but Lil' A just reacted. He grabbed the man's hand and said, "Come on," taking him into his house.

Yvette was still asleep, which was a surprise because that loud boom should have awakened her. But living in the ghetto, you always hear gun shots, sirens and car crashes. So she stayed asleep. Lil' A took the man to his room and closed the door.

The man said, "Shorty what's your name?"
He responded, "They call me, Lil' A."
The man said, "'Lil' A, go get me something to drink."

When Lil' A did that the man asked, him to go up the block to check on his friend. As he went down the stairs, the rest of the guys were waiting. They informed Lil' A that the cops came up seconds behind the man and asked if they'd seen anybody running by. Lil' A asked them what they said to the cops.

One of them replied, "We told them he ran around the block."

In the hood, the little boys knew to lie to the cops because all they wanted to do was lock everybody up. So the rule on any street was to lie. The boys walked up the block and saw the car crashed against the building and other cars. The cops had another man on the ground. As they searched the area for the missing man, Lil' A heard the cops talking. They'd lock the other man up, and continue their search. But he was safe in Lil' A's house. So the other boys wound up going home, as Lil' A went back home. He told the man that the police locked his friend up.

As the man looked upset Lil' A asked, "What's your name?"
The man said, Papi. So, Papi asked Lil' A did he have a phone? Lil' A said yeah. Papi said, "I need to use it."
Lil' A went to get the phone. The man began to speak in Spanish. Lil' A didn't understand one word. Papi asked, Lil' A the address. He told the man the address. Never did Lil' A ask the man what was in the duffel bag. A kid knows not to ask questions because people might think you are the police. But Papi already knew Lil' A wasn't the police.

Papi stayed for about an hour before they heard a horn blow outside. They saw a big truck.

Lil' A told Papi, "Yo your ride is here."
They both walked downstairs. On the way down Papi said, "Say kid you got heart. How old are you?"
Lil' A told him his age.
Papi asked, "What you doing out so late?"
"Lil' A said, "chillin', but I want a lot of money so I can take care of my mother."
Papi asked, "Are you hustling?"
Lil' A said, "I am, but it's a little something, but I want to get a lot of money.
Papi smiled, he said, "Lil' A, you got money?"
"Lil' A said, "No."
Papi got into the truck, rolled the window, down and threw Lil' A a stack of money, and gave him a phone number and said, "When you really want money like that call me."
Lil' A said, "Okay," put the money into his pocket and went back upstairs.
On the way up, he began counting the money. He made $1,000. So, the next day Lil' A called the phone number Papi

gave him and a female answered. Lil' A asked to speak to Papi.

She asked, who was calling and he told her his name. When Papi came to the phone, she told him his name.

"What's up," asked Papi.

Lil' A said, "You know you gave me a thousand? I thought you did not realize what you gave me."

Papi laughed and said, "Go and have a little fun, Lil' A, call me anytime, okay?"

That day, he went back to Yvette's mother's house. Shit, all he wanted to do was show Keisha he had a lot of money, and he did.

But Keisha was messing with this dude who Lil' A didn't like. There was a rumor that the dude and his brother had shot Lil' A's father. So he hated Keisha. After that, he got closer to Verwana. But Verwana was messing with a boy named, Kewanee. All of them grew up together. They went to the same schools.

Lil' A went and spent the money Papi gave him. Lil' A was selling drugs, but nothing major. In fact, Lil' A didn't realize that the Spanish man he saved was the biggest drug lord in Manhattan. Lil' A called Papi back. Papi knew Lil' A was a soldier and loyal. Those qualities were hard to come by. But, Lil' A still didn't know what to do with that, so one day while Lil' A was in the projects, Keisha's little boyfriend (the one who was supposed to have shot Big A) beat Keisha up one night. Lil' A was there and had to come to her rescue. But he was older and beat them both up. He beat Keisha's ass because she was money-hungry and a true ho, and he wanted her to himself. But Keisha fucked who ever had money, and she didn't want to mess with him anymore.

He made the biggest mistake by beating up Lil' A. After he beat them up, he left. Keisha said, "Boy, what's wrong with you? You know he's crazy."

Lil' A said, "Don't worry, I'm going to get him."

Keisha kissed him on his forehead and said come on. The next day "Lil' A called Papi. He told Papi he had to see him. Papi asked him what was up?

As he was about to tell him what happened, Papi stopped him. He told him to never talk his business on the phone like that. Papi said he would meet him at his mother's house. So Lil' A went to his mother's house. Papi pulled up in another type of car. Lil' A got into the car. Papi asked, "Lil' A what was up?" After Lil' A told his newfound friend what happened, Papi asked, "What do you want me to do?"

The 15-year-old responded, "All I need is a gun. I'll do it myself."

Papi smiled, thinking that Lil' A was playing. He said, "Okay, come on."

He then drove off.

They went to a store in Manhattan, and then headed to the Bronx. Papi said, "Okay, you want to become a man, so let's see what you're really made of. I'm going to park around the corner. Do what you have to do and come back." All Lil' A said was *okay*. The only thing on his mind was this man had beat him up and he was also one of the dudes that had shot his father.

They parked, Lil' A got out of the car and low and behold there on the corner was Token. That was the dude's name and he was standing on the corner with his brother. They walked toward where Papi had parked. Now Papi was testing him. He didn't think Lil' A could do it. But since he had saved Papi from being arrested, he had promised that he would do anything he could to help him.

A Father's Burden

This was a new challenge for Lil' A. He was about to step up into a new level of being on the streets. What he didn't know was that this was the beginning of a hustler's burden. As Token and his brother walked past Papi's car, Lil' A began to walk behind them. They were no more than three cars away from Papi's car. At first, he thought Lil' A was faking. Papi's friend, said in Spanish, "*Look at Lil' A.* Just as he said that, Lil' A yelled out to Token.

"Token!"

The brothers stopped. Token responded, "Little nigga, what you want?"

As Lil' A pulled out a 9-millimeter, both brothers' eyes opened wide. Lil' A let go three shots – he hit Token twice in the chest. The brother took off running. Lil' A chased after him and fired four shots, one hitting the brother in the leg. As he fell, Lil' A ran up to him and put three more shots in his head. On his way back to the car, he saw that Token was still moving. So he shot him two more times. Both men were dead as little A's new life was about to begin.

Papi sat up in the car, amazed. As Lil' A walked down the block, Papi drove past him. Lil' A didn't walk to the car. He kept walking. He wanted Papi to drive around the corner. Lil' A kept walking, and then finally got into the car further down the street. Papi was still amazed. He thought his young friend was only playing and might have only fought Token.

He asked, "Have you ever killed anyone before?"

The response was, "NO! But I think I did just now."

In Spanish, Papi's friend said, "*He's loco.*"

Papi asked his young friend how he knew not to come straight to the car.

Lil' A said, "because I had just shot those two men. How did you know to drive around the corner again to pick me up?"

Papi smiled and said, "Lil' A I love you, where's your father?"

Lil' A began telling Papi all about his father as they drove back to Manhattan.

"I know what you need. I bet you've never smoked no weed like this," Papi said as he lit up a blunt.

That was the best weed Lil' A had smoked. He pulled and inhaled. It took him to another world. Papi and his friend laughed seeing that Lil' A was high as hell. But Lil' A handled the high as if he had been doing it for years. He continued to talk about his pops. He loved his pops, but knew he was devoted to the streets. As Lil' A named the names of people his father used to run with, Papi knew Big A was getting up in age.

Lil' A said, "Let's drive through my pop's neighborhood."

Papi signaled his friend to drive toward the area where they might run up on his pops, "What makes you think he'll be out there?"

"Where else can he go? He lives in the streets," Lil' A said.

Papi just laughed and then he said, "Lil' A, you just know what to say."

Papi took a strong liking to Lil' A, not just because he saved him from going to jail forever, but because of his loyalty and intellect for his age. Now he'd become a real man by catching his first two murders. Now some would wonder what this kingpin was doing with this young boy. He felt a closeness to Lil' A for several reasons, plus witnessing him catch his first body, and not just one, but two of them.

A Father's Burden

They pulled up to Big A's projects. All the lights were out. You would think there was a blackout? If it was, it might be to just keep the police out. Allowing them to camouflage themselves as they made sales, they could hide. So even if they had to shoot somebody, such as stick up kids, or just settle a rival, they would not easily be seen. To make it clearer, they could see what and who was coming in and out. Even if the cops were to come, they could spot them a mile away.

As they drove through the projects there was a man standing in the middle of the street. Papi and his friend were kind of leery because it was so dark. As they got closer, the man was closely observing the car because the two men were white-skinned. It was hard at first, for him to tell that the two men inside were Puerto Rican.

The man in the street was Big A. As the car came to a halt, he asked, "What are you looking for?"
Lil' A yelled out, "Head Moe."
That was their father and son signal to each other.
Big A smiled and said, "Head Moe, that's you?"
His son said, "Yeah!"
Big A walked up to the car feeling more assured because he knew it was safe now.
As Papi saw the expression on Lil' A's face, he began to realize how much he loved his pops.
Big A said, "What's up?"
Lil' A said, "Head Moe, I want you to meet my friends," as he introduced everybody.
Then Big A said, "Why don't you get the car out the middle of the street."

Papi told the driver to park. After they parked, the three men got out, or as we should say, two men and Lil' A. They started talking. Big A realized he knew one of Papi's uncles from when they were locked up. So as quickly as Papi learned to like Lil' A, he could see where the young man had gotten his style. As they continued to talk, Papi got a beep.

Looking at the number on the beeper, he said, "I got to go take care of something."
Big A asked his son if he had something on him, meaning drugs.
Lil' A said, "No."

Then Papi said come with us A and I'll bless you. So you know Big A couldn't resist that. They all got into the car and headed toward the highway. They drove for a little bit, then pulled up to a major drug block in Harlem, 150th and Broadway.

Once a Puerto Rican man dropped off a big green bag of money, Big A knew that Papi was a major player. Lil' A just knew it was a lot of money.

As they pulled up in front of a cab base, Papi told Lil' A to call him in the morning. "I must take this money to my house. You know it's a million dollars. Then he asked, Lil' A, you got money?"
Lil' A said, No!" Papi reached into the bag and pulled out stacks. He counted out two thousand dollars handed it to him.
"Lil' A go to your mom's house, okay? Stay there awhile and I'll call you in a couple of days."

Now Big A knew something was up because Lil' A loved running in the projects. But he just stood quiet. Then Papi spoke in Spanish to the man who had brought him the money.

Then in English, he said, "Give him 25."

A Father's Burden

Addressing Big A, he said, "A it's nice to have met you. We can meet up again. Here, is 25 grams enough for you?" Big A said, "Yeah that's plenty."
Papi said, "This one's on me. You know your son; he's my heart."
Papi advised Big A not to worry about paying for the cab because he owned the entire cab base. He told him to just drop his son off first because it might be too hot in that area for him. As Papi gave them instructions, the Spanish man returned with the drugs for Big A. Five minutes later, the cab pulled up.

The father and son got into the cab. Seconds later Big A turned to Lil' A and said, "Head Moe, your man Papi seems like a real good dude. Plus, he's rich as a motherfucker. Lil' A turned to his father and began to tell him how he met Papi. Then he confided to his pops what he had done. He told him he had just killed two men from his projects.
Big A was not shocked, but he knew his son was now definitely a player in the game.
So once Lil' A told his pops the names, he knew who they were and said, "Fuck them. They were dirt bags. But are you alright?"
Lil' A said, "Yeah!"

Big A just sat there shocked. His little man had that look in his eye known as the eye of the tiger, which meant that he was cold-blooded. Somehow, he knew his son liked doing what he'd done, and since he himself had been a big player in the streets, that his son was likely to do it again. When the cab got to Lil' A's mother's house, Lil' A asked Big A if he was coming up.

Big A said, "No. I really don't want your mother to see this. But tell her I said hi and I love her."

Lil' A gave his pops some money and went upstairs. He knew his pops just couldn't wait to get back to the projects so he could get high on the ounce of crack Papi gave him.

But you see Big A knew so many dudes that were rich and still getting money that he always got blessed hard like that. He just had to wait until one of the rich dudes came through the hood. They make it their business to come check Big A because his word was so good. He would tell if your shit was the bomb or garbage. So you had to come check Big A.

Finally, A got back to the projects. He made a couple of sales then went to the crib to get high.

But you know what was next. He grabbed up two crack head broads to get high with him. Most of all, they wanted to get their freak on. So Big A chopped up about 7 crack rocks for them to smoke.

As Big A had flashbacks of ballin', he was listening to an oldies station. As Blue Magic plays about one hour into them all getting high, both girls got butt naked. Big A strips down too. As one girl started sucking his dick, the other young lady began eating her pussy. Big A sat back and enjoyed the fact that he still had power, or should I say crack head power.

A laid one girl on her back and the other on top, facing up. This is one of the best positions you could put the two girls in because you want to beat both pussies and butt holes together. So Big A went to work ramming both girls. He was going from pussy to butt hole, then pussy to pussy. So after he busts his first nut, he switched their positions. Now he could get the other girl in her ass hole too.
So, Big A's night went really well, good and fast...

CHAPTER Four

As Yvette wakes up the next morning, she looked as if she wasn't feeling well.

Lil' A asked, "What's wrong?"

She said, "I lost my job and I can't pay my rent. I didn't want to tell you, but I'm behind four months and I really don't know what to do. I was going to call your grandmother, but I'm tired of her helping me. But baby, I don't know what to do."

Lil' A asked, "Ma, how much you owe?"

"I owe sixteen hundred and we don't have any food," Yvette answered.

"Ma, don't worry," Lil' A assured her.

Yvette responded, "Boy I got to. You don't have a job."

He walked away and went to his room.

As he was on his way back, his mother said, "Boy don't be walking away from me while I'm talking to you…"

When Lil' A dropped the money on the table, he said, "Ma, here…, pay your rent. Get some food and keep the change so you can get around while you look for another job."

Yvette's eyes opened wide. She couldn't really say anything because a flash ran through her head. She thought of Big A and the fact that Lil' A looked just like him. She remembered how Big A used to drop money on the table or just give her anything she wanted. But now she was scared because from the little incident she knew her baby was following his father's footsteps. So as bad as she didn't want to take the money, she really needed it.

She said, "Boy get that drug money out of here."
Now she started preaching like a real mother who is worried about her child.
But he really didn't want to hear it. As Yvette went on and on, Lil' A walked away and went back into his room. After throwing on a change of clothes he went out. Lil' A had given his mother every dime he had except for the one hundred dollars he kept. Now all he wanted to do was go smoke some weed with his friends.
Before he left, his mother had asked if he was coming back. He responded was, "Yeah."
She then said, "I'll cook then."
He said, "Okay!"
Seconds later, Yvette yelled, "Boy bring your ass back here and give me a kiss and a hug."
Lil' A was mad but couldn't refuse because one thing for sure and two for certain. He loved his mother. He did what he was told. He kissed his mother and walked out.
She said, "Be safe, baby."

When Lil' A arrived at his second hood, there was a dice game going on. The game was packed. There were at least 10 people shooting dice.
He wanted to buy some weed, so he walked up to the weed spot and bought $50 worth. Some of the boys that knew Lil' A said, "What's up?"
Lil' A greeted them back with a, "What's up y'all?"

The dice game seemed to be heating up. One dude yelled out, "Fifty dollars is up on my line." Lil' A stood

A Father's Burden

around as the others dropped money. Some dropped $50 on the noise and some dropped more. One boy grabbed three dice and began to shake them in his hand. He shot them really good and yelled, "All down is a bet. Here I come. Baby needs new shoes... Mommy don't got no job. I'm too scared to rob..." As he released the dice, he hit two, two, and six. Now that's an automatic win, so the boy passed at least four times. Now the bank had to be at least seven thousand after he shot all those sixes. The boy turned to Lil' A and asked, "What are you doing. Are you scrambling or gambling...?"

Lil' A boasted, "You don't want none of me. I will shut this bank down."

His boy said, "Okay, so get down on my line." Now Lil' A knew he only had fifty dollars left, but he said to himself *fuck-it*. He was going down in a blaze anyway because he already had his weed, what else was there left to do. So Lil' A dropped his last fifty dollars into the dice game. Again, the boy said the same line he used on his last roll, "My baby needs new shoes, mommy don't got no job and I'm too scared to rob."

He then rolled the dice. The first dice dropped, and it showed a two. Then the next one fell, and it showed another two. Lil' A held his breath because all he needed was a six. But when the third dice stopped, it was a one. Now this time everybody on the line pulled back because he was throwing too many sixes. They all had the minimum on the line which was fifty dollars.

As the boy paid everyone, Lil' A looked as if he had been robbed. The crowd started to laugh. The boy said, "Okay I'm aces now, so you better double up."

The crowd was kind of hesitant, but Lil' A said, "Don't worry, I am doubling up."

He dropped the whole $100. The boy shot his shot again and rolled another ace. Lil' A now had $200. The boy remarked, "That's funny nobody else doubled up but, A."

He looked around, picking up the dice and then he said, "A, I'm going to take all your money."

"You got a long mountain to climb," Lil' A responded, using reverse psychology, and the boy was falling into his trick.

Now it was Lil' A's turn. "Okay bitches return to the dice. All I want is high numbers now...," he said, talking smack.

Lil' A took the $300 to $2,400 because the dude kept stopping his bank. He grabbed the dice shook them in his hand and said, "Okay hoes, lets race right to the top," releasing the dice.

Two ones popped up so Lil' A knew the only thing that could happen was good, but the last dice showed a two.

"I got your ass now. I hope you don't feel safe with that," his opponent responded.

Lil' A said, "Yea I do. Bet another hundred you don't beat it."

The boy jumped right on the bet. So he grabbed the dice, repeating the same steps, "Baby need new shoes, mommy don't got no job..." and rolled the dice.

This time fives popped up; the boy knew he was good. Both men waited for the third dice to stop spinning. So was the crowd, they began screaming in anticipation.

Then Lil' A yelled, "Basement hoes, basement!" The dice stopped spinning. It was a one. The dude's face dropped and Lil' A was happier than a kid on Christmas day. Now he had $4,800 plus the $100 side bet.

Afterward, Lil' A passed the bank as the dude said, "Don't worry, I got you, A. That's chump change to me."

Lil' A walked off. As he walked toward the building, shots rang out. *Boom! Boom! Boom!*

A Father's Burden

He jumped at the sound of the noise. Everybody near the dice game had taken off. Lil' A looked over to where the game had been, only to see that the dude he was gambling with had been killed. Later someone told him that the two stick-up dudes waited until he'd walked away.

Later in the week he learned that another dude who was gambling called the, Stick-up Kid, was the person who told them to wait until Lil' A had left the game. He wanted the boys to make sure he was not there.

After Lil' A left the gambling scene, he went upstairs to his girl Tiffany's house. Now Tiffany was a bad joint, meaning she was good looking. She was ready to slide with Lil' A, so they called a cab and went to Harlem. They stopped at a liquor store and bought a bottle of Moet and then headed back to his mother's house.

Once they got there, he wanted to make sure his mother was fully dressed. "Ma, are you dressed?" Lil' A asked Yvette.

She said, "Yeah, why?"

He replied, "Because I got company. Tiffany's with me."

As the two women spoke, Lil' A walked to the room. After about 20 minutes, Yvette came to his room with two plates of food. As they were eating, he asked Tiffany, who was two years younger than him, if she needed anything.

She said, "I want those new Air Maxes for girls. They cost a buck fifty...," (That means $150.) She continued, "They got two different colors."

He gave a smiling Tiffany $500 and told her to get them both, as well as an outfit to complement them. He then told her to roll up a blunt. She did as she was told. Lil' A took the plates to the kitchen and on his way back stopped by his mother's room and knocked on the door. Yvette was on the phone. She said she was talking to Big A.

Lil' A asked his mother, "Ma, you took care of your business?"

She replied, "Yeah!" He then told her he had won like $5,000 playing dice. As Yvette's eyes lit up, he asked her if she needed more money. She said, "Boy I'm good. I don't want your money."

"Okay, but just hold on to this for an emergency," he insisted as he handed her $2,000.

She stuck the money in a drawer and said, "Baby, I'm going to Jessie's house. We are going to have a drink. I might stay over, I don't know."

He kissed her and went back to his room.

Tiffany was on the bed with just a long tee on. She asked Lil' A if he wanted her to spark the blunt up. He told her yeah, and then lit a stick of incense. He popped open a bottle of Moet. This was the first time Lil' A had bought Moet since having some with Papi. That's where he learned the name, so since he won all that money, he had to front and buy a bottle. Now Tiffany and Lil' A were just fucking. She was fine, but bummy. Lil' A was on the rise to becoming a ghetto super star, and Tiffany was becoming his freak girl. The two stayed there drinking and smoking.

Holding each other tightly while wrapped up in a moment of affection Tiffany began to rub Lil' A's back. Then they kissed. Lil' A started to kiss her perfect breasts, licking all the way down to her navel. As he looked in Tiffany's eyes, he knew she was hot, and was moaning because she was enjoying their foreplay. He motioned for her to lay back. As she was leaning back, he spread her legs. Slowly licking down her inner thighs, he could see her young tight pussy getting wet. Lil' A then started licking her pussy as Tiffany moans out, *"Yes!! A! Yes!!..."* A continues to lick as Tiffany pours out cum. After twenty minutes he stops, gets up and takes another sip of the Moet.

Lil' A had fucked Tiffany many times before, but he had never eaten her pussy, just like he had never given her money. This was the first time for both. As he put the bottle down, Tiffany just laid there because her legs were quivering. She had never sucked dick before, but that night Lil' A schooled her. He told her, never use your teeth. He said lick up and down, then put it in your mouth and suck. As she did what she was told, she was beginning to get into it. She found herself sucking the head more because she saw it made him feel good. She gagged a couple of times, but Lil' A told her, "Don't choke yourself. Take your time until you get used to it."

She did what she was told. That's what Lil' A liked about Tiffany. She did what she was told and did not give much argument. He liked that she was willing to learn how to please him. Tiffany continued sucking on his dick, but Lil' A couldn't cum. It was her first time and he wanted to cum so bad. So he laid Tiffany down on her back, grabbed both of her legs, and put them on her shoulders. Lil' A's dick was big for his age. He wanted enjoyment, but he also wanted to please Tiffany and not hurt her. Sucking his dick was a special treat for him because it was Tiffany's first time. She was a virgin at it, so it was a special moment for him. But now, he wanted to cum.

He kissed her, rubbed her pussy briefly, then slowly stuck it into her. He began to pump in and out as fast as a rabbit. Tiffany was feeling it too. It felt good to her. She began scratching his back. This was a real sensual moment. The pussy felt good to Lil' A. Tiffany's hands on his back also felt good to him. Just being with her and looking into her eyes, it all felt good. He was pumping so fast that he came, but he did not stop.

Then he turned her around. He wanted her on her knees. We call it doggy style, and that was what he wanted her in the position to do. He rammed it in hard, and it seemed as if Tiffany was trying to run up the bed. But Lil' A gripped her waist so she couldn't get away. Now Tiffany was feeling the passion. She was panting and feeling the full power of his dick.

She yelled, "A don't stop! Don't stop…!" Lil' A reached another nut. Before he was tired, he came in her four times prior to her passing out.

As Lil' A rolled another blunt, he turned on the television and began flipping through the cable channels trying to find something to watch.

The phone rang. "Hello," Lil' A answered.
The voice on the other end replied, "Yeah, you at the right spot. You know the police are asking for you, or should I say looking for you." Lil' A knew the voice once it spoke because it was his pops. "Stay put, because if you don't, you're going to jail," his father cautioned.
"What's it about?" Lil' A questioned.
His father, said, "I don't know, but I'll find out. Just stay home until I call."

He hung up. The first thing he did was grab for the bottle. He took four big gulps. By the last one, he was choking. He stood up and went to the window and began pulling on a blunt.

So now Lil' A was wondering who had seen anything or who would tell. At first, he was worried. He knew he had to find out who was telling. He also knew he had to wait. Little did he know about what was about to occur, or that it would be the beginning of his rise to kingpin status. Tiffany would be his main freak, and she would become his baby's mother so another saga would continue.

He knew something had to be done, so he reached out for Papi. When Papi met up with him the next day, he finally laid down the rules to Lil' A.

He said, "Look, you're getting older now and there's one thing, or should I say there are three things I will not allow. Papi had hard and fast rules that made sense to anyone who really wanted to move to the top of the game. These would be rules that would allow Lil' A to stay focused and not get sidetracked.

Now listen, "I don't want you to ever use drugs, other than weed," he explained. "Oh yeah, there's another rule," he added with a very serious look. "Most of all, I do not want you to steal. Now if you live by these rules, there's nothing that can break our friendship."

Lil' A sat still and listened to Papi.

Then Papi said, "Look, the police really don't have anything. It's just the fact that you were the last person who had a problem with those kids, so the projects are just talking..."

This made Lil' A feel a little better. His heart had been racing and his head wasn't clear. He didn't want to be locked up. Papi made him feel a lot better. But he knew he had to be careful. Papi cared about his young friend and wanted to help him as much as he could. Lil' A had saved him from being locked up and he wanted to do the same for him.

"Now Lil' A, who did you tell about this?" Papi questioned.

"Just two people, my pops and my man, Sleepy. Those are two people I can trust," he responded.

Papi then reached into a bag and pulled out a wad of money. He said, "Now Lil' A, this is seventy-five thousand. You hide this in your house. Now God forbid you get locked up and have to pay a lawyer. You tell your mother where this money is, okay?"

Lil' A said "Yes."

Papi said, "Here's two guns. Always carry one on you. I'm giving you a hundred and fifty grams of crack, plus two-hundred bundles of dope for testers, okay? So you don't sell shit, get someone else to sell it. Put a crew together, okay?"

Lil' A wondered how he should go about putting together a crew.

Anticipating the question, Papi answered, "It's easy to set one up. You've been in the projects growing up. Man, you should have an idea who should be trustworthy. So you snatch them up. Call me when everything is done."

Lil' A took the drugs and the money to his mother's house. He hid the money in his mother's closet, in a trunk where she kept her childhood memories. When he was done he took the fifty bags of heroin to his man, Sleepy. He was four years older than Lil' A, but he was one person he knew he could trust. As the two spoke, they lit a blunt.

Sleepy was a young father he already had two kids and that's why he used to hustle so hard to support them. Sleepy had to hustle to make it. He didn't have the support system that Lil' A had. Sleepy's mother died from a heroin overdose, so he intimately knew about the danger of drugs. He kept his mother's apartment after she died, and that's where he, his children and their mother, Tank, as everyone called her, lived.

Lil' A left all two hundred bundles with Sleepy and told to him come to his house the next night to let him know if he

A Father's Burden

liked the product and felt he could move it. The two boys finished the blunt and then Lil' A left. He stopped by Tiffany's house. When he got to her door, the music was playing loudly. It turned out to be Tiffany's cousin Booberlocks, who had just come home from jail. He answered the door. As he and Lil' A made eye contact, the first thing he thought was that this guy must be Tiffany's boyfriend.

Booberlocks said, "What up, you, must be Lil' A… so, you the one who got my little cousin all in love with you?" Tiffany walked into the room. She greeted Lil' A and asked if he had met her cousin.

He said, "Yeah."

She then said, "I always tell him about you."

Lil' A smiled. He started talking to Tiffany.

Then Booberlocks asked, "So, what you into?"

Lil' A said, "To tell you the truth, I ain't into nothing. But, I'm about to go to a whole new level."

Booberlocks said, "Oh Yeah! What's that?"

Lil' A said, "Well, I really don't want to talk about it yet; I'm just trying to make things happen."

Booberlocks said, "I'm feeling that. I like the way you talk."

Then Lil' A asked if he smoked.

He responded, "Yeah!"

Lil' A gave Booberlocks the weed and said, "Roll that up for us."

As soon as he finished, he said, "Let's go upstairs. My aunt would kill me if she catches me smoking."

Once they headed for the door, Tiffany said, "Where my two favorite men going? One is my husband and the other one is my cousin."

Booberlocks said, "You know cuz, we going to smoke a blunt…"

Tiffany cut him off and said, "Save me some."

She kissed Lil' A and the two boys walked out.

They sat on the staircase smoking, bonding, and getting to know each other a little better. Booberlocks began telling him about Riker's Island. Now that's where all the bad kids and adults go in New York City when they get locked up. It's a small island with multiple buildings, a place where your time could be served if it wasn't over two years. That's called the six building. They have C74, Beacon, C95 H.D.M, a girl's unit, and many more.

Everything else is just a hold over until you finish with your case. Either you win or you go up north to do hard time. So Booberlocks was sharing his little war stories from the Island. He told Lil' A how he had to fight for phone time. He talked about how he had to beat one kid up for trying to take his sneakers. Booberlocks shared about smoking weed and how one of the C.O. broads, meaning police, liked him and he couldn't wait to get back out there to Riker's Island to get her. Then he said he wanted to buy a Benz. Lil' A wondered how much a Benz cost, so he asked Booberlocks.

Booberlocks said, "Shit, about fifty thousand."

Lil' A asked, "How long would it take you to make fifty thousand?"

Booberlocks said, "If I go hard and have the work, meaning the right amount of drugs, I could make ten thousand a week. But I would have to keep the re-up going, so I'd say about three months."

As Lil' A was listening, he began to form an idea. He began thinking that his newfound friend might be the right person to have in his new venture.

Then he said, "I'm going to help you get that."

Booberlocks wasn't convinced. So he said, "Nigga, stop faking…!"

"I'm not faking or playing," Lil' A assured him. "There are just three things you could never do to me and you will

A Father's Burden

have a real friend. But if you cross me, I will be your worst enemy," he said, as he looked Booberlocks dead in the eyes to let him know he was for real.

They both stood quiet for a few seconds.

Then Booberlocks asked, "What are the three things?"

"Lil' A then told him what Papi had told him. "Never steal from me. Never use your own supply and never snitch...," he advised.

Booberlocks said, "Shit I will never do that, or should I say none of that."

Then the two boys gave each other a handshake *(or should I say a 'high five')* and a hug started a good relationship. Then Tiffany walked in and stood by the staircase, "I know you didn't smoke all the weed," she inquired.

Lil' A passed her the blunt, and asked, "Tiffany are you coming to my crib?"

She responded that she was chilling with her cuz.

Quickly interjecting, Booberlocks said, "Shit, you'd better go with him. I'm trying to get some from your girlfriend."

Tiffany laughed and said, "Okay, let me get my jacket baby and we can be out."

She took a few pulls on the blunt and walked out.

Lil' A asked Booberlocks if he had gone shopping. He responded by saying, "Yo, I'm fucked up. I'm waiting for my aunt to give me some money and I'm going to buy me twenty grams and get my money right."

Lil' A asked Booberlocks if he had a scale, to which he replied, yes. At that point Lil' A asked if he could borrow it for a couple days, and then he added, "Yo, just go buy some clothes with the money your aunt's giving you and when Tiffany comes home, she'll have something for you."

Booberlocks was shocked, but from the way Lil' A talked, he knew it was for real. As Tiffany came out ready to go, she kissed Booberlocks on the cheek.

"I'll see you tomorrow, cuz," she said.

"Okay," he said. He gave Lil' A dap, and continued. "I'll holla at you later... But wait, let me get that for you."

Tiffany stood shocked. She was puzzled because she saw that her cousin really liked Lil' A. Maybe it was because during his whole bid she had talked about him endlessly. Booberlocks never did let his little cousin mess with boys.

He passed Lil' A the scale and they walked down the steps and on to Lil' A's mother's house.

As they were walking and talking, Lil' A questioned, "Boo, look. If I was to go to jail would you ride with me?"

Tiffany answered, "Baby, I will do whatever you want me to do." She then added, "I know you have a lot of girls, but I'm confident that I'll always be in your heart. Just like I know you'll always be in mine."

Lil' A knew Tiffany was loyal to him, but he also knew that she was into the streets. However, they were and remained cool. Plus, she listened to him and Lil' A liked that a lot. Tiffany asked him what he and her cousin Booberlocks were talking about.

Lil' A immediately replied, "None of your business. Just know we're about to make a lot of money, ma."

She smiled and said, "A, you're crazy, but I love you. You better not shit on me."

When they got upstairs, He told her to roll up a blunt. He set up the incense so the weed smell wouldn't linger out of the room. Lil' A didn't want his mom to smell it. Yvette knew Lil' A smoked weed, but he just had respect for her

A Father's Burden

like that. Yvette would never see her son pull from the blunt. But she would always see him with chinky looking eyes. As Tiffany and Lil' A sat up in the room. They were smoking the blunt and watching tv the phone rang. It was another girl, but Lil' A was so smooth and slick. He had a way with words, just like his pops.

So he said, "Hello, who's this?"
The voice on the other end said, "Nigga, where you been?" As soon as he heard that nice soft voice, he knew it was Verwana... "Why you haven't been around? I thought we were going to the movies."
Lil' A said, "Oh, I forgot" as if she could see the look on his face that he was happy.
She asked, "A, why you not really talking?"
As Lil' A said nothing, Verwana's mind went wild. Then she informed, "You know it's Quanee's birthday..."

Now Verwana already had one daughter, she was going to be two-years-old. Tiffany thought that the baby was Lil' A's because when she tried to make a little scene, Lil' A made a face and checked her. Tiffany knew it was Verwana, his so-called baby's mother.

"Oh, I'm going to call you in a couple days," Lil' A told her.
Verwana said, "A, her birthday is in one week."
He restated, "I will call you in a couple of days. I'll try to have fifteen hundred dollars for you."
"What am I going to do with all that?" Verwana responded, somewhat caught off guard.
"Throw her a big birthday party," Lil' A said.
Verwana said, "A, you don't have to play or lie to me."
He said, "Yo, I got to go. I'll call you. Just make sure you be at the house, okay?"

Now everybody always thought that Quanee was Lil' A's baby, because Lil' A kept her in his mouth. Tiffany thought it too. But the truth of the matter was Verwana and Lil' A still had never been intimate. But she was feeling Lil' A hard. Quanee's real father was a dude named Keywee. Keywee was a fraud, and a straight sucker. As a matter of fact, he was a rat too. I will explain about that later.

But Keywee and Verwana broke up because he never brought Quanee anything. Plus, he was running around the projects messing with half the girls there. What's so funny is Keywee at one point, was messing with one chic who had five kids with different guys. Her last two kids, a boy and a girl, were from a dude named, Poe.

Poe went to jail because he shot three cops.

His name was ringing bells (meaning everybody knew him), especially on Rikers Island. So, I guess Keywee was open for her. Her name was, Pokey. She used to flirt with Lil' A too, but he never fucked her. However, the word in the projects was that Pokey sucks a mean dick. Later I'm going to tell you how Poe and Lil' A were going to bump heads because everyone thought he and Pokey were fucking.

You see Verwana was young, so she probably didn't know how to suck dick, but Lil' A wound up teaching her. But in this day and time if a girl sucked a dick well, nine times out of ten she will always have her way with any man on earth. Shit, the pussy could even be whack but if a girl could swallow a nut and suck good, she would win in the end.

After Lil' A hung up the phone with Verwana, Tiffany had a slight attitude. But smooth-talking Lil' A just knew what to say.

"Tiffany cut the bullshit out. That's my baby's mother. She was just reminding me that she needed money for the baby's birthday party," Lil' A scolded.

A Father's Burden

As he grabbed Tiffany and looked deeply into her eyes, he said, "Yo, I would never disrespect you in front of no bitch, except for my kid's mother. I got the utmost respect for her, just like I would have for you if you had my kid. No one could ever stop me from talking to you, or doing for you and my child."

Tiffany replied, "I understand you Boo. I can't wait to have your child because I can see that's the only thing that honestly affects you."

"What makes you say that?" Lil' A inquired.

"Your face lights up when you talk about kids and your kid's mothers," she explained.

Lil' A knew what she said was true, but would never admit it to himself. So he shoved her off and said, "Boo, you just high...," and passed the blunt right back to her.

He thought she would take a couple of pulls and would soon forget what had just happened.

As a couple of minutes passed, their high sunk in. That's when their hormones began to rise. "Oh, I've been practicing A," Tiffany shared and then tugged at his pants.

After pulling out Lil' A's penis, she stroked it over and over. As he began to rise, Tiffany put her whole mouth on the head of his dick and bobbed up and down. She spat her saliva all over his head, then sucked it dry. While she was on her knees, she picked up the pace and was moving her head up and down with more purpose.

Lil' A sat on the edge of the bed while Tiffany's hand was pulling on his dick, messaging up and down, with her head moving in the same motion. As Lil' A leaned back in enjoyment, he began to wonder where she learned her technique from. Soon afterward, he busts off, cumming all in her mouth. Tiffany swallowed it all and she didn't stop.

Lil' A grabbed her by the waist. He told her to get up and she did. Slipping out of her outfit so fast with her perfect body, Lil' A just looked at Tiffany. She jumped right on top of his dick and started riding him hard. A was now lying on his back and Tiffany was crushing down on him, with both feet on the bed, as she bounces up and down. Tiffany was skinny with a perfect body she was well endowed in all the right places. He was certainly able to say that she was very flexible. But Lil' A could see the strain in her face because she was riding him with his dick all the way in her.

As they both relaxed after a couple hours of fucking, they eventually fell asleep. The next morning seemed to have arrived far too soon. Lil' A awakened to the sound of his mother's voice. She was yelling his name, and just walked right into his room as he was putting on his boxers. Tiffany was lying there butt naked.

"Boy, cover her up and come to my room so I can talk to you before I go," Yvette ordered.

As Lil' A got up, he threw the sheet over Tiffany's body as he smacked her on the ass. Now she was fully awake. He told Tiffany to roll a blunt and she started smiling. While Lil' A walked out of the room Tiffany continued to smile at him and he smiled back. Tiffany still looked good, even after just waking up. Let's just say she could take the sleep out of a nigga's eyes. That's how fine she was.

"Hey ma what's up? I see you didn't come home last night?" Lil' A said as he entered his mother's room.
Yvette quickly replied. "Boy I'm grown..." Then she said, "I don't see any condoms on your floor. You better hope that girl don't get pregnant."
Lil' A said, "Now ma, we alright."

A Father's Burden

Smiling at her son, Yvette counseled, "Even though I want grandbabies, I want you to be careful and find the woman you really want to be the mother of your children. I want you to respect the woman you're with and have that woman love and care about you as much as I do. I only want the best for you son."

Yvette felt she had to say something to her son. She wasn't mad that he'd brought a girl over to spend the night, but she wanted Lil' A to respect her, the woman, and the house. As Yvette grew older, she had gotten better at managing his behavior. She cared about Lil' A and some of her protective nature was coming out.

Lil' A knew his mother cared about him and wasn't trying to give him a whole lecture. He knew she was only looking out for him. He loved her very deeply. Yvette never tried to press up on him too much, and he liked that about her. He would do anything in the world to please and help her.

This was a special day for Yvette. While she felt she had to talk to her son for a short while, she was excited about herself and what she had to do that day. She knew she had to find something to do, and it had to fix her situation. She had to find another job and bring some money into the house. She did not want to depend on her son to give her money like he had just given her. Yvette knew that Lil' A would always do what he could to help her. But she had always been an independent woman. Even when Lil' A's father tried to give her money early on in their relationship, she had always strived to make her own way.

A good woman, which was someone who had a purpose and a focus, had to be able to have an endgame to that purpose. She had to know where she was going. She had to be able to take care of herself. A strong woman is an independent woman. Yvette was grown, and she had to be able to take care of herself and be able to help Lil' A too. She still felt she had an obligation to him because he was her son. At her age, she felt she did not need to be depending upon her son at this stage in her life. She had to move along quickly. She told her son the good news. She had a job interview. She was excited about the opportunity. Then she told him that she would not be back. She was spending the weekend out. She didn't tell him that because she wanted his approval to be out. She did it to let him know not to expect her.

"Are you okay?" Yvette asked.
Lil' A assured, "Ma, I'm okay. Tiffany will cook."
"Okay baby, I'll call you later and let you know how it all went. There's food in there. Plus, your ass is grown." his mother said.

Tiffany walked in with a long shirt on. "Hi Ms. Yvette, how are you this morning?" she greeted.
Yvette kissed her, and then kissed her firstborn.
Addressing Tiffany, she said, "You're beautiful. I got to go."
She was addressing her son as much as she was addressing Tiffany. They did look beautiful together. Then she walked out of the room in a rush.

Lil' A walked into the living room and turned on the stereo. He peered out the window and saw a cab. It probably was the cab for his mother. Just then he began to get hard. He turned around and looked at Tiffany's perfect ass. Seconds later he was feeling under the long shirt, he put his hands on her ass, rubbed it, and then moved his hands to the front of her body. He moved toward the couch as he lifted her body and eased forward. Tiffany responded as if she wanted him too. *She just knows what to do*, Lil' A thought.

He turned her around wanting to approach her from behind. She bent over as if she knew exactly what he wanted. Lil' A rubbed his hand and index finger on her pussy and began to stimulate her clitoris with his middle finger. Now two fingers and his whole hand were on the pussy. As soon as he felt her wetness, he slid his dick inside her ramming her back and forth. With his left hand, he began gently pulling her hair.

You could say they made love all night. But by morning it was more primal. Lil' A just wanted to fuck. He was fucking her with the same passion he would use if he were playing basketball. He was putting his energy into it. They fucked for 20 minutes, before he finally came. Sweaty and tired they shared a brief laugh confirming their moments of sexual bliss.

The phone rang. Tiffany answered in a sexy voice. She asked, "Who would you like to speak to?"

The voice on the other end was Sleepy. "It's Sleepy. Who is this? What are you doing there? he drilled, "I want to speak to Adrian."

"He's sleeping," Tiffany informed him.

Sleepy responded, "Tell him I'm on my way up there." She hung up.

Lil' A awakened and asked, "Who's that?"

Tiffany told him it was Sleepy and that he was on his way over. She smiled as she kissed him, and then told him she was going to jump in the shower.

"Okay," he said.

Ten minutes after he had sparked a blunt, the buzzer rang.

Lil' A went to the intercom, pushed the button and asked, "Who is it?"

The voice on the other end replied, "Sleepy."

Chapter Five

Lil' A buzzed Sleepy in and stood by the door to look out of the peep hole to see if anyone else was with him. It was something Lil' A had conditioned himself to do. It was just another cautious step that he had learned. As Lil' A saw Sleepy walk up, he opened the door. The two gave each other five. He closed the door and locked it behind Sleepy. They walked to the living room to sit down. Lil' A took a couple of pulls on the blunt and then passed it to Sleepy. Sleepy did the same. It was some good stuff, or *The Bomb* as we would call it.

Sleepy said, "Damn man, that shit is some killer. Where did you get that from?"

Lil' A answered, "Elliott place."

Sleepy questioned, "Damn, you got it like that?"

"Yeah, you know that Hershey Bar," said Lil' A.

As he was about to give his report on his sales venture, Sleepy said, "A, man wherever you got that dope from is crazy. Yo, I gave out only twenty-five bundles and I sold the rest. In fact, I only got about two bundles left."

Lil' A said, "Damn, that shit was fast."

Sleepy then responded, "Yo, A, wherever you get that from, you need to get a lot."

"Okay...," said Lil' A, "Just give me four hours and I'll be right back at your crib."

Sleepy counted the money out and paid Lil' A. He had the money for the extra dope he was supposed to give out as well. So he and Lil' A split the profit down the middle. They kept on smoking until turning their attention to Tiffany walking into the room with just a long shirt on, and her long hair in a ponytail. Both men stare at her, with her skin glowing and her body half damp from taking a shower. Tiffany had a big smile on her face.

"What's up, Sleepy?" Tiffany greeted.

As she walked out to a back room Sleepy said, "Damn, A, she is looking finer and finer every day. And she looks like she's getting crazy thick. I know it's because you're blazing her with that dick. It looks like she's pregnant or something."

Lil' A said, "Naw she ain't pregnant, but I am hitting her crazy with the dick though."

Both men gave each other five and began to laugh. Then Sleepy commented, "A, she a fine little broad though. You need to get her pregnant and really lock her ass down."

Taking Sleepy's advice into consideration Lil' A in agreement said, "Yeah, I'm thinking about it."

"Tiffany really does love you, A. She's always hollering your name, plus everybody's trying to get at her. But she consistently repeats, *I'm A's wife and all of you niggas is wasting your time and your lines."*

Tiffany came back into the room. First, she looks at Lil' A, then at Sleepy. After looking at them both, she glared at the table where she saw a large pile of money. She knew they had been talking business and that Sleepy had brought Lil' A the money.

Sleepy said, "Yo, A, I'm out. I'll see you later. I'm gone so I can knock off these couple of joints I got left. I'll be at my crib waiting for you." They both gave each other another five and a hug to show their love and respect for one another.

When sleepy left, Lil' A asked, Tiffany to lock the door. She did. Then he picked up the phone to call Papi.

The voice on the other end of the line said, "Hello…! Hey Lil' A, what's up…? Hold on, I'll get him for you."
It was Papi's girl. She already knew Lil' A's voice and who he was.
Papi answered, "Hey A what's popping baby?"
"Nothing, but we need to talk," Lil' A informed him.
Papi said, "I was just on my way out. So I'll be there in forty minutes. Okay?"
"Lil' A said, "Okay!"

After he hung up from talking with Papi, Tiffany glared hard into his face. It was what Lil' A thought was a *stupid look.*
He immediately told her, "Yo, cut those dirty looks out."

Lil' A didn't ask Tiffany why she was looking at him in that manner, but he could only guess that she didn't completely approve of what he was doing. However, he knew, that Tiffany loved him too much to meddle in his business. Lil' A went into his room and came back with a Timberland box. "Yo, give this to your cousin," he instructed, pulling out a 9-millimeter pistol and a big sandwich bag that had crack in it.
Tiffany stood wide-eyed and didn't say a word.

Lil' A then asserted, "Baby, I told you I'm about to be rich. If you remain loyal, you will be going places because

A Father's Burden

you're with me. We are about to see the bright lights and enjoy some of the finer things in life. You will be bright too just like the lights in Times Square..."

He finished giving Tiffany her instructions, and then told her to call him as soon as she got home.

"Then put your cousin on the phone, okay?"

"Yeah!" She answered,

Lil' A counted out some of the money. Once he counted out two thousand dollars, he told Tiffany to split it down the middle.

"Take a G apiece. Tell him it's on me and the gun is extra."

She kissed him and said, "Yes baby."

Tiffany went out the door, but knocked on it seconds after she left.

Lil' A opened the door. Stopping in his tracks he suddenly said, "Damn! What did you forget?"

Grabbing his nuts, she started kissing on his neck, and then she said, "This."

Lil' A got hard as a rock. Tiffany then went down on him. As she instantly began giving him head. He started moving back and forth as if he was fucking her pussy, but instead he was fucking her mouth. Minutes later, he bursts with a sigh. *Ahhh!* He moans, as Tiffany keeps sucking and swallowing her man's nut. She finally slows down after every drop seemed to be drained from his dick.

Tiffany got up off her knees, smiled, and said, "I love you. Thank you, baby. Call me later because it seems I'm going to be busy."

Lil' A said, "Okay!"

She wiped her mouth, stuck a piece of gum in it and kept on moving out the door.

As he locked the door behind her, Lil' A took a deep breath and remarked to himself that he has a real trooper for real. Then he relit the half-blunt he and Sleepy had been smoking on earlier. Twenty minutes later, the phone rang.

He said, "Hello. Who's this?"

"It's me, baby," Tiffany answered. She then said, "Boo, I did what you said. Here's my cousin."

Her cousin, Booberlocks greeted, "Hello! Yo, what's good?"

Lil' A responded, "Booberlocks, what's good. Yo, did Tiff give you that?"

He answered, "Yeah!"

Lil' A then expressed, "Yo, I'm trying to help you get that Benz."

Booberlocks responded, "Yeah. I see you're about that. But yo, what is this going for?"

Responding Lil' A said, "Yo, we got to pay for what it cost and all the profit we split right down the middle. So, I guess you can say we are partners."

Booberlocks agreed, "Yeah. I'm feeling that."

Lil' A then informed. "Oh, about the nine, (talking about the gun), and the frags, that's a gift. So welcome home."

Booberlocks said, "Thanks. Alright, here go Tiffany."

Tiffany took the phone and said, "Boo, I'll catch up with you later. I love you."

Lil' A said, "I love you too."

Lil' A waited for Papi to show up. A few minutes later a car horn blew. Lil' A looks out the window and sees Papi sitting in a Nissan Quest minivan. He noticed that Papi was always in a different car. He had only seen a couple of his cars twice. Lil' A walks out of his mother's house, he locks the door behind him and walks toward the van. The side door

A Father's Burden

opens. Papi is sitting in the back with two other dudes sitting in the front.

"Papi, what's up?" Lil' A greeted.

Papi, replies with a head nod and Lil' A can feel that something was wrong. It's written all over Papi's face. He gets into the car. Papi closes the sliding door and addresses Lil' A. He says, "A, we'll talk about whatever you have to talk about later. Right now, is not the time."
Lil' A caught on fast. He did not say a word.
"I want you to stay with me for a few hours, Okay?" Papi advised him.
"Yeah," was the response.
Papi asks, "Are you hungry?"
"Not really."
Papi passes Lil' A a blunt. "Here, light this up so you can work up an appetite."

Lil' A lights the blunt and Papi signals the driver to pull off. They were headed toward Washington Heights, where they wound up at a Spanish restaurant. They walked in and headed straight to the back to a special table prepared for them. A young Spanish girl walked up and greeted them, then kissed and hugged Papi. It wasn't superficial. They were really serious – the kiss and the hug. You could tell that Papi and the girl were related.

Papi then looked and turned to Lil' A and said to the woman, "This is who I want you to meet. This is Lil' A..." Turning his head toward the woman, Papi says, "Lil' A, this is my sister, Angie."
Angie smiles and says, "Hola (*hello* in Spanish)."

Lil' A could not take his eyes off her. She was beautiful. He had never seen a girl that looked so good in person. She could have been a model. When Angie looked him dead in the eyes, he seemed to be mesmerized just looking at her. She had him the first time they spoke.

Papi broke the spell when he asked Lil' A, "What's up?"
"Oh, nothing!" Lil' A replied pulling out of his temporary trance.

Papi turned to Angie and said, "You know what I like."
"Papi, are you okay," Angie asked. "You only come to eat when you are mad at somebody," she continued. She turned to address Lil' A as she said, "Don't worry, I got you. I'm going to give you your best plate of food ever."

Lil' A said, "Okay!"

Then he began thinking about what Angie said to her brother because he knew something was wrong. Angie could sense it and he could sense it too. Seconds later, out came the champagne. They all started to drink. During their session in the restaurant, Papi got up a couple of times to use the phone.

One of the guys started talking to the driver in Spanish. Lil' A did not understand what they were saying. But he somehow knew they were talking about money. One had said the word, *dinero*, which is a word for a form of currency in the Spanish language.

So now Lil' A knows Papi is mad because of some money. They stayed in the restaurant for a while. Night was beginning to pass. Angie stood behind the counter. Then without warning, Papi went to the very back of the restaurant and told Angie to go get A.

Sitting at the table, Lil' A couldn't help but to focus his eyes on Angie walking toward him. His heart began to beat from excitement because she was so bad (good looking). She

A Father's Burden

arrived at the table and whispered into his ear. "My brother wants you to come to the back."
She pulled his hand and directed him to the back. Angie didn't smell like food. She smelled like money.

Angie looks at Lil' A, and in Spanish she says, "Papi chulo."
That phrase is a compliment, meaning *pretty boy*, *good looking*, or *Mack daddy*. Angie liked Lil' A. She thought he was a nice, good looking man. Although he didn't fully understand what she said, Lil' A did get a sense that Angie liked him. He was feeling her, as much as she was feeling him. Finally, he got the heart to really talk to her, so he asked about the meal he had just eaten.

"That was a good ass meal you gave. What was it?"
Angie smiled and said, "I can't tell you."
"Why not…?"
Angie then assures him, "Don't worry. My next dish will be ten times better and it gets better and better," squeezing his hand.

Now Lil' A wasn't stupid. He knew that she was flirting with him. And when she said the meals would get better and better, that was a message indicating that they would be seeing each other in the future. Many meals meant more than once.

When they reached the back, Papi was on the phone. As Angie walked out, on the sneak tip, she grabbed Lil' A's butt. Lil' A was shocked. He turned around. Angie kept her eyes on him, gave him a wink and smiled seductively.

Now Lil' A *knew* she liked him. He thought to himself how wonderful it would be to be with her. However, little did he know that Angie was way older than him. She just looked young, and she was in the game hard. Angie was her brother's partner. He didn't know he was in for a world of surprises if he got with Angie. Lil' A had no clue whatsoever.

As a matter of fact, Angie knew more about Lil' A than Lil' A knew about her. She had known about him long before they met. Her brother had told her about him, and how he had saved him from being arrested. Another thing Lil' A didn't know was that the other guy in the car with Papi that night was her boyfriend. The guy that took all the weight for the problem that night. He tapped out and took the time receiving ten years flat. The police wanted him to tell on the passenger who got away. But he didn't and wouldn't, so they gave him fifteen years instead.

So Angie knew about Lil' A. She also knew that he had killed two dudes. So, when she first saw him, she knew he was going to be a star. Plus, he was young, so she could play mind games with him. All she had to do was suck, fuck, cook, and shower Lil' A with money. She knew he would do whatever for her. Then when she finally saw him, she was like, *Damn! This little black boy is so sexy. Oh, I must have him.* Plus, she knew that black men were known to have big dicks. She couldn't wait to perform freaky sexual positions with him. What takes the cake, the other man owed some money, so she knew that Papi wanted Lil' A to take care of it.

She had her little plan. But she knew her brother liked this boy a lot. Still, she wanted him. Papi hangs up the phone.
He says to Lil' A, "What's up?"
"Nothing, Papi..."
"You like my sister's restaurant?"
"Yeah!" Lil' A said, asking Papi if he had bought it for her.
Papi laughed. "How old you think she is?" he then asked.
Lil' A said, "I don't know."

A Father's Burden

"Guess," Papi insisted.
"25," Lil' A quickly guessed.
Papi says, "For real?"
"Yeah!" Lil' A affirms.
Then Papi started to laugh. He then tells Lil' A, "She's 35 years old."
Lil' A was in shock. Papi then mentions, "I saw that look you gave her." Giving him a serious look Papi then warns him, "A, you know I like you a lot... That's my sister, she's just like me. But she is crazy, rich, and out of control. A, you are going to go far in this game because you are a good kid. But with her, she will steer you wrong. Plus, you got that little fine girl, Tiffany. Start it with her because my sister is too much for you."

Lil' A understood what Papi was saying, but it was making him feel like a little kid and he didn't like it. But only if he would listen, Papi was trying to save him because he was really the boss, plus Angie was much wilder than Papi.

Then Lil' A states, "Papi, I finished all that dope you gave me. I need more." Papi was surprised. "I should finish the crack by tomorrow night."

Papi replied, "Yo, Lil' A, well when you go home, I will double everything I gave you and you can pay me for everything then." Papi stood quietly and then sprung the question. "Lil' A, I need a favor."

"Sure, anything..."

Papi said, "You seen that fucking guy who was sitting at the table with us..."

Lil' A interrupted the sentence with an acknowledgement. "Yeah...!"

"Well, he owes me two million dollars but only gave me half, and he says he doesn't have any more work left. He has a lot of stuff I could take, but I know his wife and kids. And I just got the word he is working with the police. That's how they knew I was coming to the Bronx that night. But I got away thanks to you."

This was a lot to hear in one short burst. First, he had to hear about Papi's sister and how she was much older than what he thought, and how she was much wilder and simply not right for him. That information made him feel young and incapable of handling himself. He wanted that older woman, maybe even more so now because he learned that she was much older than him. But he would listen to Papi at least for the time being.

And even though Papi had made him feel like a little boy while talking about his sister, he was beginning to think that Papi was about to ask him to do a big thing. Not on a level of little boy status, but to help a friend with a serious problem type thing. His friend, so he thought, sounded as if he wanted him to do a manly thing. But he did not want to jump to any conclusions.

Lil' A just stood there shocked. Then the next shocking thing came out of Papi's mouth. They were the words that Lil' A thought might come. Papi wanted him to do a major favor. An ultimate favor. One that would test their friendship.

Then Papi said the words, "Well, I need you to go with my sister. I want you to kill him and his wife."

Lil' A stood there silently for a minute. Killing the man was one thing. He had killed two guys before and didn't regret it. However, killing a female was something else. Besides, these people had not done anything to him. When he killed before, he had done so because one of the men he killed had done something to him and the man owed a debt of payback. This was different. He was certainly capable of killing, and Papi was indeed his friend. Lil' A had said he would do anything for his friend.

Doing a favor was one thing, but he really didn't want to kill a woman because he thought of his mother. But he knew he couldn't tell Papi no.

Lil' A said, "Yeah! Anything you need."

Seconds later, Angie walked in smiling. She spoke to Papi in Spanish. From the sound of her voice, you could tell they were agreeing about something. Then she yelled at Papi and walked out.

On her way out, Angie said, "A, when you are ready, come to my car in the back, it's the one to the left."

"You see, I told you my sister was crazy," Papi said to Lil' A. As he continued, "She is going with you and she is going to kill his wife."

Lil' A's eyes opened wide. Instantly expressing, "I'd rather do it myself."

Papi replied, "She wants to do it so let her do it. I told you that bitch is crazy."

One side of Lil' A was relieved. The other side was somewhat indifferent. He couldn't believe Angie was so bad. He couldn't believe she had all this money because she was a gangster bitch straight from Puerto Rico.

Then Papi said, "Lil' A, I will call you in the morning to bring you the rest of your stuff."

Lil' A said, "Okay."

Papi gave him a high five and he walked out through the back exit of the restaurant.

As he walked out, there was an all-black Mercedes Benz with dark-tinted windows. There was a little *whirr*, the sound of a power window as the driver's side window rolled down.

Angie was there with a pair of sunglasses and black leather gloves on.

She teased, "Come on, get in, or are you scared?"

Lil' A made a face as if to say, *Are you crazy?* He walked to the passenger side and Angie unlocked the door. He got in and she sped off. Angie didn't say a word. She wanted the young boy to get turned out. She then hit a button, and a familiar noise captured Lil' A's attention. Turning to see where the sound was coming from. He knew the sound well from being in the car with Papi. He knew it was the sound of a stash box opening.

Then Angie instructed, "Pull those two guns out." He did and then she closed the stash box. "Which one you want?" she casually asked.

Lil' A replies, "It doesn't matter."

Angie then decides, "Well, you take the chrome one and act like it's me. I'll take the black one and act like it's you."

She smiled after making that statement. Lil' A passed her the black gun. She took it and put it in her lap. When they came to the next red light, she pulled off one of her gloves and rubbed his face. A chill ran down Lil' A's body because he had fallen in love with this girl the first time, he laid eyes on her. Angie already knew what she was going to do with Lil' A. He quietly let his emotions run through his body. On one hand, he really loved this girl and wanted her. On the other, he felt that she could be cold-blooded. As Papi had told him, she was different. And somehow, that was a turn-on too.

This ride would be one of Lil' A's worst, or should I say, most *crucial* mistakes.

A Father's Burden

Angie's cell phone rang. Next, she began to speak in Spanish and every few seconds she would wink at Lil' A. He would just smile as wild thoughts such as how she looked naked, or who she looked like, would run through his mind. She looked like J-Lo, but her body was better than Verwana, and she favored Shakira. His mind raced through thinking of every bad Spanish girl he could recall. Then he reached into his coat pocket. He pulled out a blunt and rolled it so he could spark it up.

Angie quickly reacted. "Did I say you could light that in my car?" Lil' A made a stink face prior to her saying, "Go ahead. You can do whatever you want."

Lil' A smiled. Angie thought the face he had just made was a sexy smile. It turned her on so much she hung up the phone.

As he inhaled the smoke from the blunt, Angie asked, "When you going to pass it?"

Lil' A responded, "I didn't know you smoked."

He handed it to her.

She took three pulls and asked, "What's that?"

He said, "It's weed."

"Baby, throw that bullshit out," Angie instructed. She hit a switch; a side window came down and she told him, "Go ahead, throw that bullshit out."

He did what he was told. She rolled the window back up and hit two buttons. Another stash spot in the car opened in a different place. This time it was in the glove compartment.

Angie said, "Look in there, it should be a little black Gucci bag...." she said. A few minutes later she asked, "You got another blunt on you?"

Lil' A replied, "Yeah!"

Very coyly Angie said, "So, roll us up a nice phat one and baby when you are with your hoochie mama you smoke that bullshit. When you're with me, you'll be doing the best of everything, whether we drink, smoke, eat, or fuck..." He made another face. Lil' A was just shocked. Angie continued her brief lecture because she knew she had his full attention. Angie asked, "You understand me?"

    Lil' A replied, "Yeah, I hear you."
    Angie then inquires, "Why you making those faces?"
    Lil' A asked, "What faces?"
    She replies, "You know what I'm talking about, but I just love that face."
    He finished rolling the blunt, and then sparked it up. After the first two pulls he began to cough.
    "This that weed your brother sparked up with me."
    Angie announces, "I know, it's mine." He just looked at her shocked again.

    The two drive on the highway for a while, heading to upstate New York. She got off on the exit called, Spring Valley.

    "Okay baby, enough of the games. Now it's time for business," Angie then declares.

    They drove a couple more blocks. They pulled up to a nice house. Angie had on her sunglasses and gloves. Lil' A was wearing a leather jacket, some Timberland boots, and a black Champion hoodie. They walked up to the door. Angie rang the doorbell and a female answered.

    She said, "Hola, Angie."
    Angie answered back, "Hola."
    As they entered the house, the two women continued to speak in Spanish.

A Father's Burden

Minutes later the man who was in the car with Lil' A and Papi earlier, came out of a room. His eyes locked onto Lil' As eyes. The man had the eyes of death as if he knew he was about to die. He began to beg.

He cried, "Angie please, please!"

Angie said something in Spanish, but all Lil' A knew was she said something meaning *money*. The man continued to beg, and Lil' A knew he was begging because he knelt. His wife came back into the room. Angie reached into her bag and pulled out her gun. Lil' A followed her lead, pulling his out as well. As the man tried to jump, Lil' A pistol whipped him hard to the floor. He began to cry profusely, Lil' A hurriedly hit him again and again. Angie liked the response Lil' A had. Then she asked the man again, but this time in English.

"Where's my money?"
"Okay, okay," the crying man relented. Immediately sending his wife to get it. "Bring it all," he told her.
The couple looked at each other with tears in their eyes. The feeling in the room was that of death. The wife went upstairs to get the money. Lil' A asked Angie if she wanted him to follow her.
"No," she said. "What if she tries to get a gun," he suggested.
Angie replied, "That bitch is a square."
The man started to beg again. But this time he only begged for the life of his wife to be spared. "Angie please don't kill her. Just kill me. She's pregnant with my baby...," he said, Angie just looked at him.
Angie said, "Papi, make me happy." She then whispered into Lil' A's ear, "As soon as I see all the money, kill this piece of shit."

The woman came downstairs with two black suitcases. Angie opened them they both were full of money. She winked at Lil' A for the final frontier.

Boom! Boom! Boom!
Three shots rang out as he shot the man in his head. As blood spilled out all over the floor, the wife screamed. Crying furiously, she ran toward his body, landing right on top of her husband. Angie started laughing. The girl turned to Angie and yelled, "Bitch!" And spit in Angie's face.

Angie wiped the spit off her face, then shot the girl nine times in the head. Angie laughed with excitement as if she was having an orgasm each time, she pulled the trigger.

Lil' A was shocked at how she did it with such ease.

Angie then commanded, "Get those bags, baby."

He grabbed them and they walked out of the house. Angie hit her alarm, and the trunk opened. Lil' A put the bags in, then hopped into the front seat. They sped off headed back to New York, only stopping once to get gas. Angie told the man to fill it up, then asked Lil' A if he had another blunt. He said no, so she went inside the gas station and bought some. She came back to the car with two boxes of Philly Blunts.

She asked, "Baby, do you know how to drive?"

"Yeah," he lied.

Not wanting to look like a chump in front of Angie.

Taking him at his word, she said, "You drive baby, but roll us up one first."

He sat in the driver's seat and rolled up the blunt. Angie just stayed in the passenger seat, took off her shoes exposing her toes that were nice and neat. Her toenails were nicely polished, and she smelled so good.

As Lil' A looked at her feet, Angie asked, "Are you a virgin or something?"

He made a face and yelled, "Hell no!"

Angie directed, "So stop acting so shy."

He responded, "I'm not shy, but you look so good."

She smiled at him and said, "You do too!" Angie then asked, "Do you have a girl or any kids?"

He said, "Yeah, something like that. I got one child and a little girlfriend."

The gas station attendant signaled that he was done. She paid him and they were off. Now Lil' A had never driven before, but he always watched when people drove. He pulled right off onto the highway.

Angie said, "You look good driving."

Lil' A just blushed as he thought, *I can't wait to buy my own car.* Angie sparked up the blunt, inhaled, and then kissed A on his cheek. A chill ran down his body. She then put her tongue in his ear. Lil' A was excited and began to swerve. They started to talk. It was mostly about Lil' A. Angie wanted more insight into her new trophy. As the road sign said New York and New Jersey, she directed him to turn to the right and follow the New Jersey sign.

Lil' A asked, "Where we going?"

Angie retorted, "Stop asking me so many questions. You're with me until I say you can go."

As they came off the ramp, they rolled up to a toll booth. Angie directed him to stay in the left lane and push the button.

She said, "You know I got an Easy Pass."

He responded, "I hear that hot shit."

He pushed the button and the toll arm raised. The Benz went right through. They smoked weed and finished their conversation. Lil' A found himself driving for another four hours. Angie lived deep in New Jersey. First, they pulled up into a boat yard where multiple boats were docked. He looked in amazement. Angie knew he was young, but ready. She just had to work with him a little bit.

Chapter Six

Looking at the large boats in amazement, Lil' A inquired, "Damn! How much do these boats cost...?"

Angie quickly responded, "From $250,000 to $5 million. I own this whole dock, plus that boat over there is my yacht. It's worth $5 million."

Now Lil' A was really impressed.

After a slight gasp he remarked, "Damn ma, this shit is phat." He stared at the yacht that Angie had pointed out.

"Don't worry baby. I'm going to take you on it this summer so we can chill on it in Miami Beach, and I can fuck the shit out of you. Angie said with a smile. Now she really had him going. Angie knew Lil' A was impressed with her. She pushed up hard on him and wrapped her arms around his neck. She kissed him as he pulled back. She asked, "What's wrong?"

Lil' A stated, "Your brother! I look up to him like a father. He's my man. I can't do this." Angie didn't like those words. She got mad. She responded, "I'm the boss. He does what I say. I run the family. Without me he wouldn't have any money."

Although he was impressed and earlier had imagined himself with her, Lil' A gathered himself and showed some strength. He said, "Ma, I feel all that you're saying, but I got too much respect for him. And if he says I could then I'll do whatever you want me to do. But only if he says yes, or I won't feel right at all."

She turned away. Lil' A knew he hurt her so he wrapped his arms around her. He whispered in her ear, "Ma, I'm a soldier. I just can't go behind my man's back and do something like that, because if it were me, I would kill a man."

Angie looked skyward. What he had just said meant so much to her. She had seen Lil' A as a loyal boy who was going to go far. She thought to herself, *I got to have him.* She turned back toward him and planted a kiss on his lips and moaned, "Fine."

She opened the trunk and asked Lil' A to pull out the two suitcases. He took them out and put them on her boat. She then stopped the car in front of the parking lot and got into another Benz, a white one that was larger than the one they had ridden in. It was the two-door 500, with some 22-inch rims on it. The black Benz was a four-door 420.

She handed him the keys to the white Benz and said, "Here baby… you drive that one and follow me."

As the two cars made their way onto the highway, Lil' A switched the radio on and tuned into Hot 97. He was listening to this Funk Master Flex mix-up. He couldn't wait for his turn to shine. He knew his time was near because he had the right people around him. What he didn't know was that his only mistake would be falling in love with Angie. Why didn't he listen to Papi?

As they were driving along, thoughts ran through Angie's mind. Despite his response to her, she knew she could get him in control. She felt that she could have whatever she wanted. And now, she had made Lil' A her target. She wanted him. She thought to herself, *This little*

A Father's Burden

fine motherfucker. How is he going to deny me? Oh, I'm going to turn him out! I love his style. And I love the way he just shot that punk in the head. I want to give him a baby. I'm going to give him everything he wants. He's mine.

Angie was squarely focused on conquering Lil' A when her phone rang.
Ring. Ring. Ring.

When she answered, it was Papi. "Hello...," he greeted, The voice on the other end said, "Angie, what's up?"
She was mad. "Nothing...!" She answered.
Papi asked, "How did everything go?"
She responded, "Just the way I planned. Too bad your punk ass...!"
Papi replied, "I don't want to argue with you, where's Lil' A?"
"We're on the way to my house."
"Why are you doing this? He is a young man. I like him a lot."
"Well I do too," Angie answered with an attitude.
Papi tried to raise his voice, but she checked him right away. In Spanish she said, "Motherfucker I call the shots. You're a punk. I want him with me. I like his style, but he won't do anything unless you say it's okay."
Papi asserted, "Well I won't say anything."
Angie threatened, "Don't play with me or I will tell your wife about your other two kids, then I will kill the bitch myself. So you better not give him any sign. Shit just let him know it's okay. Do you understand me?"

He said, "Okay." Now Papi wasn't mad at Lil' A. He didn't blame him for anything. He was just more afraid of his sister. Angie, the bitch is crazy. She's killed her last three husbands. She killed the first one for cheating on her with the maid. She killed the second one because he kept going back to his other baby's mother and she killed the last one because he stole from her.

Papi thought, or should we say *knew*, that she was going to kill the one that was locked up because she feared he might snitch. Angie hated snitches. He remembered how when he and his sister were back in Puerto Rico in the San Juan jungle, the feds locked their father up because their uncle told on him. The two of them, his father's wife and his uncle, were sleeping together. Papi thought back to that night. Angie walked in the room on those two. They were fucking. He remembered how his father's own brother and wife wouldn't even talk to him.

Angie and Papi's mom died in a car accident when they were 7 and 5-years-old. Three years later is when Angie, then 10-years-old, walked up and opened the door and saw her uncle and her father's wife fucking. As her stepmother screamed, Angie closed the door and ran to her father's basement where he had a lot of guns. She grabbed a small, fully automatic Israeli Uzi, and put the clip in. Angie knew how to do it because her father had shown her how to shoot. She cocked the slide back, walked back upstairs again, and then pushed open the door. They were still fucking. This time her uncle was getting it from the backside. He was so involved that he didn't hear the door open. Angie stood there for a moment with the Uzi behind her back.
When her uncle finally turned around, he jumped up as if to run toward Angie. As soon as one foot hit the floor, Angie pulled the Uzi from behind her back. She pulled the trigger and the rapid fire sounded like a roll of firecrackers going off. Thirty shots hit her uncle. The stepmother was screaming. Papi came running to the room because he had heard the shots and the screams. He came to a stop behind Angie. He saw his uncle laid out on the floor.

A Father's Burden

He stood in shock as his stepmother laid on the bed crying and saying, "Papi, tell her to put it down!" Angie just stood there smiling.

"This is for papa you bitch," she threatened. The stepmother started to scream again. Angie let off another 30 shots. As she stood there looking at all the blood, she turned to her brother and said, "Let's go."

Papi couldn't move, so she walked out, and then came back moments later and grabbed her little brother. She went to the phone and called her father's partner. He came over and dumped the bodies the next day. The following week, the partner's wife took Angie and Papi to see their father. From that time on, she was the boss.

Angie rose to keep her father's name alive, but Papi was scared to death to kill. However, he had seen his sister kill a lot of people. She killed people who owed her father money. She even slept with older men so she could kill them. Because of her strength and cold-blooded attitude, her father made her the boss. But he told her to not let anything happen to her brother.

Your heart is like your mothers, but your brother's got brains like me. Just always give him what he wants, Okay? Her father told her.

Agreeing Angie said, "Okay."

That flashback reminded him of why Angie was really the boss. She was a cold-blooded bitch who would not stop at anything to get what she wanted.

Snapping out of his moment of daydreaming, Papi told his sister *okay*. Then Angie told him to call the phone in the white Benz. Papi knew the number, so he hung up from Angie and just sat for a few seconds wondering what Lil' A did and how he could save him because he knew his sister was crazy. For some reason, he thought it might even be too late.

He thought Lil' A could be the next superstar. Well, so be it. Papi took a deep breath and dialed the number. Lil' A was bobbing his head to the beat playing on the radio when his phone rang. It rang a couple of times before he answered, "Hello. What's up?"

Papi asked, "What you doing?"

Lil' A answered, "Nothing. I'm just following your sister in her other car."

Papi said, "Oh! I didn't know you could drive."

Lil' A responded, "To tell you the truth, I can't. I've always watched other people driving, so I picked it up quick."

Papi laughed.

Then Lil' A said, "Papi, I look at you like a pops. We've become very close...." Papi already knew Lil' As loyalty. He stopped him.

Papi said, "Just listen and make sure you listen good. You're in deep now... I mean there's still a lot you have to learn, but it will come in time. A my sister is really crazy. She's in a power struggle. She has everything, but she still seems to want more. That's why I never really wanted her to meet you. But, as you know, I had to take care of that problem you and she just handled. But A, I won't lie to you, I was scared. That's why I came to get you. But she always wanted to meet you. So that's why I couldn't keep you separated for long. And now she acts like you're in her eyesight and she wants you. A, do you hear me...?"

Lil' A responded and then Papi continued, "Don't let her sucker you no matter what from out the gate. Always stand on your own two feet. If you show signs of weakness, she will run all over you. So it's okay, you can mess with my sister."

Lil' A contested, "Papi, I just can't disrespect you..."

A Father's Burden

Papi reassured, "Don't worry, you're not. She's the boss. Let's just hope you can change her."

That last statement stayed in Lil' A's head. Then Lil' A commented, "I got the money for you."

The response was, "Baby boy, you're in too deep now. Keep that because Angie is really fucking testing your manhood. So I hope you're ready."

Lil' A said, "Okay"

Papi then said, "But you owe me a trip this summer and it might cost you about $200,000.

Lil' A quickly argued, "Papi, I don't have that type of money."

Papi's response was, "Don't worry. It's going to come fast and for the record, make sure you find a spot where nobody, *I mean nobody*, knows about. And save a lot of money. You hear me, boy?"

Lil' A exclaimed, "Yeah!"

He'd never heard Papi sound so real except for the first time he saved him from going to jail. He sounded so scared now, but ever so real. So Lil' A knew Papi wasn't playing.

Papi said, "Lil' soldier, I'll see you later. I might come over to my sister's house and smoke some of that good shit with you."

Lil' A laughed and said, "Aight! I can't wait." Then he hung up the phone. Papi then called Angie back.

"I hope you really get what you are looking for. It's done, but don't hurt my little man. I really, really, like him," Papi expressed.

Angie snapped, "Shut up punk, I got everything I want – you by my side, all the money I'll ever need, and now I'm about to make you an uncle – so shut up and stop being a punk and roll with it."

She hung up the phone.

Minutes later they were pulling up into the driveway of her mini mansion. Lil' A was amazed at how large it was. Angie had 10 bedrooms, four and-half bathrooms, two dining rooms, three living rooms, and a Jacuzzi that led into a 15ft swimming pool. The house looked like one that a rapper would have. Angie took Lil' A to her master bedroom. The room was red with white Russian carpets, a double-size king bed, a flat screen TV that was 67 inches, and three different walk-in closets.

She said, "Get comfortable baby. I got to take a shower."

As Lil' A rolled up a blunt, Angie showed him how to work the remote control. Lil' A just watched cable while smoking. About ten minutes had passed, when Angie came from out of the bathroom. She walked by just to see the amazement on this boy's face.

She said, "You act like you never seen a girl naked before."

He laughed. Thinking back to when he heard his older friend tell a story about him fucking this rich girl who was married. The wife would always sneak away just to fuck him. She gave him whatever he wanted. He remembered his friend's advice, *They like it rough, hard, and you must last for a long time.*

He said, *I'll pull your hair, bite you, scratch you and every seven minutes ask if this is my pussy. Do you like it?"*
He would ask her if she wanted it fast or slow, hard or soft.

His friend also said, *Don't eat the pussy until six months later.*

As Lil' A laughed, he thought, what the fuck, he should try it.

Angie approached Lil' A. She started kissing him. She told him to get naked. Angie slowly kissed him from head to toe, front to back. First, she started at the front. She kissed

A Father's Burden

him all the way down to his navel. Then she grabbed his dick. She thought to herself, *this little motherfucker is big,* as she began to give A head. She knew she had him from his reaction.

Lil' A thought to himself, *Tiffany doesn't suck my dick like this. She moves like a porno star.*

Seconds later, he busted off as Angie caught every drop in her mouth, and then she kept on going. She stopped and jumped on top of him as she began to ride him. She had both of her feet on the bed. She bounced up and down on this young black kid, moaning in Spanish, *Aye! Papi! Aye Papi ...!* Her screams just turned Lil' A on. He flipped her around as he began to hit Angie from the back. He rammed it harder as her screams got louder. The way she yelled must have been a turn on because he got strength out of nowhere.

He started to pull her hair, as she yelled, "Fuck me, fuck me!"

Angie thought to herself, *how does this young boy know how to fuck like this. He knows just how I like it and what I want.* As Lil' A smacked her on the ass over and over, he finally came again. He grabbed her, laid her on her back, then put her legs on top of his shoulders. As he began to long dick her, Angie scratched his back. He grabbed her hand and put it over her head. He held it down as he finished fucking her.

Time passed by so quickly, but toward the end she said, "Slow down baby, take it slow."

He did as he was told.

Now he scratched her, sucked on her neck, giving her hickeys all over her body. Angie had an orgasm like she had never had one before. When she fucked before, either it was for business, or she had to kill the person. But this time it was for pleasure, so she enjoyed it very much. She could never think in a million years that she would like this young boy so fast. Maybe her trying to be slick had backfired.

As Lil' A sparked up the blunt, they both started to smoke. Angie walked around naked, as Lil' A put on his boxers. Angie went and got some red wine.

She said, "Baby look, this bottle cost $10,000, and I wasn't going to drink it until a special night."

So Lil' A said, "What's special."

She said, "The beginning of us..."

Lil' A said, "Wait, my kid's mother...," because he had this crush on Verwana so bad.

Angie said, "That bitch doesn't have nothing on me..." Lil' A remembered what Papi told him, so he jumped up to speak.

"Wait, don't ever talk about that girl like that. You don't even know her. I grew up with her..."

From how he reacted, Angie knew he loved that girl. She saw she could press his button.

Angie said, "Okay baby, long as she's the only one. But, if you get caught with another bitch, you're going to have a beef with me."

Lil' A said, "Yeah, I hear you, but what about your husband?"

She said, "Baby, it's all about you, so whatever you want to do we'll do. If you want to kill him; I'll do whatever you say."

At that moment, Lil' A realized that this bitch was really crazy. But, she was so good looking.

Lil' A said, "Okay."

She then asked, "Well, what you working with, how many keys?"

Lil' A replied, "I just started."

A Father's Burden

Angie said, "Well just because you're just starting don't mean shit. There's no need for my baby to be standing on no street corner... What did Papi give you?"

Lil' A ran back what Papi had given him. Then they just fucked and talked the night away.

The next morning Angie brought A breakfast in bed and she did whatever he wanted. She asked if he wanted more juice, then brought him another glass.

After that all they did was fuck, drink, and smoke. They had such a good time that before you knew it, a week had passed by. Everybody was looking for Lil' A – Sleepy, Booberlocks, Tiffany, Verwana and most of all, Yvette. It was a Sunday night, going into Monday morning when Lil' A said he had to go take care of business.

Angie said, "Why you don't want to stay with me?"

He said, "Yeah, but I have to take care of my mother, and my daughter's birthday just passed."

Inside Lil' A knew Verwana was going to be so mad, but he also knew that money would make her smile.

Angie said, "Okay! Well, this is what I'm going to do. First, you move your mom into her own house, but you keep that apartment she lives in for a few months until money starts rolling in on your side. Then you just keep it as a crib. And I'm going to give you two keys of coke and two keys of heroin." Lil' A was caught totally off guard at what she was saying. He listened carefully as she continued, "You could sell it, weight or whatever, but the heroin goes for top dollar. You could get from $50,000 to $75,000 for each one. Now the coke you can do whatever you want from $8,000 to $30,000. You can do what you want because I got coke like I have panties," she smiled. "So baby, I'm going to go out of town for one week, so move your mother and we are going to stay with each other for another week straight, okay? Oh, you can drive that Benz you got, so let me show you how to work that secret compartment..."

So she did. As Angie handed Lil' A all the work, he put it into the stash box.

She said, "Oh wait, here's a going away present for you."

She began giving him oral sex. He came in less than a minute and Lil' A knew he was way out of his league.

Angie went back inside her house and Lil' A couldn't wait to get back to New York to front. He thought to himself, *Damn, I'm about to rule the world.* As Lil' A was about to pull off, he hit the brakes. Angie came back out.

Lil' A said, "Ma, I don't have no money on me."

Angie smiled and said, "You just make the sexiest faces. Just wait right there, baby."

She ran back into the house. When she came out, she threw a stack of money into the car. Lil' A didn't even count it. He smiled as she blew him a kiss. Then he took off.

He came through the Holland tunnel into midtown Manhattan. He pulled up to a record store. Once inside, he brought so many CDs including one of his favorite rappers, Jay-Z. The bill came to $200. He had slow jams and all. He picked up the phone to call Verwana. Then he hung up the phone so fast before he could dial the number. He thought that Angie would have Verwana's number if he called from the car phone and he never wanted the two to meet under any circumstance. So he drove the car to a car wash.

The man washing the car admired it so much, he asked, "Boy, how old are you?" Lil' A smiled and said, "None of your business."

Another attendant said, "I know a hustler when I see one. Can I get a job?"

Lil' A said, "Nah! I'm a rapper!"

A Father's Burden

With that said he walked off because they were asking too many questions. He stopped at the pay phone; put 25 cents in and dialed.

Ring! Ring! Ring! Ring!
The phone rang four times.
"Hello, may I speak to Verwana...?"
The voice on the other end of the line replied, "Hold on let me see if she's in." Lil' A waited and began bracing himself because he knew she was going to be mad. The voice on the end asked, "May I ask who's speaking?"
"It's A."
The person said, "Okay. Hold on."
Seconds later, Verwana came to the phone.
"Yeah nigga, what's up?"
He said, "Okay, wait... I know you're mad at me, but I had to leave town for a couple of days."
"Yeah...! You just lied to me again," was Verwana's answer.
He said, "No I didn't."
"A, I got to take care of something for the baby."
"Okay, but before you go, did she have a nice birthday?"
"Well, I did what I could; you know her father ain't shit. Plus, my mom's is driving me crazy. I got to get my own place."
He asked, "So why don't you?"
"A, I don't have that type of money. Plus, the Section 8 people didn't call me back yet. I'm on the waiting list."
"Well, I don't mean to cut you off, but my car is ready."
Verwana asked, "What car?"
He replied, "Don't worry, you'll see it, but first I got to take care of a few things. What time does the kids store close?"
"About 5:00 or 6:00 o'clock," she answered.

"Okay, well I should be done by 4:00 o'clock. So meet me by the side of the building. I'll be in a white car with tented windows, okay?"

Verwana asked, "Are you playing or lying again?"

He said, "I'll be there, okay? Just be ready..., I got to go."

She said, alright and hung up. Lil' A walked to the car, and people were still gawking. He didn't say a word.

He gave the attendant a twenty-dollar bill and said, "Y'all split that."

Then he jumped into the Benz, turned up the music and drove off.

He was headed toward the Westside Highway so he could get to the Bronx. He lit a blunt and cruised along smoking. When he finally reached the Bronx, he ran upstairs to Sleepy's house, but he wasn't there.

Sleepy's girl said, "A, his cousins from New Orleans is here. In fact, they're driving around in a red truck.

"Oh, okay."

He went back downstairs and as soon as he walked out the building, a truck pulled up. Sleepy and his cousin got out. Lil' A sparked up another blunt and walked toward the two.

"Yo A, man what's up? Where you been? This shit been dry. Plus, Tiffany has been going crazy..., he added, Yo, these are my cousins. They been here for two days and they are trying to buy some heroin."

Lil' A asked, "Well what they trying to spend?"

"Well I don't know exactly, but they getting money. You know how these country boys roll... let me introduce you."

Sleepy turned to his cousins and started to introduce them. "Yo, Lil' Bone and B.C, this is my man Lil' A."

They gave each other five.

"Yo, what's up y'all?" Lil' A asked as he looked into their eyes. Lil' Bone was the one talking, so he knew he had the brains.

Lil' Bone said, "I'm just trying to score. And if the shit is raw, we could get rich."

Lil' A replied, "Well, what you trying to cop?"

Lil' Bone said, "Yo, I got $50,000 on me now. And I really need some boy."

Lil' A hadn't heard that term before. He asked, "What's, boy?"

The response was, "Dawg food is heroin. And girl is coke powder..."

Lil' Bone then said, "This is my last because our connect in my town got locked up. So we finally caught up to cuz so we could find another one."

Lil' A said, "Well you did, so don't worry. I got you."

Lil' Bone looked at Lil' A kind of funny. But Lil' A knew that look it was the same look that Booberlocks gave him. He was thinking how someone so young could move like that. They stood there talking and smoking weed. Lil' A had a plan. He asked Sleepy if he finished that other thing.

Sleepy said, "Yeah. I got it all. But I had to pay my rent, so I'm short about $750."

Lil' A said, "Don't worry about it. I have a big come up for you, but only if you come back with my money."

Sleepy said okay and asked, "What you want me to do?"

Lil' A said, "Give me a second... Yo, Lil' Bone, how long will it take you to move a key?"

Lil' A then told Sleepy to meet him at his house at 10 P.M. and to bring the money. Sleepy asked if he also wanted him to bring his cousin's money. Lil' A said, yes. Lil' A rushed up the block to catch up with Booberlocks. As he walked, he saw Tiffany getting out of a cab with her mother.

As he said, "Hey Boo...," she turned around and smiled. She looked happy, but she was also somewhat mad. The look on Tiffany's mother's face, however, was kind of weird. He couldn't pinpoint it at the time. It did look as if she did not want him to speak.

Lil' A spoke anyway. "How are you doing, Ms. Walker?"

She responded, "Fine, and yourself...? A, I would like to talk to you so before you leave. please, make sure we all sit down and talk, me, you, and Tiffany."

Lil' A agreed, "Okay, ma."

Then Tiffany butted in. "We'll talk later." As Ms. Walker walked upstairs, Tiffany hugged him. Then she asked him, "Nigga, where you been?"

"I had to take care of a few things, but what's up with you?" Lil' A inquired.

"Me missing you, that what's up with me. I missed you so much and Booberlocks was looking for you. In fact, he gave me some money to hold for you. He also said that he took a little out to flip. He said he'll explain it later."

Lil' A said, "Okay, well, go upstairs and get that. Meet me right back here. I got something I want to show you. And I got to make a few runs, so hurry up."

Tiffany just looked at him. Lil' A asked her if she had Booberlocks's number on her.

Tiffany said, "Yeah."

Lil' A said, "Okay," turning as he hurried to walk down the block to the car.

He walked up to the Benz, knocked on the door lock and jumped into the car. Lil' A pushed the CD button and put on some Tupac. He pulled off. As he pulled up to a stop light, he saw Tiffany standing in front of the building. He liked looking at her light skinned body. But it looked as if she was

A Father's Burden

getting bigger. He pulled up near her and hit the horn. But she paid it no mind. She didn't know who it was.

Then Lil' A rolled down the passenger side window. "Yo, are you deaf or blind?" he asked. Her eyes opened wide, as she came toward the car. Lil' A said, "Get in." She did. As they pulled off, he said, "Call Booberlocks." She dialed his girlfriend's house, but nobody answered. Lil' A said, "Don't worry, you can try him back later." Lil' A then instructed, "Yo, dial my number." She did.

His mother answered. "Hey, it's Tiffany."
The voice on the other end, responded, "What's up girl? Did you run into that boy yet?"
"I'm with him now..." Tiffany answered,
"Well let me talk to him."
He picked up the receiver and spoke to his mother, "Hello ma. What's up with you?"
"Don't what's up with me...," she said angrily. "Why didn't you call me? I was worried sick about you. You know all I wanted was one phone call."
"I know ma. I'm sorry. I just wasn't at a good spot to call. But anyway, are you dressed?"
"Yeah, why...?"
"Well come downstairs. I want to show you something."
"Boy, let me come down in like five minutes. Okay?"
Tiffany just sat in the front seat looking at, A.
Lil' A asked, "Girl, what's up with you?"
Her response was, "Nothing."
"Yo, do you want to go shopping?"
"Yeah baby... A, I do have to tell you something."
"So tell me," he said.
"Nah, it can wait."
"Okay, so let it wait. Oh, open that glove compartment," he said as he pointed to it.
She opened it. He told her to roll a blunt.

"I just got to holla at my moms for a few seconds."

Yvette was standing in front of her building when the big white Benz pulled up. Her little ass son jumped out the car. Yvette's heart could have dropped. She just didn't want to believe it.

Yvette could not say a word when Lil' A asked, "What's up?"
She stood still and began remembering when she and Lil' A's father, Big A, walked up to a white car that cost more than both of their apartments. Yvette couldn't move or speak. The car was nice, but she did not want her son caught up like this. Yvette had seen how the streets had pulled her and Big A apart.
"Ma, ma, what's wrong...?"
"Nothing...!" Yvette snapped back. "Boy, whose car is that?" As Lil' A was about to speak, his mother stopped him. "Never mind, I know good and well what this visit is for. It's just to show me the car. And of course, we got to move now."
Lil' A was shocked now himself. He asked, "Ma, how you know all of this?"
Yvette scolded, "Boy, you just like your father, and I'm tired of busting my ass to take care of us and you still following his footsteps."
"Well ma, you ain't going to have to bust your ass no more," he said.

Tiffany got out the car and greeted Yvette. She said hi to Tiffany and continued talking to Lil' A.

"You just can't see it yet. You're about to be in a world of trouble, pain, and a broken heart," Yvette said prophetically.

A Father's Burden

Lil' A told Tiffany to get back into the car. As she did, he followed behind his mother upstairs. He didn't know why his mother flipped out like she did outside. Lil' A probably would never really understand what his mom was thinking, unless he went through the storm that she'd been through with his father. Yvette felt that just as fast as her son's world was rising, it would surely fall apart just as quick.

"Ma, what's wrong," Lil' A asked.

"Nothing's wrong," she retorted. "But, if you don't take the time to see who is really in your corner, you're going to miss out. Those streets don't really love you. It's a dirty game, and that game is not for you. It's kill or be killed. And if you ever listened to whatever I've said, history repeats itself baby. It's your turn now. So be careful. Your heart is too good."

Yvette began to cry. Lil' A hugged his mother tight.

"Momma, don't cry, I'm going to be careful, okay?"

Yvette just held her only son tight, as her mind raced back to the time when she went to that condo with her son's father. She remembered hugging his father the same way. She remembered him broke, and she remembered him rich. With Yvette hugging him so tightly, Lil' A could feel some of her pain, but really couldn't understand it.

"Ma...," he spoke into her ear as she eased the grip. "Listen ma, I need you to stay at Wizzes house for a couple of days."

"Why, what's wrong?" she asked.

He took control. He walked to the closet and pulled out the box of money Papi had given him in case he got locked up for that murder.

"Here Ma...! Take this money and go put it on a house for you and go buy a car. And then I'll give you some money to finish paying it off, okay? But you must do it now. Try to move somewhere you like, right outside New York."

"Where," his mother asked.

"At least two hours away so you can drive back and forth to work."

"Okay baby! But are you alright?" she asked.

"Yeah, I'm good. I just want to make sure you're okay. Now here goes the cell number to the car. Call me when you've done it all, the house and a car, okay?"

"Well, what about this place?"

"We'll pay the rent for this crib," Lil' A answered.

Yvette asked, "You're not going to make this no drug spot."

Lil' A responded, "No, but a few of my friends will come by and I really don't want you nowhere around that. Plus, I might bring a couple of girls around. Just call me when you're done in a couple of days. Here's the number, 201-555-1328."

Yvette asked, "Where's that number to?"

Lil' A said, "Jersey…" and then smiled. "Oh, and I got an older Spanish girl. She looks like a model."

Yvette turned to him and asked, "Boy, what you mean older?"

"Well, she's a few years younger than you, don't worry you'll meet her, okay?"

"Yeah, I do want to meet her."

"Ma, I got to go, so call me in a couple of days when you finished taking care of your business."

Lil' A kissed her and walked out.

"Boy, be careful. I love you."

"I love you too momma," Lil' A said as he was headed out the door.

He closed the door behind him.

As he got downstairs, Tiffany asked, "A are you okay? Why did your mother say that?"

A Father's Burden

He replied, "I don't know. She's just going through it right now. But never mind her; how are you?"

"I'm good. Just thinking about you," Tiffany said.

"Yeah, whatever..., Yo, spark that blunt up." Tiffany did what he asked. She lit the blunt. The first two pulls had her coughing.

Lil' A said, "Pass that before you hurt yourself."

He hit it like a champ now and laughed as she was still coughing.

Chapter Seven

Yo, try your cousin's number again. This time Booberlocks answered.
"Hey cuz, what's up?" she greeted. "A is trying to holla at you."
"Oh word, put him on..., what's good baby?'
"You..."
"Yo, where you been?"
"I had to make a run, but I'm back now."
"Yo, did Tiff give you that?"
"Oh yeah, she did"
Booberlocks said, "Yo, I used a little bit of your money with mine, so I could keep the spot moving, word."
"So what you got now?"
"Well I got ten thousand. We can split that."
"Okay, well where you at. I got a surprise for you."
"Oh, yeah...? Tiffany knows how to get here!" Booberlocks said with excitement.
"I'll be through! I'll see you in about half an hour."
They hung up and Lil' A asked Tiffany where he could hook up with Booberlocks. "Tiff where is he?"
"He's on 189th and Broadway."
Lil' A headed to the highway.
"Well, who are you to meet?"

A Father's Burden

"Look Boo. I know. I know. Don't get mad at me and don't ask questions."

Lil' A passed her the blunt, and then he turned up the radio and merged onto the highway. He was in the Bronx, on his way to Manhattan. Lil' A was speeding because he had to go check on his money. He was happy to catch up with Tiffany, but he was in love with Angie now. She was his murder mami. Plus, she was rich. But he also loved him some Verwana. There was something about her. The two just matched. He couldn't pinpoint it, but he loved her, and he couldn't have her upset with him twice.

They finally reached Manhattan. They were on 180th street. He told Tiffany to let her cousin know that they were downstairs and for him to come down. Booberlocks was already downstairs waiting. His eyes opened wide when he saw the car. Lil' A told Tiffany to open the door.

Booberlocks got in and said, "Damn homie. You took my dream ride."

"Nah. It ain't nothing like that. It's a friend's car. He just let me hold it to make some runs in it for a few days. You know you my partner. When you're ready to buy your car, I will buy my first car. Plus, I got a hook up on the car dealer. I can get you anything you want."

Booberlocks responded, "Word. So let's go next month."

"Okay, whenever you're ready because I'm already ready. Yo, Booberlocks, I really don't want to rush you, but I have to go take care of something."

"Okay. I don't want to hold you up. Here's half of the money in fact here's two more thousand from the money I used."

Lil' A turned to Tiffany and said, "Okay, Tiffany take out the two thousand and you keep the rest. Go buy yourself a lot of clothes and buy me two beepers okay. Make sure one is a 1-800 number so you can get in touch with me out of town. Yo, here go the keys to my house. After you're done shopping, meet me there. Okay?"

"Where are you going?"

"I have to take care of something real important, so I'm going to drop you off at the store."

Tiffany said, "Fine. So drop me off at 125th Street."

Then Booberlocks remarked, "Homie, I don't want to get into your business, but you just gave my cousin all your money."

"Don't worry dawg, we about to be rich. Just stick by me and we'll go far."

Booberlocks responded, "Dawg, that's why I dig you, I knew you was good money from the start. No wonder my little cousin is in love with you... Yo, I know you got to go, but did you forget me?

Lil' A responded, "Come on homie, I told you I got you."

They made small talk for a while, then he hit the button. There was a noise.

Booberlocks jumped and asked, "What's that?"

Lil' A started laughing then asked, "You scared dawg?"

He reached into the glove compartment and pulled out two keys. Since he had to make sure he'd been given the right work, he only gave Booberlocks one of the kilos.

Booberlocks said, "Homie, you just be coming up with work out of nowhere. Yo, what I owe you on this?"

Lil' A said, "Well it cost $20,000 and I paid for it so all you have to do is give me back the $20,000 and the rest we split. Okay?"

Booberlocks said, "Okay homie."

"Yo, I'll call you tonight, but I got to run."

Booberlocks jumped out of the back of the car.

Booberlocks said, "Cuz, I'll see you later."

Tiffany said, "Alright."

A Father's Burden

Lil' A pulled off and he began to talk with Tiffany.
"Now don't forget to do everything I said, Boo."
"I heard you the first time, boy" she said with a smile. He jumped back onto the highway. She said, "I want to go get my hair done. All the girls always talk about it so drop me off there and I'll meet you back at your mother's house. It's on 137th Street."

Lil' A drove for a bit, and then pulled up to the shop. There were a lot of cars outside, almost just as many as there were hoes on the inside. So, he had to front for his baby. The Benz was a top of the line one. There were only a handful of these made, or should we say, on the streets, and he was driving one.

So Lil' A told Tiffany, "Wait here... Let me see what's going on in this spot. I might have to shoot one of these niggas for messing with my baby because you look too good."

When Lil' A made that statement, Tiffany laughed. Well, she really blushed because she had not seen him in a week. She missed him, but she was kind of mad that he was dropping her off like that. He pushed a button and grabbed a gun out of the stash box. Tiffany eyes opened wide, being that she was really seeing a different side of A. As Lil' A got out, he turned up the music in the Benz, and the system was so loud that the bass had the whole store rattling. Lil' A opened the door as all the girls just looked at this little boy. He wasn't even dressed up for real, no type of jewelry on or nothing. But Lil' A's car cost more than a house, so every girl in there knew he had to be a baller. So he walked on in.

Lil' A inquired, "Is the owner here?"
One girl said, "No. Little boy, how old are you?"
Lil' A responded, "Are you a cop?"
She answered, "Baby, my man got life in the federal pen, so I don't condone that."

"Oh okay, I'm feeling that, well how many girls you got?"

She said, "Baby, I'm booked up..."

As Lil' A started to think, he asked, "Well how much do you charge?"

She answered again, "Two hundred dollars. Why are you asking all these questions?"

"Well, my girlfriend needs her hair done, plus she got to go shopping, and I got to go meet my kid's mother for my daughter's birthday so I could get her to the store. And my baby just heard about this spot, so she made me bring her. So here go $500..." Lil' A was really rolling. He was making the big play and was going to follow through. He continued, "She's next and from now on she's going to come to you. Here go $100 for whoever is next. What's your name?"

"Well they call me Red."

"Baby, my name is A. I'll holla at you next week when I bring my girl in to get her hair done."

Red said, "Okay baby, send her in."

Lil' A didn't know that Red was the owner. He also didn't know that her man was a dude named, Lou Sims. He was the leader of a crew out of Harlem called, Lynch Mob. But Red just knew the look. She knew that this little boy was either rich, or on his way to the top. Now she just had to get close to him before he got run out (meaning all the girls fucking or sucking him up) Red repeated herself.

"Okay A, send her in."

"Alright Red, thank you..."

Red countered, "No thank you, baby" and smiled.

A smiled back. Red thought to herself, *He got one of the sexiest smiles in the world.* As Lil' A headed toward the car, he knocked on the passenger side window. Tiffany was bobbing her head to the music. She turned to see a smiling Lil' A. so she got out.

A Father's Burden

Lil' A smiled as he said, "Boo, you're next to get your hair done. Don't forget what I told you and I'll be home later. Okay?" They hugged and kissed each other.

Tiffany said, "Don't take too long."

He said, "Okay. Oh, the girl Red is going to do your hair. I'll see you later."

As Tiffany walked toward the salon, Red peered out the window to see this little perfectly shaped girl. She knew now that, A and Tiffany, were young. And she knew too that A wasn't really as tough as he sounded. She had to do some investigating.

Lil' A pulled off. Now it's about 3:45. He stepped on the gas pedal. He was flying. He had to be in the Bronx within 15 minutes. When he made it to the Bronx, there was a minor traffic accident holding up traffic. Lil' A then called Verwanas house. The phone rang several times before anyone answered. Finally, someone answered.

"Hello, may I speak to Verwana? The person's response was, "She's not here. May I ask who's calling?"

"This is A."

The voice on the other end said, "What's up nigga?"

"Who is this, Keisha? Yo, what's up?"

Then Keisha informed him, "Yo, you know the police are looking for you?"

"Yeah, I know but fuck them," Lil' A replied brushing it off.

Keisha explained, "Well they been pressing me, but all I keep saying is I don't know shit because I don't."

"Well, that's good Keisha just keep to the story line."

"I know. Well, I'll tell Verwana you called..."

"Yo, tell her I'm 10 minutes away. And Keisha, I'm going to send you something up there with her."

Keisha asked, "Boy, what are you going to send?"
"Don't worry. She'll have it, just wait and see. Okay?"
"Alright nigga, peace out..."
"Peace."

***

It's 4:15. Lil' A beeped the horn and both girls looked. For some reason, Verwana knew that it was Lil' A.

Verwana motioned, "Come on Nicky..." Nicky asked, "Verwana, who is that?"
"That's Lil' A" They walked up to the Benz.
Verwana asked, "Is this car stolen...?"
"Girl, what's wrong with you. That ain't my style. Come on; get in so we can catch the stores."
So, Verwana got in and told her friend, "Nicky, I'll catch up to you later. Call me."

As they pulled off, Lil' A asked, "What's up?"
Verwana responded, "Nothing. What's up with you...? You know everyone in the projects keep saying that you were the one who killed those two brothers."
"Well they don't know what they're talking about. I didn't do anything," Lil' A replied.
"A, I don't want you to get into any trouble," Verwana said very concerned.
"Oh, you don't?"
"No! Don't act like these crackers won't lock you up for life."
"Well, I won't ever give them a chance," Lil' A boasted,
"A, where did you get this car from...?"
"It belongs to a friend of mine. I didn't get a chance to get mine yet."
Verwana then inquired, "Where you getting all this money to buy all this stuff?"

"Damn girl, what you don't trust me or something? I'm just trying to make a living for you and Quantiah. Why are you asking me all these questions? Are you really for me, or what?"

"Yeah, why you ask that?" Verwana reassured him.

"I mean Verwana. I'm really in love with you and I'm ready to settle down."

She seemed a little surprised.

"A, I hope you know what you're saying because that's a big step. I have a child. I'm trying to get my own place."

Lil' A then asked, "So, how much have you saved?"

"I had about a $1,000, but I had to buy some things for Quanee."

Lil' A looked at her and said, "I need you to be truthful with me. Do you want to be with me?" Verwana took a deep breath and looked Lil' A straight in the eyes.

"Yeah!" Verwana answered,

Lil' A then stated, "You and Quantiah won't need for nothing. I'm going to take care of you and her like she's my child."

Verwana said, "I hope you not playing. Shit, you don't know how many years I've wanted this. So why did you used to flirt with my sister?"

"I don't know, but I love you, Verwana..." She just stood there and looked at Lil' A.

"What store you trying to catch?"

She replied, "Let's go to Macy's down on 34th Street in Manhattan."

A headed toward the highway.

He asked, "Oh! How much will it cost you for your apartment?"

Verwana replied, "It depends on where I move."

"Well, just don't move to where no drug dealers are. Make sure you move somewhere where white people live. I mean a nice quiet block."

Verwana said, "A, I don't have no money for nothing like that."

Lil' A replied, "Yes you do. As long as I have it, you'll never need anything again."

She asked, "What you got?"

He said, "In a few months, I will be worth a million."

Verwana started to laugh.

Verwana joked, "I knew you was fronting."

Lil' A looked at her like she was crazy.

By the time they reached downtown, all the stores were closed or just about to close. So instead, they decided to go to the movies. Later they talked and smoked weed. As the night passed, he knew he had to meet Sleepy and his cousins. After taking care of that little bit of business, he could bullshit around. But, oh so bad did Lil' A want to spend the night with Verwana. He didn't want to rush it because he truly liked her. So after the movie, he took her to eat. They ate, talked, and had fun.

Lil' A said, "Okay Verwana, here's $5,000 so you can look for your apartment... Here's $3,000 so you can buy Quantiah a lot of clothes... Here's $3,000 so you can buy clothes... Here's $2,000, give it to your sister Keisha, okay? She'll know what it's for. And here go $2,000 just in case you need it."

Verwanas eyes popped open wide. She was in shock.

Lil' A then smirked, "Now you see, I ain't playing."

Verwana was about to ask, "A where did you..."

He stopped her in mid-sentence. "Verwana, no more questions, and no more games... Don't worry about shit, I got you. Just make sure you move somewhere low-key and quiet, okay?"

"Yes," Verwana agreed.

Then Lil' A said, "Verwana, I got to take care of something real important."

Verwana asked, "What are you going to do, mess with some girls?"

Lil' A made it clear, "Look, I really don't have no time for girls."

Verwana extended, "Well I got a babysitter, so stay with me."

Lil' A declined, "Verwana, I would love to, but I got to take care of this. Just call me when you get your new apartment. Tomorrow, I'll call you to give you my beeper number, okay?"

He paid for the food and left a tip. The two youngsters then got up and headed home. They were holding hands. Lil' A had to rush back to the Bronx to drop Verwana off then go take care of business. On the way back to the Bronx, he lit up a blunt of that fire green. Now, Verwana was smoking weed whenever she got a chance. So they smoked and talked. The way Verwana carried herself turned Lil' A on more and more. On the ride back home Lil' A realized why he loved her so much. Verwana reminded him of his mother, Yvette.

He remembered some time ago when he first met her. He admired how she put her daughter first. Right then, he knew he could give her a baby. From that day on Lil' A wanted Verwana in his life. But, for some reason, he knew Verwana didn't feel the same way. He just had a gut feeling. All Verwana cared about was herself or should we say as long as she was getting money. Because Verwana came from a low-class family, she never got what she wanted. She couldn't afford it. You can say she was *money-hungry*. But just because she was money-hungry didn't mean she would sleep with a thousand dudes for money. Verwana did have respect for herself. But on the inside, she was full of shit.

They finally reached the Bronx and Lil' A told her he would call her in the morning to give her the number. He also asked Verwana what time she would be going out shopping.

She answered, "Around 12:00 P.M."

Lil' A stated, "Okay, I will call around that time."

Verwana reached over and kissed Lil' A. That kiss seemed like the kiss of love, or the start of a wonderful life, or could it be? The two kissed for about five minutes straight. Finally, they stopped, and Lil' A watched Verwana walk back to the building. While he was there, Lil' A saw his pops. They greeted each other, and his father looked impressed with the car. Then his father told him how this all reminded him of himself 15 years ago. Big A told his son about the white Benz he once had.

"This is really nice. I know how nice it drives because I had one 15 years ago."

Lil' A said with excitement, "You did pops?"

His father responded, "Yeah! In fact, I remember the first time I pulled up to get your mother. She was shocked as hell."

"Word pops?"

Lil' A just sat there and listened to his pop's story. Now he could see why his moms started to cry when he pulled up. Now he knew why his moms said, *history repeats itself.* Now it was all coming together. Then Lil' A thought of Verwana. He felt a little tear coming.

Lil' A stated, "Head Moe. Yo, I really don't want to cut you short, but I got to take care of something."

His father replied understandingly, "Okay, you just be careful."

A Father's Burden

The father and son gave each other five. Then Lil' A pulled off.

The phone rang. "Hello" The voice on the other end said, "What's up, what are you doing...?" Lil' A knew it was Angie from her accent. He replied, "I just hollered at my pops. Now, I'm on my way to sell this work."

"Yeah baby, well what have you been doing all day? Did you go see your baby mother?"

"Yeah, I did." Angie was shocked, but she liked the fact that he didn't lie.

"Well did you give your daughter money?"

"Yeah, but I told her I'd holla at her later."

"Well, I wish you'd hurry up."

"Oh yeah...? Why?"

"*Because I want you to come beat this pussy up,*" she said.

Lil' A laughed. "Yeah, I can't wait either, so I can beat that pussy up."

They talked on the phone all the time it took for him to get back to his mother's house. It was around 12:45 a.m. and Lil' A was so late. As he was pulling up, Lil' A saw Sleepy and his cousins sitting in the red truck. He blocked them in. Hit the horn and rolled down the window. At first, they were spooked.

Lil' Bone said, "Man, you so late I thought you were bullshitting."

Lil' A cleared up, "Yo, I never bullshit. I'm a man of my word. I just got caught up with my kids' mother."

Lil' A drove around the block, came back and parked. Sleepy and his cousins were in the truck in front of the building. Lil' A drove around the block because as he told Sleepy, he thought somebody might have been trying to ambush them. Lil' A was getting more paranoid now. He knew he had to really be careful because the police were looking for him, and some friends of the brothers he shot might have been looking for him. Sleepy was cautious too.

Sleepy said, "I got this 45 Caliber."
Lil' A responded, "I know we have to be careful. That's why I got this 9 MM Beretta."

Both parties strolled forward in order to take care of their business. They headed for the building. They walked upstairs. Sleepy was curious about Lil' A's new wheels.

Sleepy asked, "A, where did you get that?"
Lil' A replied, "That's my Spanish mami's car. I'm just using it to make my runs until my car is ready."
Sleepy said, "You're full of surprises."

They went back to the crib where Tiffany was waiting. She looked mad, but she'd missed Lil' A. She looked good with her new hairdo. *It really was worth the cost,* he thought. Lil' A reassured Lil' Bone again.

"See, I'm a man of my word," he said.

Chapter Eight

Little Bone passed the $50,000 to Lil' A, who gave him three keys – two keys of heroin, and one key of cocaine. Lil' Bone was happy. His trip to New York had been well worth it. Now he had a new source, at least for now. Lil' A told Tiffany to roll them a blunt. As Lil' A was talking with Sleepy and his cousins, Tiffany handed her boyfriend his beepers. Then he gave Sleepy and Lil' Bone his number. Lil' A instructed Tiffany to call Booberlocks and to give him the numbers.

Lil' A turned to Lil' Bone and said, "Yo, I'll see you in a week."

He responded, "A, I see that you're for real and we about to be rich."

"Yeah, I know."

Sleepy, Little Bone, and G.B. left. Leaving Lil' A and Tiffany in the apartment alone for the night. She was horny, but Lil' A was tired, so they played music and fell asleep. First thing in the morning Tiffany woke up and took a shower. Then she asked Lil' A if he wanted her to cook.

Lil' A responded, "No, I'm going out to eat." He asked her to get ready and run him some bath water. She did as she was told.

Lil' A jumped into the bathtub. While in the tub, he sparked up another blunt. Lil' A sat and finally had time to think to himself. So many things were hitting him at once. First, he thought of his moms and how she cried over him. He thought of how he wanted her to have a better life. He was trying to give her that. Then he thought of his pops, but what stuck out the most was what his mother had said about him, how *history repeats itself.*

Lil' A's thoughts then turned to Angie and how she was a good fuck, but also that the bitch was crazy. He also was thinking how they had just killed those two people upstate. His thoughts also turned to Papi and what he'd said about his sister. Lil' A figured that he had to get to the bottom of Papi and Angie's relationship. His thoughts switched back to his mother. He really wanted to know what made his mother break down like that. What was funny was, he wasn't even thinking about Tiffany. For some reason, he had her on smash, she was head over heels for him.

From the start Lil' A was down for Tiffany, but when the smoke cleared, he would see who was really in his corner. After he jumped out of the tub, Lil' A snapped out of his trance. He dried off and got dressed. Finally, he grabbed his final accessory a 9 MM Beretta that he slid in his waistband.

He asked, "Tiffany are you ready…?"
She responded, "Yeah!"
As they walked out, she locked the door behind her. They walked around the corner to the parking garage to the Benz.

In the garage, they saw the Spanish man who lived in Lil' A's mother's building. He was used to seeing him a lot. So they were cool as they spoke.

A Father's Burden

The man said, "That's a nice car."

"Yeah, thank you. I'll see you later."

As the two youngsters got into the car, Lil' A said he felt like some Red Lobster, so they jetted down to Midtown. He had learned that when you have money, you hang out where all the white people hang out because police really won't mess with you. However, if you drive around in the projects, the cops will harass you all day by assuming; *Yeah, he's a drug dealer.* Every time they saw your car, they pull you over, or every time you'd be on the block, they follow you. So, Lil' A knew to hang out where he wouldn't be hassled.

Like the older people often would say, *Don't shit where you eat.*

So, a lot of people did not see Lil' A in the Benz. He was a low-key type of dude. In fact, he still hadn't bought himself anything yet. In Lil' A's mind, he just had to wait. At least he was getting money now.

They finally arrived at Red Lobster. Tiffany just loved her some Lil' A. They sat and talked. After the waiter brought out their food, they started eating and making small talk. Tiffany began telling him about Red from the beauty salon. She told him that Red wanted to know where they were from and how old they were.

Lil' A asked, "What did you tell her?

"Come on Boo. I'm from the projects. I talked a little, but got a lot out of her."

"Tell me what you talked about."

"Well, I said you'd be going out of town and basically that's it."

"Oh! Okay and what do you know about her?"

"Well, she owns the beauty salon."

"Oh, she does," Lil' A commented as he thought of how Red had played him, or out talked him.

"Red said her man was running the whole Harlem at one point. The Feds just locked him up. She has two kids from him and she has a BMW. Red also said that her baby father had done over 25 murders," Tiffany said as she disclosed more information about Red.

"Oh yea...?" Lil' A said.

"She invited us to a party."

"Really, what party?"

"It's called a Final Four party. And she said if your shit ain't right, don't come. I guess she means as far as clothes, cars, you know, straight shining."

"Are you going to go?"

"I don't know. My mom wants me to go to my grandmother's funeral next week and that's when the party is taking place. I gotta get my hair done before then. Red gave me her cell number and asked how many V.I.P. passes I needed. Boo, I want you to go represent for us."

"I don't know, Tiffany. I might go. So, did you spend all your money?"

"Yes. I bought school clothes, plus an outfit to wear when I go to my grandmother's funeral."

"Well as long as you got everything you needed, that's cool."

The day went by fast. After he dropped Tiffany off, he found himself thinking about Verwana, but he went back to Angie. She was just so street smart. Angie was able to school Lil' A to the game. Sexually, she took care of him more and more. She fucked, sucked, and turned Lil' A out. Everything seemed to be going well. He disappeared again from everybody – Tiffany and Verwana, as he stayed with Angie.

Lil' A never answered his beeper. He was only waiting for one phone call, and it was from an out of town number. He was waiting for that big money. Lil' A had close to

$200,000 coming. When the calls came, they all came at once. First, his mother Yvette called.

"Hey baby, what's up…? Oh, you're going to love the house I bought. When are we going to meet up so I can show you?"

Lil' A responded, "Ma, we could meet downtown later. So in the meantime, go pick out your furniture."

"Baby, I did everything already."

"Okay, give me four days ma and then we can meet up, okay? Just stay at your house until we meet because I'm trying to find you a car."

She said, "I'm okay. We need to have a real talk because I need to know where you are getting all this money."

"Okay ma. Just don't worry; I'm going to let you go. I'll see you in four days, okay?"

"Okay baby, be safe."

Then his beeper went off again. *404! Yes!* That was the call he'd been waiting on. Lil' A dialed the number back, 404-555-4004.

"Hello! Yo, what's up, A?"

"Yo, what's up, Sleepy? Yo man, I'm telling you I'm moving out here, the shit out here is crazy, A. The girls, money, it's just different…"

"Well you know you got a baby mother?"

"Yeah I know, that's why I'm having fun while she's not here."

"Okay, I'm feeling that."

"Yo, I'm coming in tomorrow night. I'll be at the Amtrak station on 34th Street. So, be there to pick me up, okay?"

"Okay!"

"Yo, A, wait. Lil' Bone is trying to holla at you."

"Okay, put him on… Yo Bone what's good?"

"Yo, A, I really don't want to talk on this phone right now, but my cousin will be there tomorrow night. I'm going to take my time, because we about to come up. Yo, we'll talk about it later..."

"Yo Bone, there's a party here I want us all to go to, but it's supposed to be a dress to impress kind of thing."

"Word...? Yeah, I like that. We could do that. I'll be there."

When he hung up the phone Angie asked who he had been talking to.

He replied, "That's my man. He's someone that's about to be down with my team."

"Oh yeah...! Well I hope I'm a part of your team," Angie said.

They then sparked up a blunt. As they got horny, they fucked the night away. The next day came, but they did not really get out of bed until around 4 P.M. He couldn't believe he had slept so long. When he looked at his beeper, he saw that Verwana had called five times. Tiffany had called three times. Booberlocks's number was on it twice. Since Angie was right next to him, he knew he couldn't call any of the girls back. So, he called his dude, Booberlocks.

"Yo Locks, what's good?"

"Ain't nothing, A... Yo, I got that money for you. I still got enough work. I just want to take care of you. But I could wait a couple days before you hit me."

"Okay that's good. Yo, are you at your girl's house?"

"Yeah...!"

"Well I'll be there in about two hours."

"Okay, just call me when you get downstairs and I will come down."

"Okay, I'll see you in a few."

As Angie got out of bed butt naked, she grabbed Lil' A's hands and pulled him in the direction of the shower. They got in. Angie washed him and herself. Then she gently sucked his dick. Lil' A got off right inside her mouth. Then Angie turned around, reaching her hands to her feet, as he grabbed her long hair and started banging her from the back. Before you knew it, an hour had passed by. They both got out as Angie dried them both off and applied cocoa butter lotion to their bodies.

And for the first time, Angie was ready for something different. As she bent over, he went to put his dick into her pussy. However, Angie countered, "No baby! You're ready. Now put it in my ass."

At first Lil' A hesitated but did what he was told. He worked it a little while and then came all in her ass hole. She turned around and smiled and Lil' A couldn't believe what had just happened. But it was so, so good. They got dressed.

Angie said, "Baby, only drive the Benz when you're hanging out or once in a blue moon. And drive it when you pick up or drop off. Other than that, drive an everyday car."

He just listened before informing her of his plans. "Well I'm about to buy me a few cars because I've got to have my own. I really don't want to keep driving your car."

Angie said, "Okay!"

Then Lil' A said, "I need you to take me to go get those stash boxes though."

Angie said, "Baby, anything I have access to, you'll soon have. You can have them put in whenever you find the time to sit still."

Lil' A said, "Ma, you know I'm trying to get my weight up. So you can sit back and I take care of you."

Angie just smiled. She said, "Baby, drive that Quest van."

Lil' A asked, "Which one?"

"The red one."

Lil' A went to the garage through the basement of the house. Angie came out and showed him how to work the stash box. Lil' A found out that the van had three stash boxes. One for a gun up front, a big one in the back to hold 200 keys, and the middle one could hold up to one million in cash.

Lil' A liked the minivan. It had a TV and VCR in it. There was also a PlayStation and a loud music system. He kissed Angie and left. Shortly after he left, she called his cell phone. When Lil' A answered she said, "Oh baby, I forgot to tell you, write down this number 646-555-8013."

"Who's this?"

"His name is Slick. He knows you're going to be calling. He's the one who has that shit we like to smoke."

Lil' A asked, "What do I have to give him?"

Angie answered, "Nothing. Just take enough to spread around. That's for us to smoke off, okay?"

"I hope he ain't one of your little flunkies, or somebody that you fucking because I might have to do something to him," Lil' A joked.

Angie laughed and said, "Please baby. He ain't about nothing. He's Spanish and he's a sucker. I can't fuck no suckers." After a moment of silence, she added, "Baby let me find out you jealous."

Now Lil' A started to laugh. "No. I just have to keep an eye on you because you think like me and I got love for you," he responded.

Ending the call before hanging up Angie said, "Okay baby. I love you too."

Angie thought to herself, *This boy is really sharp. No wonder my brother likes him so much.*

A Father's Burden

Lil' A thought to himself how slick Angie was. She was so-so slick. But one side of him still really loved and cared about her, despite her slick and crazy characteristics.

Lil' A was back in the city. He shot up to 189th Street in Manhattan. He picked up the phone and called Booberlocks. Within a few minutes Booberlocks was downstairs with the bag of money. He was impressed with his homie.

"Damn, Lil' A, where you keep getting these cars?" Lil' A assured him that it wasn't his car.

He then said, "Don't worry. When I go by my first car, you'll be going with me. In fact, we're going in a week. Will you be ready?"

"Yeah! I'll see how much money I have in my safe tonight."

"Okay, so we'll go in a week."

Booberlocks then said, "My cousin is looking for you."

"Yeah, I know, but I have to take care of a few things. I'll catch up with her later. I'll see you later."

Then Lil' A pulled off.

He was about to jump on the highway, but instead the broad Red ran across his mind. He really didn't like the fact that she was thinking ahead of him. So instead of jumping on the highway, Lil' A was heading to Manhattan. He shot downtown to Red's shop. As he pulled up in front of the shop, his cell phone rang. It was Angie.

She said, "Baby, I don't mean to bother you, but Slick just called me and said he was leaving town. He said he is waiting for you, or can he meet up with you?"

Lil' A answered, "Okay, I just got off the highway. I'm on 128th Street and Eighth Avenue in front of a beauty shop. Tell him I'm going to wait for him there."

"Okay baby, I'll call you right back." Angie called Slick and then she called Lil' A back. "He said he will be on the east side of the street. He can be there in about 15 minutes. He said he will be in a yellow Hummer."

"Okay, I'll be waiting," Lil' A said.

"Baby, don't stay out too late. I want to smoke, plus I cooked something real good for you," Angie told him.

Lil' A asked, "What?"

"You'll see when you get here."

Lil' A knew she could cook her ass off, so he said, "Okay."

He looked at the front of the salon and called the number. The phone rang and a girl answered.

She said, "Hello, who is this?"
Lil' A asked, "Is Red there?"
"May I ask whose calling?"
"Tell her it's a secret, alright?"
"I'm not telling her that."
"Well, she won't be able to get her gift if you don't."

The girl on the other end of the line hesitated. However, Lil' A knew she would fold because all girls, or as he believed, that the average girl was out for material things. He was right.

"Hold on for a few seconds," the young woman said.

Red picked up the phone. In a snappy voice, she questioned. "Hello, who is this...?"

"Woah! Woah! What's up with the attitude?"
"Well, who is this?"
"Yo, this is A."
"Who?"
"Damn, you meet that many dudes you can't remember?"

"Well, A doesn't sound too familiar." Then Red thought for a moment and asked, "Is this Tiffany's A, the one with the Benz? Yeah boy, what's wrong with you?"

"Nothing at all, I was really trying to holla at the owner."

Red laughed. She then confessed, "Well you got her."

"Yeah, I know."

"Red said, "So you think you are the only smart one?"

"Not at all."

"Boy, where do you get off coming like this? Nobody knows you..."

"Well that's good. I don't want to be known."

"Where you at…?"

"In front of the shop."

Red looked out the window. She said, "I don't see your car."

"What, you think that's the only car I got?"

"Boy, what color car you in?"

"I'm in a minivan. It's red."

"Oh. I see it. I'm coming out to holla at you."

"Well, you do that."

As she hung up the phone, she came out. On her way out, she thought to herself, *I have to get this boy.* She came out with a tight outfit on, looking good.

Red walked up to the van and said, "What's up A, where's your girl Tiffany?"

"Come on, that ain't right."

Red asked confused, "What?"

"Look, we don't ever have to talk about her if she's not around. I just hate talking behind people's back."

"Okay, whatever you say. So, what's up with you?"

"Well, to tell you the truth, I'm trying to see what's up with your party that's coming up."

"Oh, Tiffany told you about that. I got the door and the bar."

"Well I need ten tickets."

"Damn boy, that's how you're rolling"

"What, I roll thicker than that. But my crew from out of town is coming through and I just want them to have a good time and spend a little money."

Lil' A smiled and Red smiled back. Then, she said, "You remind me of somebody."

He didn't ask her who. He was interested in making some more points with her.

Out of nowhere, Lil' A inquired, "Who's your baby's daddy?"

Red was shocked. She thought to herself, *What's he up to?* Instantly her curiosity took over and in a loud voice she asked. "What made you ask that?"

He responded, "I guess the look in your eye." As Red blushed Lil' A asked, "Well anyway, how much are the tickets?"

She said, "Fifty dollars and you must dress up."

Then he said, "I don't dress." He pulled out a stack of money and counted out $1,000.

She quickly said, "That's too much."

Lil' A said, "Nah! I just need a cell number from you, so I can call you when we are out front, so me and my crew can just come right on in."

Now Red really understood what time it was. This young man was making a big play and wasn't too subtle about it.

She said, "Okay." Red gave him her number and said, "Call and check on a girl sometimes too. Don't be a stranger."

Now she was the one making a play. Lil' A had played a card and she responded. Now Red was putting the ball back in his court. If he was going to make a play, then she could play the game too. She just hoped he would bite.

Lil' A said, "Okay. I just hope I don't run into none of your jealous boyfriends."

"Oh, wait baby, ain't none of that. All these dudes out here are too scared."

"Well I'm not."

"I can see that," she replied.

As Red got out of the minivan, Lil' A asked if he could use her cell phone.

"My dude is supposed to be here. I want to know what's taking him so long."

"Boy, as long as you're not talking about drugs or killing somebody."

Red walked toward the salon.

Lil' A said, "Wait!" He hopped out of the van and walked toward Red. Just as they were about to walk into the salon, the yellow Hummer pulled up. Red's eyes opened wide. "Never mind. Red, I'll call you later," Lil' A told her.

She said, "Yeah, you do that."

She walked into the salon and stared out the window.

Lil' A pushed up on the Spanish dude. "Yo Slick, what's up?"

"Oh, so you're A. I've heard a lot about you."

"Oh, did you? Well I heard a little about you."

Slick seemed a little scared because Lil' A had a hood on and his eyes looked too scary.

Slick said, "I got ten pounds of purple haze for Angie,"

"Okay," Lil' A said.

A Honda Civic pulled up behind two other cars. Slicked explained about the car. Then Lil' A asked him to tell the driver to meet him around the corner. Lil' A jumped into the Quest and pulled off. Slick jumped into the Hummer and went on about his business too. Lil' A got the weed from the girls in the Honda Civic. They also gave him three ounces of some new hydro weed to try out. Lil' A took it, and then put the 10 pounds in the stash box. Then he pulled up in front of a store where he bought some blunts. Since it was getting late, he had to pick Sleepy up at the Amtrak station. He decided to call Red while he waited.

"Hello" he said, "What's up?"
"Hey, A!" Red greeted.
"How did you know it was me?"
"Because I was thinking about you too..."
Then Lil' A asked, "Can you take a ride with me?"
She replied, "Yeah, my sister can close up."
"Okay, well come on," Lil' A said as he pulled back around to the shop. Red came out. She got in and they pulled off.
Red remarked, "To be so young, you're into a lot of big things."
"Nah, not yet," Lil' A said. "What's really good with you, Red?"

As the questions came out, Red answered them in rapid fire fashion as if she was being interviewed by a news reporter. Some of the questions got real personal. He asked her if she was still fucking with her baby's father. If she was dating anyone. How old she was? What her kids' names were and how old they were? He also asked how many cars she had, what she likes to eat and where she hangs out. He got everything out of her and his final question was, whether she smoked weed or not.

Red said, "Yeah, I smoke a little here and there." Lil' A began rolling a blunt. They began to smoke and talk. Red exclaimed, "That shit is fire…!"

Lil' A jumped back onto the highway. He was halfway downtown when his beeper went off. Sleepy's train had

A Father's Burden

gotten in a little early. He was calling to let Lil' A know he was back and waiting at the train station. A few minutes later, Lil' A was downtown. Sleepy was standing outside the Amtrak station. When Lil' A beeped the horn Sleepy walked over to the van and got in.

Lil' A said, "Yo Sleepy, this is, Red." Turning to Red he said, "This is my man, Sleepy." As they talked, Lil' A gave Sleepy a hand full of weed and Sleepy rolled it up. Sleepy had a whole bunch of bags.

Sleepy said, "Yo, I got too much money on me."

Lil' A asked, "So, what you got?"

Sleepy replied, "I got $300,000." Red's eyes opened wide, but she sat still. Now she really knew that this young man was getting big. In reality, Lil' A wanted Red to hear what she'd just heard; but he didn't want to dwell on it for too long. He quickly changed the subject.

Next, they were on the way back to Uptown. Lil' A asked Red, "Are you hungry?"

She answered, "No."

Sleepy asked Lil' A if he could stop at a store. He said, "Yo, just stop real quick, so I can buy my baby's mother these sneakers she wanted. It's right on 144th and Broadway. It's called K.P. Con."

Lil' A drove to the store. Sleepy got out to make his purchase. Meanwhile, Lil' A and Red sat and flirted. When Sleepy returned, Lil' A dropped Red back at her car, then he headed out to take Sleepy home.

Before Sleepy exited the car, he said, "Ay man, thank you. This is the most money I've ever made on my own and held on to. I just want to thank you because I'm eating, so that means my kids and baby's mother are eating." They shook hands and Sleepy wanted to cry.

Lil' A said, "I'm with you to the end. Rich or poor, I'm a loyal friend."

"I know, dawg," Sleepy said. "I know. I love you man."

Sleepy got out of the car. Lil' A headed back to Jersey to his Spanish mami's house. As he thought of her, he really wanted to show her that he was capable of getting money too.

Finally, when Lil' A reached Jersey, Angie had laid a path of red roses from the doorstep all the way up the stairs, to the bed in the master bedroom. She was really a romantic. The roses were a very nice touch. Angie wasn't subtle at all. She wanted to impress her new man and she was not bashful about it. When Lil' A walked into the bedroom, Angie was lying on the bed butt naked. She had blue wine on ice that she poured in crystal glasses for them both. As Lil' A sipped his wine, Angie served her baby his food. With as hot as she was looking, Angie was still concerned about feeding her man. She fed him fork after fork of food until it was finished. Then Angie wiped his mouth.

Lil' A sparked up a blunt as they got high and talked. He told her what he'd made, having profited close to $250,000.

"Damn, baby. You made all of that?"
"Yeah," he said.
Angie replied, "You surprise me more and more every day. I'm going to take you to all my car connects so you can buy a fleet of cars and where you can have a whole bunch of pictures taken. Then you will be able to have a fake license. You will need about ten of them."
"Why so many?" Lil' A asked.

A Father's Burden

Angie answered, "Baby, you never know when you may have to switch up your identity. Anything can happen and you have to be ready"

Later, Angie ran his bath water and put some bubble bath in it. The bubbles looked very inviting. Lil' A got in. Then she asked if everything was in the car. As he sat and soaked, Angie went out to the car to get all the weed and money. She put the money into her safe and went back into the bathroom to wash him up. After that she dried him off, and proceeded to doing what she liked to do. She was about to make some mad love to him. First, she gave him oral sex. He came within seconds of her putting her hot lips on his dick. Angie kept on sucking his dick causing him to get two more nuts. She was impressed that her young horse could last so long. After Lil' A busted his second nut, Angie asked him to put his dick in her ass and to ram it hard.

Lil' A loved that position. When they were done Angie wiped his dick off with a soapy rag before they engaged in more oral sex. After that, Angie put her legs on his shoulders and Lil' A hit it from the front. After he nutted a few more times, he let her take control. Angie began riding him, she screamed loudly from having so many orgasms. She held on to his arms and started shaking. Lil' A didn't know what the fuck was going on since she was shaking so much.

Later when she stopped, he asked, "Ma, what's wrong with you?
Angie responded. "Baby, that's that good dick of yours. You make me cum. I haven't had one of those in seven years. Boy, I love you."

Lil' A thought Angie was bugging out. But only if he knew she wasn't. As the night went on, they continued sleeping through the day and into the next night. Needless to say they were tired, and that heavy sex had them both exhausted. It didn't mean anything because Angie got what she wanted. Lil' A loved it because she treated him like a king. It was all in Angie's plan to turn this boy out and have him under her web.

Before they knew it, two days had passed. It seemed that whenever Lil' A was with Angie in her house, he was being treated as he had never been treated before. Angie pampered him, made mad love to him, and somehow time just seemed to quickly pass by in her presence. It was as if they were in a timeless period where no one cared what time it was and day would seamlessly melt into night. Somehow, time didn't mean anything to them. What mattered most was them being together and enjoying every minute of it.

Finally, the two sex-crazed lovers made it out of the house. Angie showed Lil' A how to buy the cars he wanted. Then she schooled him on where to get the stash boxes made. She showed him the real tricks of the trade. She showed him how to get tagged cars, and cars that had been crashed. You buy a crashed-up car, then steal another car, switch parts, and the crashed car is brand new again.

She explained that he could do all that for $7,000 to $15,000. *Oh, you won't believe what you can do with your money if you set your mind to use it in the right way.* More and more Angie introduced Lil' A the other side of the world. Or shall I say the major money side.

Chapter Nine

Lil' A finally met Harry, the car dealer, who could do more than find him a car. Harry could get almost anything including apartments and houses. But Angie never bought property from him. However, Lil' A knew he could buy some and could use them as fuck houses just to take different girls there. Harry liked A from the beginning. Angie let the men be men. She didn't try to interfere with their interaction. Lil' A told Harry he would be back with his man and that they would buy a couple of cars. He put in an order for 10 cars. He gave Harry $20,000 for himself to make sure he would always get what he wanted. Lil' A and Harry talked a little more and Harry secured $120,000 up front.

Harry knew Lil' A was young and was about to buy a fleet of cars. *Most young dudes always bought a bunch of cars*, he thought. Harry understood their needs and realized that they would be good people to do business with. Lil' A and Angie left the Long Island car lot. They realized that Harry had the hookup as long as you had the cash. He would do the paperwork so that the police nor the IRS wouldn't harass you. So everything was taken care of. The next day, Lil' A called one of Angie's drivers to drive him around all day.

Lil' A went to get Booberlocks. They smoked and chilled on the ride to Long Island. He asked Booberlocks how much money he had for a car.

Booberlocks said, "$50,000."

They arrived at Harry's car lot. As soon as Harry saw Lil' A his eyes lit up.

"A, my friend, I thought you were never going to show."

"Why did you think that?" asked a surprised Lil' A.

"Come on, come on. I just got five new models in. I got a family car, a Volvo station wagon. It's brand new. I have two Benzes. I got a Nissan Z Twin Turbo, and a BMW 325."

"Oh word? Let me see them."

Booberlocks was amazed. He couldn't believe he was about to buy his first car, the Benz he always wanted. Lil' A had another $30,000 on him. But, Booberlocks didn't know Lil' A had already given Harry $120,000. So off the top, Booberlocks finally bought his first Benz. Lil' A told Harry he wanted the Nissan Z and the BMW for himself. Lil' A also wanted the brand-new Volvo. So that's three cars he bought. Lil' A instructed Harry where to send the two cars, so he could get work done to them. He wanted them to be souped up fast. So, Lil' A got work done to the engine, and had a stash box installed.

Booberlocks had to front. He didn't want it to go to any shop yet. Lil' A kept the BMW so he could drive around. Now nobody on the streets had these cars yet. So they were the first ones to bust out with these whips. Lil' A bought the other Benz.

Booberlocks asked, "Damn A, what are you going to do with four cars?"

Lil' A responded, "Well, three are mine and one is for a friend. Next week, I'm going to surprise Tiffany with her

A Father's Burden

own car. I don't know what I'm going to buy her. So, I'm going to see what she wants."

Harry called Lil' A back into the office. Lil' A told Booberlocks to give Harry $40,000 and he did. When Lil' A walked back into the office, Harry made out what he owed for the rest of the cars. In fact, he gave him six months to pay and Harry would do the paperwork to make it look like he was paying monthly. Harry told Lil' A he owed him $150,000 more. He said fine and gave him $70,000 more. Harry looked as if to say, *Boy where are you getting this money*. Of course, he had a very good idea where the money was coming from and he did not really care as long as he was making sales. He liked doing business with Lil' A because he didn't have to hard sell him. Lil' A had ready money so Harry didn't have to dick with him about the price.

Harry said, "No wonder Angie loves you. She said you are her husband."

"Yeah," Lil' A said. Smiling he confirmed his balance, "I owe you $80,000, right?"

"Yeah," Harry replied, and then Lil' A stated, "Just make the paperwork out so both Benzes and the station wagon are paid for."

Harry nodded his head and said, "Okay, I got you."

As a surprise to Harry, Lil' A said, "I'm putting in an order for 10 more cars next month. I want three up-to-date cars and seven cars I want like Hondas, Camry's, and minivan types. Like $20,000 and under type of cars, okay? I will pay for half in two weeks when I come bring the $80,000, I owe."

Harry in good faith said, "I going to throw in two cars on the strength of your credit, but they can't be over $50,000."

"Yeah, I hear you Harry" as they shook hands. Then Lil' A walked out of the office to his man, Booberlocks.

Booberlocks asked, "How much do I owe?"

"Don't worry about it dawg. I took care of it. And I also bought the other Benz, so we'll be back."

"Man, I don't know what you doing, but you're doing it big."

"I'm keeping the BMW for the day until the other cars are ready and I can put this one in the shop."

"Well I'm just going hard A," Booberlocks said.

But Lil' A knew he couldn't slip.

While they waited for the paperwork to be completed, Lil' A asked Harry if he could use the phone. He called Papi, but he wasn't there. So Lil' A told his girl he needed to talk to him. He asked if she knew where he was.

Papi's girl said, "He's out of town."

Lil' A told her he had a surprise for her from him. He said he picked it up. Papi's girl knew Lil' A was good people. She had met him and knew that Papi liked him a lot.

Lil' A asked her to have Papi call him as soon as he got in and that he misses him and loves him.

She said, "Okay."

He hung up and told Harry that a girl was coming to pick up the station wagon and for Harry to wait for her no matter how long she took and to make sure the car was ready to go.

Harry said, "Okay, anything for you, A."

He made sure, or shall I say doubled checked, the other address to send the Benz and Nissan to was right.

So the next thing you know, the Benz pulled up shiny and black. The BMW came up money green with beige leather. Booberlocks jumped straight into his Benz. Lil' A told the driver who had brought him to the dealership to go ahead and leave as he jumped into his first owned car. Next, as the two cars were about to pull off, they stopped side-by-side. Lil' A rolled down his window.

A Father's Burden

Booberlocks said, "Man, I don't even know how to get back."

Lil' A started to laugh and then jumped out of the car leaving his door open.

He said, "Booberlocks, I don't have any money on me. Let me hold something."

He gave Lil' A $5,000.

Lil' A said, "You know we got to drive around all of Harlem and the Bronx." Then Lil' A added, "And I got to go see my baby's mother and take her to get something to eat."

Booberlocks said, "Okay A, let's ride."

The two jumped onto the highway and headed toward the city. As they were driving back to back in a two-car convoy, they rode through 102nd Street and Third Avenue. Then they drove through 110th Street and Second Avenue up to Lenox Avenue. Then they drove through 112th Street. 113th Street and 114th Street toward 125th Street as everybody was looking because they were the newest cars on the streets.

They were taking the grand tour showing off their new possessions. They were proud of their cars because they felt they had worked hard to get what they had dreamed of for so long. They felt good as people on the streets gawked at them. They could tell that some people actually thought they were something special. That was a very good feeling. Girls pulled up beside them. On their tour, Booberlocks grabbed so many numbers, but Lil' A was low key. He had dark tints on his car. Booberlocks just had to show off, so they stopped on 125th Street and Broadway. At the front of a store, both cars parked side-by-side.

Lil' A said, "Yo, come with me to shit on this broad. Then after that, I'm going to meet up with my baby's mother. Okay?"

Lil' A was talking about Red's salon. He told Booberlocks that Red owned the salon on 128th Street and Seventh Avenue.

Booberlocks said, "Yo, my girl wants to go there. They say all the ballers girls go there to get their hair done."

Lil' A said, "Yeah, the owner is sweating me, plus I'm sending Tiffany there to get her hair done."

"You see A, I told you. You surprise me every day, dawg."

"Yo, you know they say bad boys move in silent ways."

They both laughed and pulled off. They finally pulled up in front of the salon. It was crowded as hell with mad honeys. Both Lil' A and Booberlocks left their cars doubled parked on the street. Now everyone was gawking at their cars. They were just stopping to look and commenting on how nice they were. Then both Lil' A and Booberlocks walked into the salon.

"Hey, Red…,"

She smiled, showing signs of her blushing. Red's sister sat there watching knowing that her sister was up to no good.

Red said, "Hey. What's up, A?"

He replied, "Yo, this is my man, Booberlocks, Tiff's cousin."

She hesitated and then said, "Yo, what's up? What are you doing, just chillin'?"

"I just wanted to show you my new car. It's a BMW like yours."

Red said, "Oh it is…?" She looked out the window. "Oh man, that's the new 325 joint. I heard it's on back order for one year. And that other car, that's your man's car…?"

"Yeah," said Lil' A

Red said, "You just wanted to show off that you got a car I would love to have."

A Father's Burden

Lil' A started laughing and said, "In fact, we just bought 10 new cars."

Red's eyes popped wide open. Meanwhile, Booberlocks was on the side hollering at Red's sister.

Red said, "Come on let me see how it looks on the inside." She got in and Lil' A got into the driver's seat. Red said, "Damn boy, this shit is crazy."

"Yeah I know. When the car dealer told me, they didn't have these cars out yet, I had to jump on it."

Red said, "What's really good?"

He asked, "What do you mean?"

Red then said, "Look, I know about your little girl, Tiff. But you probably got a lot of bitches. But look, I'm starting to fall for your little ass."

"Whoa! Wait up. Ain't nothing little about me."

"Yeah I know, but we got to get together."

"Sure, whenever."

Red said, "Look I'm a woman and I don't have no time for games. But I'm trying to fuck. I haven't fucked in about five years, ever since my baby's father got locked up. But I'm feeling you, A."

It was hard for him to believe she had not fucked in five years. A woman this good looking, and as savvy as she appeared to be, would be hit on all the time. Certainly, she would have given in to someone.

"I'm feeling you too," Lil' A said.

Red said, "I'm on my period and I'll be done, soon. But I need at least one more day so I can douche good for you. You know, before I put it on your lil' ass."

Lil' A made one of his little slick faces and said, "You sure it won't be the other way around."

Red smiled and asked, "On another note, are you still coming to my party?"

"Yeah, I'm coming through thick with my whole crew."

"Oh, finally you're going to show your hand."

"Nah, just a few fingers," he revealed as they both laughed.

Red's sister and Booberlocks made their way out of the salon toward his new car. The two looked as if they were hitting it off.

Red said, "Okay low-key player. Let me hold something before all those hoes out there get you."

"That's a slick line, but I don't fuck with hoes, so I don't have to worry about them getting me. But, aren't you a woman…?"

"Yes, I am," Red answered.

"So I'm good then, but it ain't nothing to me though because I might need a favor back."

"Sure, anything you want, A."

"So, what do you need to hold?

Red replied, "Well, I want you to take me shopping, so after we could go fuck."

"Oh yeah?" said Lil' A. After evaluating her comment, he added, "So, when you want me to take you?"

"Well you're the busy one. So you give me a date," Red retorted.

"How about we link up in two days? Is that's good for you?" offered Lil' A.

"Yeah, that's good. I'll call you," she said. "And don't forget that the party is coming up in two weeks."

"Yeah, I know. Don't worry, I'm ready."

She leaned over and gave A a kiss on his cheeks. "Call me," Red said.

"Okay," he said as she got out of the car.

Lil' A made his way around to the driver's seat of Booberlocks's car.

"A, where are you trying to go now?"

A Father's Burden

Lil' A replied, "Remember I told you I had to go holla at my baby's mother. So I'll call you tomorrow."

"Okay, I'll drive around and keep shitting on them. Plus, one of them broads I just met I'm about to go fuck," said Booberlocks. "I'm going to need some more work."

Lil' A said, "Okay, I'll be ready."

"I'll call you later," Booberlocks responded, before they parted ways.

Then Lil' A jumped onto the highway and headed toward the Bronx. As he got off on the Rosedale exit, he pulled over into a gas station. Lil' A used the phone to call Angie and told her he was going to go take care of a few things with his mother.

Since Lil' A wasn't coming home, Angie figured she would fly out of town for a few days. She told him to meet her at the house in five days.

Agreeing to her suggestion he said, "Okay."

Angie said, "I love you baby."

Lil' A repeated her sentiment. "I love you too," he said.

Lil' A called Verwana's house, but she wasn't there. Verwana's family told him she was at Nicky's. So he drove up to the projects and knocked on Nicky's door.

When Verwana came out, she didn't look very happy to see him. "Nigga, where you been, you got that Benz and now you can't ever be found," she snapped.

"Nah, it ain't like that," he explained.

Verwana said, "Well, I got the condo. It's way uptown in Bedford Park. I want to show you the crib. I bought beds and everything else. All I need is about two thousand dollars more and I can fill the house up."

Lil' A said, "Okay. Well let's go. You can show me now. Are you hungry?"

"Yeah," she answered.

"Alright, let's go."

So Verwana went back inside to say goodbye to everyone, while he waited out in the hallway. Lil' A sparked up a blunt. When Verwana came back out, she said, "Come on, let's go."

"So what's up, Verwana?"

"Nothing, I've been overwhelmed with concern thinking about you."

"Why? I'm okay."

"You know the cops came by my house asking my sister questions again. They're looking for you hard."

"Oh word? Well fuck the police. Boo, how are you and the baby?"

"We're fine. Finally, we got our own crib. Oh, it's your own crib."

"Shut up. It's yours too," Lil' A replied.

"Oh, I didn't know. Sike, you know I'm just trying to make fun of you."

As they walked outside the building, a crackhead saw Lil' A and said, "What's up…?" Lil' A looked up. It was Bee-Bee. "Nigga where you been?" Bee-Bee asked.

Lil' A replied, "Man, I've been staying low key."

The next thing Bee-Bee did was hit A up for some money. "Let me hold something."

A's response was a quick one. "Yo, I don't got nothing on me right now, but here go twenty dollars. I'll see you later."

"Okay, good looking A," Bee-Bee said, as he walked off toward the projects.

Verwana and A walked over to the BMW. She asked, "Where you get this car from?"

"I just bought it today."

"Word...? Verwana said. "How much did it cost you?"

Verwana was full of questions. She was a good for asking all the business. She seemed to question him whenever they were together.

A Father's Burden

Lil' A answered. "Not much, like $40,000."
"A, are you okay?"
"Yeah, let's get out of here."

They both got into the car and pulled off. Lil' A lit a blunt. Then he turned on some Mary J. Blige. They talked and smoked. Somehow Lil' A felt like a child whenever he was in Verwana's presence. They laughed and joked as she told him where the apartment was located. Verwana expressed her thoughts and that she felt like he was playing. She explained that she really liked him because he thought of her child as if she were his. They talked about growing up.

Finally, they got to the condo. It was big. At first Lil' A didn't like it. He never let Verwana know this because he had seen how happy she was just for the mere fact that she was able to get her own crib. They chilled. They finally locked eyes as Verwana kissed A. This kiss felt so different. It was like his first kiss ever. Lil' A really couldn't believe it. He kissed her again as she touched him.

She must have felt he was holding back as she screamed at him, "Nigga, you scared!"
"Shit, never that."
"So act like you been with a girl."

Then Lil' A started to take charge. Verwana was different from Angie, a woman who knew how to make him happy. She was a woman who could take charge of him and guide him to do whatever she wanted him to do, or what she wanted him to do for her. Yes, Verwana was his baby's mother, but she was much different.

He loved her very much too. He lifted up her shirt. Verwana's breasts were so nice and soft. As he took off his shirt, the two kept on kissing. Lil' A pulled down her pants.

She had the softest legs ever, all black and smooth. Lil' A pulled down his pants and then tugged at her panties until he had them off. Wasting no time, he quickly pulled down his boxers. He was so hard he could not control himself. She grabbed for his dick and put it in her pussy. It was so hard.

Lil' A rubbed the head of his dick up and down against Verwana's pussy. It felt so good. Lil' A knew Verwana hadn't fucked anyone in almost a year. So, she was ready to go, but after about ten pumps up and down, Lil' A exploded. His dick went weak. Verwana's pussy was just too wet for him. Lil' A was so amazed that he finally was making love to her, but he couldn't control himself in the moment. He came all in her. She felt the warm nut all inside her. Lil' A felt so ashamed. Verwana laughed.

She said, "Don't worry, baby. It's our first time. It'll get better the next time."

Lil' A couldn't say anything as Verwana got dressed. Even though his erection didn't last long but it still felt good to Verwana. It was just that he had cum too fast. Verwana had really wanted to go all night.

Lil' A gave Verwana $3,000. Verwana responded, "I only need $2,000." Lil' A retorted, "I know that. That's just in case you need more."

Verwana laughed and said, "Next time you'd better last longer."

Shame came all over Lil' A again. Lil' A boasted, "Don't worry. I'll be ready. Cause the next time I'm going to eat that pussy too."

Verwana questioned, "Can you do that?"

Lil' A confidently stated, "I sure can. Just you wait and see."

Verwana started laughing and said, "Come on let's go, I got to pick up the baby. Plus, the lights will be on next week and I want you to stay here with me?"

They locked the crib and headed for the garage. Seeing the smirk on Verwana's face he felt like a kid.

Verwana asked Lil' A if he had any more weed.
Lil' A answered, "Yeah."
"Let me roll one up," Verwana requested.
As soon as she finished, she sparked up the blunt. Thinking about their brief sexual encounter and in a sort of playful manner, Verwana said, "Don't worry. You will have a couple of days to redeem yourself."
Then they both started laughing.
He said, "Okay. You got this one on me. I got you though. Watch, you'll see the next time."

As she looked up at him, Lil' A jumped on the highway and took Verwana home. After dropping her off, he went back to his mother's old house. He finally met up with Tiffany. They just chilled. Lil' A sort of lost touch with Tiffany, he didn't even fuck her anymore. Tiffany just kept sucking his dick. But Lil' A just couldn't get Verwana off his mind. He was so mad that he wasn't able to fuck the shit out of her when he had the chance.

Chapter Ten

The next day, Yvette came to the house. When Lil' A left Tiffany's, he took time to show his mom his new car. The shop called to tell him that his Z was ready. So Lil' A went to get it. He left the BMW there to be worked on, meaning the sound system and the stash box.

Yvette showed her son where their new house was located. She too had bought herself a new car. Lil' A told her not to come to the old apartment anymore.

Yvette said, "Okay."

Lil' A told his mother he would not be selling drugs out of there.

Yvette just smiled and said, "I know, and I trust you."

Lil' A took Yvette to the apartment he bought for Verwana.

Yvette commented, "Finally you're getting for real."

Lil' A got a call from Papi, who said to meet him at Angie's store. Lil' A had his mother with him, so he would have to drop her off first. When he got there, they hugged and gave each other five.

Papi said, "I was out of town. My girl told me you gave her a new car."

"Yeah, does she like it?"

"Boy, you didn't have to do that."

"Nah Papi. You're my man. I finally bought my first car."

Papi said, "I have to buy you something. A, man, you're a good dude. You're going to be a good soldier."

Then Papi moved on to another topic. This one he felt was an important one, but it was already too late to make a difference.

"My sister is bad news and it seems like it's too late on the personal relationship front, but as a business partner that arrangement might be a good one....," Papi told him, taking a seat before continuing, "My sister likes you a lot. She brags about you already saying, you move 1,000 keys a month. She said that during the next six months, you should be able to move double that amount…"

"Let's go eat, drink and catch up a little," Papi suggested, getting up so they could leave.

After relocating to Papi's house they ordered food, had drinks, smoked weed and had much fun. Papi's girlfriend really liked A because he had helped her boyfriend avoid jail time and he'd just bought her a new car.

Enjoying the party atmosphere, they started to get a little wild. Out of the blue, Lil' A asked Papi if he had ever been with a black girl.

Papi said, "Yeah, but it's been over five years and I do need one." Lil' A explained to Papi that he was going to do it big that night. Papi said, "Well, big is my middle and last name."

They both started to laugh. Then they began playing PlayStation. Lil' A and Papi played over and over, all night. Until A eventually fell asleep on Papi.

As morning came, Lil' A told Papi he would see him later. But before he left, he said, "I got a surprise for you too."

Papi replied, "Man, you really don't have to give me anything. The car you got my girl was enough."

Lil' A said, "Nah, I will always want to do things for you," he hugged Papi and then walked off.

Later, A caught up with his mother. Yvette showed her son where her new house was located. Lil' A told his mother where he bought Verwana's house.

Yvette said, "Boy you really like that girl Verwana don't you? I remember when you were young, and you used to chase her around. All she had to do was yell your name and you'd come running to her. You beat up all the boys who liked her." Lil' A began to blush. Yvette continued, "I remember when she had that baby. Your world almost ended. You didn't talk to her for almost a year. But you finally turned it around."

Lil' A called Verwana. "Hello! What's up?"
"Hey A, what are you doing?"
"Nothing, just chillin' with my mom's..."
"Oh, tell her I said hi and ask her how she's doing."
Lil' A repeated the message to his mother.
"Boy, let me get that phone," Yvette ordered, as she grabbed it from her son.
Both women talked for a while.
Then Yvette said, "Let me give the phone back to A because if looks could kill, I'd be dead or is it a look of love?"

Later, Lil' A talked with Verwana again. She wanted to know more about the conversation with his mother. Did

A Father's Burden

Yvette say anything else to him about her? How does Yvette feel about her? Verwana was full of questions once again. Lil' A could tell this was going to be a real serious phone conversation. Verwana sensed that Yvette liked her, and really saw her as that *someone special* for her son. Talking to Yvette, however, gave Verwana a funny feeling. She wondered what was in store for her in the future with Lil' A.

After the phone conversation, Verwana thought a lot about Lil' A, their relationship, and the role his mother would play in them being together.

Verwana asked Lil' A, "Boy what was your mother talking about?

Lil' A brushed her off, "I don't know. She's crazy."

Verwana then asked Lil' A, "Do you love me?"

Lil' A was a little surprised by the question, so he asked, "Why did you ask me that?"

Verwana stated, "Because I want to know."

So Lil' A answered, "Yeah of course. Why do you think I want the best for you?"

In a tone that suggested she was not fully convinced, Verwana asked, "Oh you do, but that does not mean you love me."

Lil' A responded by making Verwana remember that he was the father of her daughter. In his mind, this was the reason he had a strong tie to Verwana; therefore, he loved her at least for that fact.

"I do because you got a daughter to take care of as well. As long as I'm alive, I'm going to always do for the both of you."

That thought began to sink into Verwana's head. For the time being at least, that would suffice. That was somewhat reassuring. Besides, Lil' A had made it possible for her to realize the dream of having her own house. He had been a very good provider and took care of her and her daughter. Even though, he seemed to have some periods when he would disappear, Lil' A did always come back strong for her. The two love birds continued talking for a few more hours. Finally, Verwana asked if he was coming back to the house later to spend the night.

"Yeah," Lil' A confirmed. Then he followed that by saying he had some things to do before he came. "Verwana, I got to make a move, but I will call you later. Okay?"

She responded by saying, "Well, in a couple of days the lights will be on, so make sure you're ready to spend the night with me because A, you know you got to redeem yourself from that one-minute fashion you pulled. Okay?"

"You can make jokes now, but don't worry. I got you, okay? Next time you won't forget or be able to laugh at me no more," Lil' A retorted.

Verwana said, "Okay. I'm holding you to that."

They both laughed and said, "I love you," before they hung up.

There was a lot to think about. Lil' A had taken part in two very serious conversations with two very important women in his life. They both meant a lot to him and he wanted to make sure he fully understood them knowing he would do anything to help them in any way that he could.

Now it was time to head back to Jersey. It had been a good day. Lil' A had enjoyed spending time with his mother and talking with Verwana. So, he jumped onto the highway and shot back to Angie's house. She was waiting for him. When Lil' A walked into the house, Angie was walking around naked with only a long shirt on. As usual, she looked very sexy and inviting.

"Hey baby, how are you?" Angie greeted.
"Chillin'," Lil' A responded.

Angie then informed him, "Hey, tomorrow we have to go take care of something, okay?"
Lil' A answered, "Whatever."

She asked if he was hungry. His answer was, yeah. Angie went straight to the kitchen to cook, asking A to roll up a blunt as she walked away. When dinner was done, they ate, smoked weed, and had a few drinks. This was all preliminary for what she really wanted to do with Lil' A. She was anxious for some lovemaking, or shall we say, good sex.

Angie started out by giving him oral sex. She worked the whole program. She took Lil' A's clothes off, then began massaging his dick with her long, slender fingers. Angie worked them up and down the shaft of his dick. It grew and became harder. Now she was ready to put her lips on it. She licked up and down the shaft. Then out came the tongue. She licked up and down his dick playing with its head to arouse him even more. Angie put her fingers around his pubic area, massaging the area while she licked and sucked. Then she moved to the next stage. She turned around and let Lil' A fuck her in the butt because she knew he liked doing that with her. It was special for him because he had not done it with any of the other women he had been with.

After that bit of first and second stage sex, they fucked the rest of the night away. Angie liked when he came inside of her. She asked him to do so. For some reason, she really got off on that. It made her feel really good and it somehow helped her to cum too. Lil' A liked when she came. It made him feel good and confirmed he was working it well. Too bad he had misfired with Verwana.

It was a good evening. They had fun. They made love as only two people could dream of having. After their vigorous workout they fell asleep.

The next morning, they got up and went to where Angie docked her boat. Lil' A finally met the man who supplied the whole East Coast with narcotics. Ricco was his name. Lil' A was amazed to see him because he thought of how powerful the man must be to have such control over such a large area and be able to move so much stuff. Without him, guys like him, Papi, and others would not be able to make as much money as they were able to make.

Angie and Ricco spoke to each other in Spanish. After a few words of introduction and greeting, Angie told Ricco that she was going to marry A, and that she was ready to take a big shipment. Angie put in an order for 10,000 keys of coke and 10,000 keys of heroin. If you do the math, the number of keys and the amount of money that can be made from the sale of the keys, amounts to a billion dollars. *Yes, a billion dollars with a B.*

Ricco had worked with Angie before. He knew what she was capable of producing. She was no novice. She could do what she said she could do. Ricco knew that. He believed it and he respected her ability to do that. He didn't worry about the money because he knew Angie was more than capable of paying for it. However, this was a lot of work. So, Ricco said he would want $5,000 for each key of coke and $10,000 for each key of heroin. Meaning Angie owed Ricco $100 million dollars. *Like I said, this was a lot of work.* No matter how she sold it. That was what she owed Ricco. She, however, could triple her money.

Ricco said it would be there in 48 hours.
He told her, "Have half of the money in two months and I will pick up the next half two months from that day."
She said, "Okay!"

This was an experience for Lil' A, this was really the big leagues. He was impressed with Angie's confidence.

A Father's Burden

Shit. He was impressed just hearing the numbers. This was some real work. This was Lil' A's proof that Angie was no bullshit broad. She was thorough, confident, and cold-blooded. After the meeting with Ricco, Angie, and Lil' A went out to eat at a restaurant in New Jersey. It was a good meal. They didn't rush; they just enjoyed eating the different courses. Angie really knew how to do things big. Lil' A was getting a good lesson in being cool. He was learning very much from her.

Angie really enjoyed schooling Lil' A. She was molding him in the way she wanted him to be. She was teaching him class. She was teaching him how to live nicely. She was teaching him how to be a good love maker. She was teaching him about cars. And she was teaching him about power. Most of all, Angie was teaching Lil' A how much she wanted him to be a part of whatever she was building. She did not have to take him to the meeting with Ricco, but Angie wanted to impress Lil' A and let him in on what she was doing. She was not hiding anything from him. *Would there be consequences later?*

After the nice meal, they went back to the crib to indulge in serious sex, drink, and smoke some more.

Chapter Eleven

Two days later, the drugs came in. Angie left all the drugs in a warehouse for safekeeping.

Red's party in the City was coming up in two days. Things were happening fast. There was a lot to do.

Angie had managed Lil' A's growth. She liked the transformation she was seeing in him.

"Well, baby you're no longer young and dumb. You're growing fast and you are dealing with a lot of money. All kinds of bitches are going to be on you now. I might not be able to stop the hoes. Just keep them away from me or we are going to fall out," Angie said, expressing her thoughts.

Lil' A said, "Look, I don't want to hear that shit..."

Angie was shocked and immediately replied, "Okay gangster, the only one that's exempt is your baby's mother. You just got to be careful, baby."

Lil' A said, "I know how to move around in this snake pit full of snakes. If you don't trust me, why are we doing it?"

Angie said, "You're right."

Lil' A then headed back to the city. He had work to do and people to contact. He called Booberlocks and asked him

A Father's Burden

how much money he had. Booberlocks said he had $50,000 on hand. So Lil' A asked him to bring it down.

Of course, his response was, "Okay."

So he brought the money and they both talked for a while.

Booberlocks told Lil' A he'd ran into a man who knew him from Riker's Island. He said he thought the man might be a good connection. Lil' A asked if he thought the man and his people were good dudes. Booberlocks gave them a vote of confidence. He asked Lil' A if they could drive through their block to check them out. He said they were on 105th and Second Avenue.

As Lil' A drove toward their destination, he saw the dope line. From that, he knew the block was getting money. Booberlocks saw his man out there too.

He called him to the car, "Yo Kay."

Kay walked over to the car. "Yo, Booberlocks," he responded. "What's good? I thought you forgot?"

Booberlocks' responded, "Nah! My man just got back in town. Get in, Kay."

The man got into the car. He yelled at someone on the block, "Yo! Hold it down. I'll be back."

Booberlocks' introduced Kay to Lil' A. He said, "This is my man A."

Kay, said, "Yo. What's up, A?"

Lil' A replied, "Yo, What's up, Kay?"

Kay said that he had heard Lil' A's name before but could not recall where he'd heard it. He was trying hard to remember.

Kay then expressed, "Yo, Booberlocks. What's good? I'm trying to find that plug. want to cop something tonight."

Booberlocks' replied, "Word. Well you got the plug, my man A. That's why we're here."
Kay asked, "What are the tickets going for?"
Lil' A answered. "That depends on how many being bought."
Kay just jumps straight to the point. He knew A meant business.
He said, "Yo, man. I got paper. I just need it for the low, low. Right now, my block is doing $50,000 a day. It used to do $100,000, but my source got pinched. So, I'm off and on."

Lil' A knew from the look of the block that there was money to be made.
Booberlocks' passed Kay a blunt.

Kay drew on it and said, "Yo. That shit smell like some fire. He hit it again. This time, Kay choked. "Damn, I knew that shit was some fire. I just need the work to be fire..."
Lil' A cut him off.
With intensity he said, "Dawg, all my shit is guaranteed!"
Kay said, "I'm feeling that."
Lil' A asked, "What are you trying to get?"
He said, "Well, I need one ticket of heroin, and at least two tickets of coke."
Lil' A said, "No problem." Continuing he said, "The ticket of heroin is $70,000 and that shit can hold up to anything."
Kay's eyes opened wide and then he said, "Word?"
Lil' A responded with more business talk. "The tickets for the coke are $20,000 each."
Kay said, "Yeah. That shit is cheap."
Lil' A then said, "Yo dawg. If you are my man's man, then you're my man. I just mean business. You burn me one time that's it. You're gone. So, the choice is yours. Now if you can move the work in a week, whatever you buy I will

match it for the same price. But you have to get me out the way first."

"Word A," Kay said. "Yeah. I'm feeling you. So make that two and two of each and there'll be no problems on this end, dawg"

"Cool, so when you ready, call this number," advised Lil' A as he gave Kay his phone number. "And make sure you don't talk on the phone. Just say A, what's good and I'll tell you where to meet me. Okay?"

"Can you bring it to me? I have a stash crib in Queens by Randall Island?"

"Okay. No problem."

Kay said, "I'll call you in two hours. Aight? I'll see you then... So you will have double?"

Lil' A said, "My word is my bond."

"Okay. I'll see you later. I'll be calling you in a few."

Kay then turned to Booberlocks and said, "Good looking out, man. I'll see you later."

Kay got out after they pulled around the block. Lil' A and Booberlocks drove off and they went back to Booberlocks's crib.

On the way back, Booberlocks said, "Boy, you surprise me more and more."

Lil' A said, "Yo dawg, we about to make more money than ever. I'm about to flood you. So, sell weight too, and make all rocks bigger than ever. Okay?"

As they pulled up to Booberlocks crib, Lil' A said. "Now, for that $50,000, here go four keys. You know our style, or should I say, the way we do, so here go one more key. I just want $15,000 back on that, so when you bust it down you keep all the extra. Okay?"

"Damn A you definitely flooding me."

"Nah dawg, let's just get money. I'm with you... Take that upstairs."

Booberlocks did what he was told.

Then Lil' A asked, "Yo, you have any work cooked up already?"

Booberlocks said, "Yeah."

"Bring down 28 grams, so I can give it to someone."

As Booberlocks got out of the minivan and went upstairs, Lil' A began mental accounting of the money and work he had on the street. Let's see. There's $50,000 already. He was about to pick up $180,000 more with another $180,000 on the street. There was at least $80,000 more from Booberlocks coming in. Plus, when B.C. came back from out of town, they were going to cop heavy.

Two hours went by fast. True to his word Kay called in the time frame he stipulated. "Yo, A, what's good "B"?"

The response was, "Nothing dawg."

"Yo. Meet me at my stash crib."

Lil' A said, "Nah, there's been a change of plan. Meet me at this hair salon on 127th Street."

"Oh, I know where that's at," Kay replied. Then he said, A, don't you want to count the money?"

"Of course, I do, but not now. When I get to my crib, I'll handle it. Plus, I trust you. I told you before, you burn me one time, and your ass is cut off. And if I feel any disrespect, put yourself in a box. You feel me, Kay?"

Kay said, "I feel you A. So, how long will it take you to get there?"

"About 25 minutes."

"Okay. I'll be there."

Lil' A called Red. "Yo, what's up stranger?" Red said.

"You ready to go out and get your outfit?" he asked.

"Yeah."

A Father's Burden

"So be ready. I'll be there in about 25 minutes," he said.
"Okay, I'll be waiting for you."

Lil' A sparked up another blunt and made his way toward Red's salon. His cell phone rang. It was Kay.

"Yo, I'm here. I'm stuck at a red light. I got too much money on me."

Lil' A pulled up and hit the horn. He had a Smith & Wesson 9-millimeter on his lap. Kay got out of a nice-looking car. But Lil' A didn't really pay much attention to the car. He was looking at the black book bag he had in his hand. Kay got into the van.

"Yo, what's up?"

Lil' A responded "Nothing."

Kay took the bag and dumped all the money in the backseat. Lil' A reached under the floor panel and pulled out eight keys – four heroin keys and four coke keys. Kay hurried to put it in the bag.

Kay said, "Yo A, man if this shit is the bomb, you about to get half of Harlem's money. I hope you can handle it."

"I can handle anything that comes my way." Lil' A reassured.

As Kay jumped out, Lil' A said, "Holla when you're ready."

Seconds later, Red came out. She had just missed Kay. Since she did not see him, Red wasn't able to realize that they knew each other. As she got into the minivan, she kissed A on the cheek. She noticed the gun on his lap, and then she turned around and saw all the money on the back seat.

Red asked, "Boy, why are you driving around with all that money?"

"Stop questioning me and you won't get lied to," Lil' A instructed her.

Red smiled and said, "You and that slick mouth."

"So, where are we off to," Lil' A asked Red.

Red answered, "To the Christian Dior store."

"Okay, tell me how to get there," he remarked.

"Jump on the Westside Highway," she replied.

Lil' A did as she directed and they smoked all the way there.

When they got to the Christian Dior store, Red said, "I know men don't have the patience to shop. I already know what I want."

She described what she wanted. There were two dresses, a dress bag, and shoes. The shoes were $5,000, and so was the bag. The dresses cost $10,000. Red said she bought both outfits in different colors. She went in and tried everything on.

Meanwhile, Lil' A called Verwana to ask her shoe and dress sizes. She told Lil' A, and then Verwana asked him why he was asking.

Lil' A said, "Chill ma. I'll show you later."

So Lil' A told the lady at the store to get him a second order. It was funny because both sizes were there and ready. It all came up to $40,000. So Lil' A paid for both. He gave the lady a $1,000 tip. She was very happy.

Red got back into the minivan and they pulled off. Red asked, "A, who is this other dress for, Tiff?"

He smirked and said, "Yeah."

After shopping, they went to get something to eat. They decided on Benihana, where they cook the food right in front of you on the grill. At the restaurant they talked, got a little tipsy and ate their entire meal. Lil' A was starting to really

A Father's Burden

like, Red. But she had a funny look in her eye, so Lil' A had a bad feeling about her. By the time they finished it had gotten darker, indicating it was time to be on their way. Lil' A was going to drop her off back at her shop. He told Red he would see her at the party.

He pulled off and went to pick Tiffany up because he had been playing her lately, so he felt as if they weren't together. After visiting he dropped Tiff and her mother off at the bus station. He gave her money to keep on hand and to go shopping. Lil' A told her if she needed more money, she should call him.

Then, Tiffany looked him directly in the eye and asked him straight up, "A, you don't love me no more?"
Lil' A quickly responded, "Why you ask that?"
Tiffany replied, "Because it seems the more money you're getting, the more distance there is between us."
"Nah, Tiff! It ain't like that, Boo. I'm just real busy."
Tiffany retorted, "I know, Boo...! But we really need to talk."
Lil' A said, "Whenever you're ready."
Tiffany began to cry which initiated him asking, "Why are you crying, Boo?"

Tiffany's mother said, "They're ready. The bus will leave in 10 minutes."

Lil' A said, "Well, you have to go. Just call me, okay?"

They kissed and Tiff walked off with her mother. As he pulled off, Tiffany's mother asked, "Baby, did you tell him?"
Her daughter answered, "No mom. The time wasn't right."
Her mother then said, "Girl, you're about to have a baby. You don't have anywhere to stay or nothing. No job.

No money. What does he do; because he has a lot of cars? So he's got to be dealing a lot of drugs. I'm no fool. That doesn't last forever."

Tiffany told her mother, "I really don't want to talk about it."

"But girl you have to."

Then Tiffany said, "If I want to get an apartment, all I have to do is tell him and A will give me whatever I want. Look… He just gave me like $8,000 just to spend."

Her mother wisely assumes, "You see. I told you he's a drug dealer."

Lil' A jumped back onto the highway heading toward the Bronx. He was wondering what Tiff wanted to talk with him about. He did not know that she was six months pregnant. He didn't even notice how big she was getting. Her breast, legs and everything were getting bigger. Lil' A was too busy handling his business to know.

In fact, Lil' A was getting bigger in many ways himself. His business was getting bigger, his status was getting bigger, and he was even getting a bigger head. He was so focused on himself and what he was doing that he couldn't really pay attention to others. He was living by a motto of: *Have fun and fuck the bitches.*

Back in the Bronx, Lil' A finally got to settle down. And out of everybody he loved to chill with, his favorite was Verwana. So Lil' A went to their apartment. Verwana cooked him something to eat while he took a shower and they cuddled up to watch TV. After they ate, Verwana wanted something to drink, so he ran to the liquor store. Lil' A bought two bottle of Hennessy and two bottles of Moet so there would be something at the house.

As he got back to the apartment, Lil' A walked to the garage and pulled out the outfit he bought for Verwana. As he went back upstairs, he got to the door and heard Verwana say to someone on the phone, "Wait hold on. He's right here."

He wondered who it could be. He had not given anyone this number except for his mother.

When he got inside, Lil' A asked who was on the phone. Verwana replied, "Your pops."

Lil' A smiled, picked up the receiver and said, "Hey Big A. What's up?"

His father said, "You son. Where have you been? I haven't seen you in a while."

Lil' A replied, "I've been laying low."

His father then said, "I can see that."

"Yo pops. Have the cops been messing with you?"

Big A answered, "Well not like that, but there is one cop who always messes with me and it seems like he's always going to mess with you because you're my son."

Lil' A replied, "Well fuck those pigs. I might split one of their wigs wide open." They both laughed. Lil' A said, "Yo, pops. I'm in the house for the night, but if you want to come up, you can. I got something for you, anyway."

"Man, you need to get that to me," Big A said.

Lil' A reiterated, "I don't think you heard me. I'm in for the night. But, if you want to grab a cab and come by, I'll pay for it back and forth. But you need to call a cab from another area and chill for a second then break out. Okay?"

Big A asked, "What's the address?"

His son replied, "It's 2070 Villa Ave. between Bedford Park..."

Before he was able to finish, his father said, "Damn son. That's a nice area."

"Yeah, I know. Just come so you can check out my new crib. Okay? It's apartment 6-B."

Big A said, "I'll be there in an hour."

Lil' A replied, "I'll see you when you get here."

***

Lil' A took out the dress he bought for Verwana.
"Here's something I bought for you. Try it on. Tell me if you like it."
Verwana grabbed the bags, looked at them, and said, "This is Christian Dior."
Verwana was impressed. This was the kind of dress she had always dreamed of having. She had seen pictures of them in the fashion magazines. Now this was big time classy.
"Oh, I see you know your designer names," Verwana joked with a big smile on her face. Her voice was full of joy.

Lil' A rolled up a blunt while Verwana got dressed. As he sparked up the blunt, she came out looking like a million bucks. Lil' A's eyes opened wide as she said, "How do I look, baby?"
Lil' A answered, "You look very, very good. Verwana gave him a big kiss and a tight hug. Within seconds they were tongue kissing, so Verwana went and took off her new outfit to keep it looking crisp.
She had seen the receipt in the bag, but Verwana asked anyway. "How much did you pay for this outfit?"
Lil' A lied. "Well, I got it for half price. I paid $1,000 for it. Verwana knew he was lying because she had seen the receipt for $40,000, but she didn't want to ask who he bought the other dress for. Verwana figured that she had better leave it alone, she'd find out later it was meant to be.
A couple of minutes passed, Verwana came out and served Lil' A his food. As he started to eat, the phone rang. It was the door man.

He said, "Ms. Parks, there is someone here to see you and he said to send the money down for the cab."

A Father's Burden

Verwana told Lil' A, "Your pops is here."

"Tell the door man to pay for it and I will come down to give his money back." The door man did as he was told and knocked on the door a few seconds later.

When Lil' A answered the door, he gave the doorman two $20 bills and said, "Yes, that's my pops. I'll let you know when to get him a cab to leave. Okay?"

The door man said, "Mr. Parks, but the cab only was $10."

Lil' A responded saying, "Yes, I know. That's just a small tip for taking care of the cab."

Lil' A smiled at the door man.

Big A walked in, gave his son a handshake, and greeted Verwana. She already knew of Big A because he was a legend. He used to be rich, plus he had all the game in the world. Big A was a man who was easy to fall in love with. He was a man who people seemed to like. Anyone who met him would easily gravitate toward him because of his magnetic personality.

As he walked through the apartment giving himself a tour of his son's crib, Big A said, "Boy, you coming up. This shit is so fly."

Lil' A finished up his food. They relaxed in the living room watching the big screen TV. and Lil' A sparked up a blunt for his father. Verwana opened a bottle of Hennessy for the three of them to drink, while they sat there and talked. Big A had his son and Verwana laughing with his stories and jokes. The night was passing quickly.

Verwana got up from the couch, gave Lil' A a kiss and said, "I'm going to take a shower and get in the bed." Then she whispered into his ear. "Don't take too long. I'll be waiting naked in bed for you because you owe me."

As her sexy black self-moved toward their bedroom, she said bye to Big A. He returned the gesture.

Big A said, "Verwana, you need to give me a grandbaby. She laughed and kept on walking. Then Big A turned to his son and advised, "Baby boy, she's a winner. That's the one for you because she has good housekeeping skills. That's the type you want to have raise your kids."

Lil' A's response was, "Yeah. I know. I'm trying to make that happen."

A few minutes later, you could hear the shower running. Big A asked, "Yo. You got that for me?"

"Yeah man. Damn, you thirsty? Chill for a little while."

"Shit boy. I've been chillin' long enough. I need that. Okay?"

"Hold up, pops, wait until this blunt is over." Then Lil' A asked his father, "Pops, have the cops still been messing with you looking for me?"

"Yeah, I told you it's only one cop."

Lil' A knew his pops wanted some crack. He put the blunt out and said, "Come on," as they both got up and went toward the front door to get to the elevator.

Chapter Twelve

Lil' A pulled out his cell phone and called Red just to see what she was up to. As father and son got onto the elevator, they pressed the button marked, "G" for garage.

Red answered, "Hello... Hey, what's up player?"
Lil' A responded, "Nothing. What's up with you?" He couldn't tell her the truth. Lil' A didn't want her to know he was with another woman, his baby's mother. "I'm downtown at my man's loft and I'm in the elevator."
Red asked, "What are you about to do?"
Lil' A answered, "Get drunk."
As they got to the bottom floor, father and son got off and walked out toward the minivan. Lil' A spoke into the phone. "Red just talk!"
So she did. Red told him about her friend who was in love with some dude from the East Side but had a wife and family at home.

Lil' A told her to hold on for a second and he put the phone on mute. He and his pops got into the van. There was a half clip of a blunt in the ashtray, so he sparked it up and opened the stash box. Lil' A found the 28 grams for his pops. He still had a couple keys in the van too. Big A was finally getting what he wanted, and he was happy.

"Do a little bit of it here," Lil' A requested of his father.

Pops didn't have to be told twice. Big A did not waste any time. He got started as Lil' A leaned the passenger seat all the way back, while he continued talking on the phone.

Lil' A smoked his weed and talked to Red. She continued telling him about this married dude and her friend. Red described how her friend really liked the dude, or shall we say *loved* the dude. Lil' A didn't know who the dude was because Red never said his name. But little did he know that Red was talking about Kay, the dude he had seen earlier and given the work to. Lil' A would find out about that later.

Red said, "Don't worry A, you will meet him because he will be at the party."

"Oh word?" he said. Before he knew it a whole hour and a half had passed with them talking on the phone. The cell phone battery was low. The battery light started to blink, so Lil' A ended the conversation, "Red. Yo. I'm tired. I'll call you when I wake up."

Now Big A was high as a kite in the back. He hadn't said a word after he got what he came after. Big A was silent the entire time his son had been on the phone.

Lil' A said, "Damn pop. Why did you let all this time go by without saying a word…?" He was a little mad at his pops. "You don't give a fuck as long as you get what you wanted."

Big A said, "Boy, you were into Shorty. I couldn't say anything. Plus, I'm high as a kite." With that said he said, "Son, let me hold a couple dollars."

A Father's Burden

Lil' A was still somewhat mad. So his next comment was, "Shit, man you got an ounce of crack, Nigga, you could make a thousand dollars…"

Big A went to open his mouth, but Lil' A just pulled out two $20 bills and gave it to him.

Lil' A went straight back upstairs as Big A got off on the lobby floor. When the door man saw Big A he called him a cab.

As Lil' A opened the door to their place, all of the lights were off. Music played in the background. Sade was playing. It was nice, romantic, mood-setting music. Other than the music, the house was quiet. It smelled good. He walked into the bedroom and took off his clothes except for his boxers. Verwana was lying in bed. Her naked black body looked so good. She was only wearing a short T-shirt.

Lil' A could see her thick black legs and then there was that phat pussy. Easing up to her. Lil' A went straight for the pussy. He slowly opened her legs and began to lick. Verwana was half asleep; she had been waiting patiently for him while he was outside with his father. By now, of course, she was a little drowsy. As Lil' A licked, Verwana began to moan. He opened her legs wider as he kept on licking. Verwana finally awakened fully. Her head was all the way back on the pillow.

During all of this, two love songs had finished playing. Finally, her pussy squirts out cum. Verwana had just climaxed. Lil' A hesitated, freezing in his tracks because he had never seen that.

Then Verwana whispered softly, "Baby don't stop. I'm cumming again."

Realizing what had just happened, Lil' A kept on going because he had seen how much she liked it. Minutes later, she had another orgasm, the cum began oozing from her pussy again. So much so that it was as if she was squirting. The bed was so wet from her climaxing and discharging her pussy juices four different times.

Verwana put his head back in place. Lil' A rose up and laid on the other side of Verwana because the bed was so wet on her side.

Verwana pulled off Lil' A's boxers and she went down on him. She began give him oral sex. After a few minutes of being pleasured and oral stimulation, Lil' A was about to cum. He lifted Verwana's head and came in his hand. He immediately reached for a towel beside the bed and wiped his hands.

Lil' A thought to himself how he really wanted to cum in Verwana's mouth, but he couldn't because he felt as if she was going to be the mother of his kids and she would have to kiss the kids with those same lips. So that's why he came in his hand. If it had been any other girl, Lil' A would have cum right in her mouth.

After he wiped his hand, he laid Verwana on her back. Lil' A put both of her thick legs on his shoulders as he slid his shaft inside her vagina. Her pussy was so hot and wet. She grabbed his back as he started to move. Lil' A pushed his dick in and out, all the way in and all the way out. Verwana just made facial expressions that suggested she was in sexual bliss.

Verwana moaned, "Faster, faster." So Lil' A began to go faster.

He let out a nut and came right inside of her. She vigorously grabbed his back scratching and tugging. Lil' A finally let her legs down, his dick was still hard. This time he was still going strong because she was nice and wet. Verwana turned around and got on her knees and raised up so that Lil' A could hit it from the back. He inserted his dick and started hitting it from behind, doggy style. They fucked and made love for at least three hours. Lil' A was redeeming himself for his previous misfire with Verwana. He wanted to do all that he could to give her a good time and make her experience a feeling of sexual bliss. He was more concerned about pleasing her than himself, but he too was having a good time.

They stopped and sparked a blunt. They began to talk. Verwana said, "You came in me, right?" Lil' A responded, "Yeah." She just looked in his eyes as she passed the blunt. They fell asleep.

As morning rolled around, they finally got up. Verwana cooked Lil' A some breakfast and then had to go to work. She kissed him goodbye and then left. Verwana had to go pick up Quanee because this was the weekend, she was finally going to move in.

Chapter Thirteen

The day of the party arrived. Kay called him and said, "Yo A, man you were right. I'm about to run the whole Harlem to you. In fact, my man wants to buy some of both."

Being that they were on the phone, Kay used a code like three pairs of sneakers each. Lil' A told him to meet him at his mom's old apartment. When they met, Lil' A sold him six more keys; 3 heroin for $210,000, and 3 cocaine for $60,000. Kay just copped and left after they agreed they would meet up later.

Sleepy wound up buying one key of coke. His cousin came back to New York. He paid the money he owed and had money left over to spend.

B.C. came back with $250,000. B.C. had his girl and her friends with him because he wanted her to drive the drugs back. Now Lil' A was going to hit him hard this trip, but he had to make sure the drugs got back safely. So, Lil' A loaded up one of the Quest vans and let B.C.'s girl transport it back. He didn't have to worry because nobody knew how to open the stash box. So at least he knew the drugs would make it to their destination safely while all the guys got ready for the party.

A Father's Burden

Lil' A got his cars ready for the party. He brought out his Benz and BMW. Booberlocks pulled his Benz out. Papi came with his 911 Porsche letting two of his men drive the Acura and Hummer. Lil' A drove his Benz, and let Sleepy drive his BMW. He let B.C. drive the Hummer. B.C. and his mob were feeling real good. Lil' A rode alone because he was young and coming up.

Everybody was suited and booted, but Lil' A had on a regular Polo style jean suit with some Nike Air Maxes. Papi had to have on at least a million dollars' worth of jewelry. The Bronx mob made a statement as well. Red's party was off the hook.

She rented out Club New York. She called Lil' A and asked, "Where are you?"
Lil' A replied, "I'm on my way."
Red asked, "How far from here are you?"
His answer was, "About seven minutes out."
"Okay. I'm waiting for you because it is so packed out here and I got to make sure you get in, okay," Red expressed feeling reassured.

Since everybody was ready, and Lil' A had his pops with him, they were about to have a nice time. Pops was wearing the same type of outfit that his son had on. Although Lil' A's father was a legend, somehow, he did not seem as big as he once was. Now, Big A was just your regular everyday crack head. On the way to the party, he kept telling Lil' A, "Son, you're doing it real big…" as all the cars raced on the FDR Drive highway. The little convoy was at least eight cars long. All those cars together were worth a cool million. Finally, they pulled up in front of the club. Red was standing out in front in the Christian Dior dress. From head to toe, she was looking so good.

The music from all the car stereo systems had the whole block rocking. People were looking. It was a least 1,300 people outside. They all seemed to grow quiet at once as they looked over at the cars. Everybody started to point saying, 'Damn who the fuck are those cats?' As well as other comments.

Red picked up the cell phone and called Lil' A back.
"Baby, where are you?"
"I'm right in front of you," he replied,

She hung up the phone and walked toward the cars. He hit the button to open the power window. He wanted to make sure she saw him because he had the darkest tint ever.

Red walked up smiling from ear to ear. "Oh, you just had to show off."
"Nah, what makes you say that?"
Red inquired, "Who are these people?"
Lil' A replied, "This is my clique."
Red then asked another question, "You got cars that are not even on the streets yet. And who is this with you?"
Lil' A answered, "This is my pops, Big A and I'm Lil' A."

"Hi! How are you doing? Your sons got a lot of mess with him."
"Yeah, I know," pops said.
"Boy, you look just like your father..."
"Yeah I know."
Red looked at Lil' A's outfit and said, "I told you to let me pick out an outfit for you..."

Lil' A got mad and cut her off. She was about to diss how he was dressed, and he did not want to hear it.
"I said no... What are you saying? I can't get in?"

A Father's Burden

Red replied, "I'm throwing this party, but you two – father and son – are going to be the only ones wearing sneakers and jeans."

Lil' A brushed her off, "Yeah, so what?"

"Ooh boy, you and that mouth. Well I don't want to argue with you. And how's your crew dressed? Like you?"

"No! They are suited and booted."

"Okay smarty pants. You just have to be different. Well park around the corner. Here's two V.I.P. passes. You come right in the side doors. How many of your crew are there?"

"There are eight us."

"What's the latest hot car, your Caravan?"

"Nah Boo, come here... The Hummer is the last one."

Red said, "Okay.

She walked to all the cars and gave each of those in the cars V.I.P. passes as she introduced herself. "Hi, I'm Red. Thank you for coming. Welcome to the party.

When she finished, she walked back to Lil' A's car and said, "You brought those Puerto Ricans with you?"

"Yeah, that's my man."

"Boy you crazy and you got some old country boys with you."

"Yeah and you're going to learn how to respect million-dollar niggas."

"And what about you...?"

"Well I'm about $1,000,000 short from my first million."

Red smiled and said, "Baby, why don't you go park so you can come in."

They all rolled down the block, back to back.

One of the bouncers asked Red, "Who the hell are those dudes. They're doing it."

Red replied, "Yeah, I know. Look, only two of them got on jeans and sneakers. That's my little Boo and his pops. So he's good – him and his pops."
The bouncer said, "Pops?"
She replied, "Yeah! You know he's rich, young, and full of cum."
They both laughed.

Everyone in Lil' A's crew parked their car. Lil' A tucked the Tech 9 under his shirt with about four extra clips on him.

Papi got out with all his diamonds. He asked Lil' A, "Who's the woman."
"Red," Lil' A replied.
"Oh, she is fine."
Then Papi said, "Lil' A, you sure know how to pick them. I know you got man's best friend on you."
"Is an elephant heavy?" Lil' A asked sarcastically.
Papi started to laugh and remarked, "Oh, I should have known."
At that point Papi revealed all his jewelry. Everyone in Lil' A's party said, "Damn! What the fuck he got on."

Papi thought that he had so much jewelry on that someone might try to rob him, but if Lil' A had his gun, he knew he would be protected.
As they all walked up the block, the bouncer said, "You must be A?"
Lil' A acknowledged, "Yeah." Then he pulled the bouncer to the side and asked, "What's good. Since you know my name, what's yours?"
The bouncer said, "Well, I'm T.O."
Then Lil' A said, "Okay, this is for you."
He gave him $1,000.
T.O. asked, "What's this for?"

Lil' A answered, "Because me and my Spanish man don't get searched."

Jokingly the bouncer asked, "Who is your Spanish man, the hood Roc-A-Fella?"

Lil' A said, "I'm the only one dirty." He flashed on him and said, "I never leave home without it."

T.O. then said, "Dawg, I got you and don't worry. I'm the bouncer for all the top parties. You will never have a problem with that. Okay?"

Papi smiled then Lil' A said, "Let's go."

"The rest of your crew can go through the door," T.O. informed him.

As they walked through the door, Papi thought Lil' A certainly had a mouthpiece on him. B.C., Booberlocks, and Sleepy were really starting to understand how much power Lil' A had. Inside, they all met up and Red ran over to them.

She looked at Papi and said, "Damn baby, ain't you scared with all of that jewelry on?" Papi reassured her that he was okay with it and not worried. There were all kinds of people at the party; some were rappers, some were ballplayers, some were hustlers, and then you had some of the finest women there that the crew had ever seen. Everyone was fly. Lil' A was on one side next to his pops. On the other side, Papi was standing. And across from them were some hoes that were looking at them trying to figure out who the hell they were?

Lil' A sparked up a blunt and the waitress was taking too long to come back with their drink order. So, Lil' A and Papi went straight up to the bar. Lil' A made a bold move.

"Yo, I want every bottle in here," he requested. The bartender looked at him as if he thought he had not heard him correctly. So, Lil' A made his request again, "Are you deaf? I want every bottle in here, I mean every single one.

Moet, Hennessy XO, Courvoisier. If it's in a bottle, I want it. And tell me the total!"

The bartender said, "Hold on. I have to get my boss."

Lil' A said, "Get whomever. Just don't take too long." Finally, the manager walked up. Lil' A asked, "How much do I owe you?"

The manager was somewhat surprised, but he answered, "$75,000."

Lil' A then said, "Okay, here's $80,000. We'll be over there in the V.I.P. section."

Shortly afterward, the bartender started coming over with bucket after bucket of ice and mad bottles. Booberlocks sat there in amazement. B.C. was just having a great time. They had girls surrounding them. Big A, Lil' A, and Papi sat at the table with at least six bottles of each type of liquor in front of them. It didn't take long for Red to come over because they had just stolen the party. Now the party was really in the V.I.P. section. Red was puzzled.

Red asked, "What are you doing, Boo?"

Lil' A answered, "I'm just having a good time."

Red started to introduce some of her friends, particularly one of her friends named, China. Now China was crazy bad. Lil' A told Red to tell China to go next to Papi and do whatever he asks.

Red asked, "What do you think she is a hoe?"

Lil' A remembered the conversation he had with Papi some time ago. At the time, Papi said he had never been with a black girl. So, Lil' A wanted to provide his friend with this opportunity no matter the cost.

He responded to Red, "Nah, but as long as she does whatever he says, I will give her $10,000 for one night."

Red's eyes opened wide. Lil' A said, "That's my man. He just flew in from Puerto Rico and he's never been with a black girl. I want her to do everything in her power to turn him out – head, ass, whatever he wants."

Red grabbed China's hand and dragged her over beside Papi. Papi looked at Lil' A and gave him a wink. He was having a good time and it was about to get even better, or so it seemed. Big A was drunk. Lil' A was taking sips from a bottle of XO. He was having a good time as well, but he had to be on point because everybody else was getting drunk. As Red and China came back, China went to stand next to Papi and whispered in his ear.

"Hey Papi, you got me all to yourself, just for one night, so don't be scared."

Papi looked shocked, but he filled up a glass and gave it to China. Papi looked at Lil' A and gave him another wink. Lil' A lifted the bottle of XO to solute him and to let him know what time it was.

Red said, "You learn something new every day," as she cuddled under Lil' A and started to get her drink on. T.O., the bouncer, came over and told Red that someone up front wanted to see her. She looked at Lil' A and said, "Baby, I'll be right back."

Lil' A said, "Okay." Turning to T.O. he asked, "What's up, are you good?"

T.O. responded, "Yeah. I see you're doing it real big." He continued, "Nobody does it that big. Not your average street player."

"Well I'm different. Do you want a bottle?" Lil' A was passing T.O. a brand-new bottle.

"Nah," T.O. declined.

Before she left the area, Lil' A told Red," Send back ten more girls for my crew. Tell them free drinks and tell one of the bartenders to come back this way, okay."

"Okay baby, whatever you say."

As Red got up to the front, it was Kay and his East Side boys. They had been looking for Red. They also were mad because they couldn't get any bottles from the bar. The bartender said all the liquor was sold out and the only thing left was beer and punch drinks, so Kay was irritated. He asked who was back in the V.I. P. section.

"Who's back there, Puff Daddy?"

Red inquired, "Nah, but come on. I want you to meet somebody."

Kay went with Red toward the V.I.P. section. It was crowded. When they reached the back there were some girls from 3333 Broadway, a complex that was full of some of the baddest bitches in Harlem. Lil' A knew one of the hoes, Felicia. So, as Felicia was all over Lil' A, Red tapped his shoulder. Kay turned around and was talking to Red's friend who was all in love with him.

Then Red said, "Oh, I can see where you're at, having a good time."

Lil' A turned around and said, "Oh. What's up Boo…? Excuse me Felicia. I'll be back."

Both girls gave each other dirty looks. Red said, "I see you can find the sluts."

Lil' A laughed and said, "I don't like sticking my dick in shit."

Red then said, "I want you to meet a real good dude…" as she tapped Kay on his shoulder. He turned around.

As soon as Lil' A caught his eye, Kay yelled, "A, what's up, baby. What the hell you doing in here?"
Red stood there in shock. So she asked, "You know each other?"

Red just stood back because since she was from the streets, she knew that Lil' A was fucking with Kay. Now she knew this would get back to her real Boo who was locked up.

Kay asked, "Where is Booberlocks?"
"Yo, he's over there somewhere."
Lil' A invited Kay to bring his people back to their table or to take some bottles back to his crew.
"We got all the bottles back here."
"No wonder I couldn't buy a drink."
"Take however many you want."

Kay went back to the other side to get his crew. Finally, seeing Booberlocks Kay ran up to him, so they walked to the other side of the club together.

Her curiosity eating away at her, Red finally asked, "Baby, where did you meet, Kay?"
Lil' A said, "I know him, why?"
"I'm just asking because he's from the East Side."
"Yeah, I know. Well, remember I was telling you about my girlfriend that's in love with someone, but he got a wife?"
"Yeah…"
"Well, that was, Kay."
Lil' A asked if Kay was getting a lot of money.
Red said, "He's just above water A because after my husband got locked up nobody could hit him like that."
"Oh, so you know Kay very well!"
"Yeah, he's a good dude…"

Lil' A let her talk, as he was taking in all the info. His mind was racing with all kinds of thoughts. Kay came back to the V.I.P. section, everyone enjoyed themselves. Lil' A got the whole party drunk. Meanwhile, Big A was ready to go. He wanted to get high. The longer Big A stayed at the party the more he reflected on how big he used to be, and now he saw his son doing it just like he did.

Papi was ready to do whatever Lil' A wanted to do. Papi asked if anything was wrong. Lil' A said no, reminding him that China was his for the night.

Lil' A asked the remainder of the crew what they wanted to do. They all said they wanted to stay, so Lil' A said he would call them in the morning.

He said goodbye to Kay who responded by saying, "Yo man, Red is very good peoples. She might feel funny because we know each other really well, but she's a good judge of character..."

Lil' A cut him off and said, "Yo, we'll talk about that later."

Then Lil' A broke for the door. Following him was his pops, Papi, his Spanish man, China and Red. They all walked toward the garage. Papi was so drunk, so he let China drive. Lil' A said he was going to follow him until he got indoors.

Papi said he had a fuck crib, a condo up in Riverdale. So, they shot uptown deep in the Bronx. They finished drinking and chilled. They were all comfortable, the doorbell rang. It was Angie. She knew Lil' A was there because she saw his car in the driveway. Red wondered who it could be ringing the doorbell at this time. She finally thought she had Lil' A to herself. Angie walked in. Papi's eyes opened wide because he knew his sister would act a fool.

A Father's Burden

Next, Angie walked over to Lil' A and before she could speak, Lil' A asked her, "What made you come out this late?"

Angie replied, "I'm coming to get my man because he's starting to pick up bad habits. Which one of these bitches you fucking?"

Angie's head turned to Red because she was dressed the nicest. Red was about to say something, but Lil' A stopped her and told her to chill.

Angie was mad and getting hotter by the minute. She put her bag on the mini bar. The handle of her gun stuck out of it. Papi spoke something to her in Spanish. China looked shocked as the other Spanish dude just sat quietly. Big A knew this woman was there for his son. Angie thought Lil' A was there with this girl and her brother had her friend. But they had just gotten there. They were finished drinking and were about to fuck.

Angie looked at Lil' A and said, "If you're not doing anything, I'm ready to go."

Lil' A was mad. He was mad that Angie had come in and put on such a show before everyone. Lil' A threw his pops the keys, gave him $500 cash and told him to give Red his car.

"Tell her I'll come for it later" Then he turned to Papi and said he would see him later. Now Papi really was hot.

Lil' A said to Red, "Nice meeting you." And then he walked out.

Lil' A grabbed Angie by the neck and said, "I just wanted to make sure that Papi got home safely. He had been drinking and was drunk, so I wanted to make sure he was alright."

Angie asked, "Why you so mad? What, you want to go back in there and run a train on those bitches? A, baby you could be telling the truth, but Papi just got that crib so he can fuck bitches in it. I was on my way home, but Papi's wife was looking for him and said you were together and had been gone all day. He had on a lot of jewelry, so she was worried." Giving him a crazy look, Angie added, "Yes, I'm the type that would spy on you. So I came to one of my brother's fuck cribs. And yes, I saw your car. I knew you were in my brother's fuck crib, so I decided to stop by."

"Well inspector gadget, don't ever come nowhere making a scene like that ever. My pops was there."

"Oh baby. I'm sorry, but I told you don't play me. Do you want to go back up there with your pops?"

"No, it's too late," Lil' A scoffed

They got into Angie's big Benz. By the time she pulled out her spot Lil' A was rolling a blunt. He was distracted as they passed the entryway, noticing Red and Pops coming out. Red was about to drive Lil' A's car. Angie looked over at Red and glared at her. She just had that look. Even Big A could see in her eyes that Angie wanted to bust a cap in Red's ass.

Stopping her car in front of them, Angie sucked on the blunt and said, "Big A., I'm sorry you had to meet me like this, but I had to come get what's mine."

Big A replied, "Sweetheart, you didn't do anything wrong."

Angie said, "I can see where A gets his looks and smarts."

On the ride home, "Lil' A thought about almost getting busted. Angie had shown him her gun. He knew she always carried a piece, but he never thought she would think of using it if she wasn't taking care of work-related business.

A Father's Burden

He knew Angie meant business when it came down to him and protecting her property. Her frame of mind was that she was Lil' A's property and he was certainly hers and hers alone.

Then Lil' A also thought of Red. She didn't seem too happy. She seemed to bristle when Angie came into the house. He felt that Angie and Red were staring each other down. Inside Red was boiling. She wanted to beat Angie's ass, but Red didn't know that Angie might be able to fight as well as she could, and that she was a vicious murderer. So, Red would have lost.

They headed toward Jersey. Meanwhile in Lil' A's car, Red and Big A were talking. She couldn't wait to start asking Big A questions about his son. This was also a chance for him to ask Red for some money.

"Red let me hold a couple hundred?" She gave him $500. Then he said, "My son said for you to hold on to the car until he comes to get it."

Using the opportunity to get information Red asked, "So who is Angie and what does she mean to Lil' A." Thinking what else she should try to get out of Big A she asked, "Is that woman his baby's mother?"

He lied and said, "Yeah she is. That's the crazy one. She's from San Juan, that bitch from the jungle."

"Oh, she is. Well I'm from the hood, the projects," said Red.

They had a brief laugh. Seconds later Big A began talking on a more serious note. "Red, baby," he said. "That's not any average girl. You see how close she kept her bag. I've been in the street game for a long time, baby. I know how to judge a man and a woman, but I just got a bad feeling about her," he cautioned.

Red listened quietly. She was soaking up all that he was telling her. Music played in the background, but Red was all ears.

Big A just thought to himself for a moment. *How could a brother sit there and just let his sister bust up in his place and talk to people the way she did.* Big A knew she was not only crazy, but powerful.

Red got to the Bronx in no time. She dropped Big A off and said. "Okay, Big A, it was nice meeting you…"

She was off to her girlfriend's house, but was mad as hell. Not only was she mad at that bitch Angie, but she was mad because she fucked her nut up for the night. She had plans for the night. She couldn't wait for this night to come and her expectations were high. She wanted to fuck Lil' A's young ass so bad. As Red pulled up in front of her girlfriend's house, Kay was leaving. He had to get home to his wife. Her girlfriend just stood in the doorway wearing a bathrobe.

Kay asked, "Red, what brings you by here this time of night…"

"Nothing, Kay… Let me ask you something, how long have you known Lil' A?"

"That's me and Booberlocks's man. You know Booberlocks and me were on Rikers Island together, so that's how I got the hook up. Man, on the first deal, he blessed me with 10 joints. Shit, it kind of reminded me of when Lou was home…" Red just listened. She hung onto every word. Her eyes stared down his mouth. Kay then said, "I don't know where that nigga came from, but he was shining at your party. All the hoes wanted to know who he was. Even my little stink hoes wanted to know who he was. Red, you saw his little mob. They're getting money. I mean

A Father's Burden

crazy money. Shit, I should have another meal ticket in 200 days if Lil' A keep flooding me."

Then Kay said, "Red I got to go. I'll come through tomorrow." As he was getting ready to jump in his car, he couldn't help but to notice that she was driving Lil' A's new Benz.

"Oh, you got his car. Look those 600s just came out and he's letting you whip it already?"

"Well you wouldn't believe how I got it, his little baby mother came on the scene, some Spanish bitch, talking all funny, plus she was driving one too."

Kay said, "Red, it looks like you got a big fish on your hand or should I say another."

"Shut up boy...!" They both laughed. "See you later!"

Kay drove off, Red and her friend went inside to talk so Red could tell her what happen.

Meanwhile, back at the hotel, Booberlocks, B.C., Sleepy and them had all scooped up a hoe, and she was fucking the rest of the boys as the night went by. Another girl, one from Italy was at the party. She ended up getting drunk in the V.I.P. with them and had given Booberlocks her cell phone number to give to Lil' A. She told Booberlocks she was an A & R at Sony Records. They were throwing a big party next week and she wanted them to come through, but Booberlocks forgot to give the number to A.

Angie got home and jumped in the Jacuzzi to calm down. She called for Lil' A to join her. He hesitated at first, but he wound up joining her. After they drank and smoked, they fucked in their usual manner the rest of the night. Lil' A anger finally subsided, Angie had just drained his young ass; she let him get his ass shots from the back, to her giving him head, then him cumming all in her.

Early the next morning, Lil' A woke up and heard Angie in the bathroom throwing up. Now she couldn't keep any food down. Lil' A didn't really know what was going on, but remembered what a friend told him. Finally, Angie got her wish. She was pregnant. They went to the hospital that day to confirm it, and indeed Angie was pregnant. So now Lil' A was really happy. He went to celebrate with Papi.

Lil' A and Papi drank and talked about how Papi was feeling China. They went to pick her up on 114th and Eighth Avenue. Come to find out, China had a twin sister, Brandy. So the four of them went to get something to eat. Later, they had their first gang-bang together, with China and Brandy switching. Papi even videotaped them.

Days later, Papi bought China a car, she was his little personal freak.

As drug business was growing, Lil' A doubled everybody back up and they all hit the streets again. Lil' A finally caught up with Red a week later. She had fun with the car, and when Booberlocks dropped Lil' A off, he could see in Red's face that she was still mad at him, but that she also wanted to fuck his young ass so bad. All she could do was hug and kiss him. Then she made a smart remark. "Oh, your little Spanish baby mother finally let you out."

"Red, look I'm sorry about that, I just left because that hoe ain't got it all. I could have gone upside her head, but for what. That's what she wanted me to do, plus the bitch busses her gun like she a nigga."

Red said "Look A, cut her off. I'll make it up to you okay. Let's go away to an island somewhere. I've never been to one."

Lil' A cut her off then said, "Okay, because I've never even been to one with my baby mother."

They both laughed.

"Which one…?" Red asked.
Lil' A offered, "Any one."
Red quickly responded, "Okay, let's go to Hawaii."
"Fine, we'll go next week."
"Okay?" Red kissed Lil' A.
Lil' A looked at Red and asked if she was okay and did she need anything.
Red said, "Nah, I'm okay. You're not going to treat me like those little hoes. Thank you, but I'm alright. Well, your keys are in my jacket.
A walked towards her jacket.
"Are you okay, do I need to drive you home."
"No, I'm okay, so call me later."
"Okay! Later Boo."

Chapter Fourteen

As time was winding down, Kay started running Lil' A all types of money from Harlem. This Bronx bomber was becoming a kingpin, Lil' A ran through the first shipment of coke and heroin very quickly. He was able to do it a month and a half earlier than expected.

Lil' A started to deal with Ricco by himself because Angie was getting deeper in her pregnancy.

In the meantime, everything seemed to be fine with Tiffany. She continuously tried to get in touch with A, but they kept missing each other. Lil' A sent Tiffany money once a week. Eventually, Tiffany felt that she had lost her connection to him, so she decided to stay away from him and attend college elsewhere.

Finally, Tiff's mother came back to New York and Booberlocks picked her up. Tiff's mom told him to take her straight to Lil' A. Booberlocks didn't want to argue with his aunt, and he knew Lil' A was with Papi at the restaurant.

When they walked in, Lil' A was drunk as hell.

Tiffany's mother didn't like what she saw at all. She said, "Oh, so this is what you're doing while my baby is out there stressing over you. You don't even know that she is eight months pregnant."

As soon as he heard that, Lil' A's eyes opened wide and Tiffany's mom walked out. Due to the respect he had for older people, he ran behind her, but she did not want to talk with him.

A then told Booberlocks, "Yo, I'll call you later."
"Alright homie," Booberlocks' responded.

Later that day, Lil' A finally got in touch with Tiffany.
"Yo! What the fuck is going on?" he asked her.
"Nothing."
"Why didn't you tell me?"
Tiffany sighed, "A, I've been trying to tell you for the past eight months, but you were always too busy."
"Yo, when are you due?"
"I'm due in 40 days, but anything can happen."
"Well come back home."
"Well I want to, but I've decided to stay here and finish school. Plus, why should I come back when all of New York is talking about you, who you fucking, what new cars you got... It's better that I stay here away from all that."
Lil' A flipped; he was really mad.
He said, "Look, I don't want to hear that you're not coming back here shit..." Thinking for a moment Lil' A said, "Fine. I'm just going to set you up where you're at, because I'm not going to kiss your ass! You're grown. You're going to do what you want."
A, why are you talking to me like that...?"
"I'll call you in a couple of days. Love ya."
Then he hung up the phone and Tiffany started to cry.

Lil' A had not realized that he had been dogging Tiffany for some time now. Now he was caught between three girls;

Angie, Tiffany, and Verwana. Lil' A further realized that he was spending a lot of time with Red too.

Another month passed; Tiffany called Booberlocks to tell him that she was going into labor. As Tiff gave birth to a baby boy, Booberlocks finally caught up with Lil' A. Unfortunately, he couldn't be there for Tiffany because he'd been in the house with Angie who was moving deeper into her pregnancy.

As soon as he could, Lil' A flew out to see Tiffany. He called B.C. because he was only about 6 hours away. Lil' A needed B.C. to bring him $100,000, because he couldn't travel with so much money.

When Lil' A finally got to the hospital, Tiffany's mother was there. Tiffany's mother said, "Boy! It's a damn shame you weren't here to see your own child born."

"Yeah. I know. You're right ma." Lil' A agreed brushing her off, not wanting to argue.

Tiffany was glad to see him. As he held her hand, Lil' A said, "Baby, I've been running around like a chicken with its head cut off."

Tiffany said, "Baby, don't worry. We'll talk about that later."

Lil' A was more like his father than he really knew. Big A had been too busy to be himself when Yvette delivered Lil' A.

The nurse came in, "Are you ready to feed your baby?" she asked Tiffany,
"Yes."
"You must be the father?"
Lil' A said, "Yeah that's me."
Tiffany said, "Are you ready to feed your son?"

A Father's Burden

"Of course." Lil' A was excited, "Who does the baby looked like, and what complexion is he?" Lil' A asked.

"Mine," Tiff responded.

Tiff was a high yellow girl, also known as a *redbone*.

The nurse brought the baby in. He was looking high yellow and shit with Lil' A's nose and ears. A was in amazement, as he was rocking his son. Tiffany's mother stood outside the door, looking in, and she could tell her daughter loved Lil' A. They spent the entire day in Tiffany's hospital room relaxing and fussing over the baby.

Eventually, Lil' A left with Tiffany's mother, as they went to her car they talked. Lil' A was a smooth talker, and could feel that Tiffany's mom held a deep grudge against him.

"Look Ma, you don't really know me, so you can't judge me," he said.

Tiffany's Mom said, "Look Baby..."

Lil' A said, "Wait, please let me have the floor. I will never disrespect you or Tiff. I have a mother, and I grew up without my father because he fell victim to the streets. Well Ma, basically what I'm saying is, I know I'm in a game that won't last forever... Tiff wants to stay out here, so I'm going to buy you and her your own house. I want you to start your own business, too."

"Okay."

"And I'm going to put Tiff threw college and give you some extra money for my son and his other brother and sister."

"Now, Tiffany only knows about one child, but I may be having another one. I know this sounds crazy, but I can't tell her now because it would hurt her. I want her to finish school. I don't want anything to stop her. If something happens to me, I just want my son to never need for anything.

Just promise me you will reach out to his other brother and sister."

"Okay?"

Tiff's mom couldn't say a word. She was shocked to see this young man open up to her. So A finished talking.

"Ma for some reason, I just feel like my luck is about to change. Please Ma, don't tell Tiffany because…"

"Baby I won't ever tell her, okay."

Two days later Tiffany's mom and Lil' A went looking for a house. She found a nice three-bedroom home down south for $150,000. Lil' A dropped $50,000 on the house and had Tiffany's mom get rid of her old hooptie and bought her a new car.

When Tiffany got out of the hospital, she went to her mother's new house. "Ma, how did you get this," she questioned.

"Oh, my son-in-law bought the house and car for me."

When she heard her mom's response Tiffany knew her mother was full of shit

Lil' A had more money sent to him, which he used to purchase Tiffany an even bigger house, two cars, plus he paid her college tuition in full.

Tiffany's mother opened a store; on one side she operated a restaurant, and on the other, there was a game room.

In time, it would become one of the best restaurants out with leather couches, TV's, surround sound system, and all. As the restaurant business grew Lil' A would come set up new locations, but he would return to New York as soon as it was finished.

* * *

A Father's Burden

Back in New York Angie was getting huge, but she had to go to Puerto Rico for two months. So Lil' A went back out to see Tiffany, because he missed her and his newborn son. The baby was growing, and Tiffany and A had reconnected and were fucking during the entire two months.

Down south, Tiffany was Lil' A's star. The little hustlers out there were gunning for her, because she drove a brand-new Land Rover and had a BMW, but Tiffany never talked to anybody, only at the store.

Tiffany's mother knew how to flip the money Lil' A gave her. She bought a little building and rented it out, bought another clothing store, and her businesses were growing, while Tiff finished school to be a lawyer.

As time passed, Lil' A gave Tiffany's mom $250,000 for her to put away, and $50,000 to go in a bank account. Tiffany didn't know that her mom was Lil' A's partner.

* * *

Now Lil' A was moving more drugs than ever. He stood Red up again, but he sent Red, her sister, and a friend on a little trip to make up for it. While they were away, Lil' A was running around freaking off with China's twin sister Brandy. But Brandy had a baby father name Mel Murder. He was some young kid that was making a name for himself in the streets.

Mel Murder would beat Brandy's ass every time she stayed out late with Lil' A. One night, Lil' A came from getting his dick sucked. Parked right outside of Brandy's building, she was sucking his dick. Mel caught her getting out of Lil' A's car. Mel was there with his man, both were strapped and so was Lil' A. As soon as Brandy got out of the car, Mel started beating Brandy's ass real bad.

Finally, Lil' A got out of the car. "Yo dawg, at least do that shit inside the house!" He yelled.

"Who's this fucking clown you fucking?" Mel asked Brandy, pulling out his gun.

Lil' A was caught off guard, even though he had a gun on him, Mel drew his first. Lil' A said, "Alright dog." and backed up.

Mel's man hit A in the back of the head. Lil' A fell to the ground. Mel dragged Brandy into the building. Mel's man jumped in A's Benz. He went to roll him over, but A pulled his gun and shot him.

"Bang... Bang...Bang!"

Lil' A let out three shots, Mel's boy fell, and Lil' A stood over him and finished him off. By this time, Mel-Murder came out of the building, but ran into a hail of gunfire as Lil' A emptied out his last 10 shots on him. He jumped in the Benz and took off.

Hearing all the gunshots, the cops were not far away and didn't take long to get to the scene. So, when Lil' A sped off, the cops were already on his ass. He was trying to make it toward the highway. Lil' A ran a red light, just missing a car as he weaved around it. He was three blocks away from the highway, but a girl pushing a baby carriage was in the middle of the street. It was either run them over or turn away.

A couldn't live with the fact that he ran over a mother and child, so he hit a sharp right.

"Boom!"
He hits a police car head on.

A hit his head on the steering wheel, and was dizzy as fuck, but he had to get up and out of there. He jumps out the car and starts running, throwing his gun in a sewer as he did. In the middle of Harlem, there were no projects around. Lil' A was fast, but not that fast. He got like two and a half blocks away from where he threw the gun. Suddenly, every cop in the area was surrounding him with their guns drawn. Three of the cops started to whip A's ass.

Finally, when they got to the precinct. Lil' A tried to give a fake name, but a warrant popped up on him. He was wanted in the Bronx for two murders and now he was being charged with two more. The officers in the precinct were happy. They'd caught a big collar that night.

One cop said, "You killed Mel-Murder, boy. You're going to have mad beef now, but you saved us some police work, because he was wanted for murder too. In fact, for three murders. Mel was one of Manhattan's most wanted..."

As this incident hit the news, Lil' A called Booberlocks first. He told his partner to go snatch up Brandy and make sure she keeps her mouth shut. Booberlocks got right on it. Lil' A also asked Booberlocks to not tell Tiffany that he was locked up.
So Booberlocks ducked her.

The Bronx Police Department came and took custody of Lil' A. He didn't say a word, so they sent him back into the bullpen with another dude from around A's projects, named Bronx Dale, who was also in the pin.

He said, "Damn Dog, you been charged with all those murders."
A looked at him and asked, "What are you in for, meth or something?"
"Nah kid. But do you got a lawyer?"
"Nah, but I got one."

"Shit you better get this lawyer I fuck with. He just beat a murder for me."
"So what you locked up for now?"
"Driving without a license. They just be sweating me for nothing."
"Word."
"What's his name?"
"Wiggins."
"You got his number?"
"Yeah. Just tell him Petey gave you the number."
"Okay."

Later, Lil' A asked Booberlocks to call a lawyer he'd heard about. He called this lawyer, Wiggins.
"Hello."
"May I speak to Wiggins?"
"Yes, please hold."
"Yeah hello."
"Yes, Wiggins this is A. I got your number from a friend."
"Well what's your friend's name?"
"Petey."
"Oh, okay. Well, where are you?"
"I'm in the Bronx."
"They got me for two murders and two more in Manhattan."
"Okay. Well, you didn't say nothing right?"
"Nah."
"I'll be there in an hour. Make sure you got 30,000 for me."
"Okay sure."

As he hung up Booberlocks said, "What you want me to do?"
"Meet Wiggins at the jail."
"How much money you got?"

"I got that $30,000 on the nose."
"Okay."

Booberlocks and Wiggins showed up at the precinct at the same time. Booberlocks gave Wiggins the money. Wiggins went to the back to talk to Lil' A.
"A what's up?"
"Ain't nothing."
"I just wanted to see how good you are."
"Shit. I'm good."
"Well, just as long as you got the money."
"Well money ain't my problem."
"And beating cases ain't mine."

The two talked about what happened. Wiggins was asking questions and Lil' A asked questions too; he wanted to know if this lawyer could really help him.

Wiggins said, "Look son, I know you're in the streets, but you got to trust me. Look I'll be back. Let me see what they talking about."

They took A back into the bullpen, Petey said, "A yo dog, Wiggins is a good dude. All five boroughs are scared of him, plus you could trust him."

A had to believe him, "Yo! How much does he charge?"

"Oh, he's going to charge you top dollar, but he's worth it."

"Word."

Another hour passed; by the time Wiggins came back. He said, "Look, I got good news and bad news, so which do you want first?"

"Give me the bad news."

"Well you're going to have to sit for a couple of months and go through the process for those murders in Harlem, but that case looks real, real weak, because the two guys had guns on them. One of them had a warrant for 3 murders, but I can beat that and get you bail. But that's more money. It seems like these two murders in the Bronx don't got nobody who knows shit. But some girl named Keisha is here and they want you in a line up."

"What Keisha here for?"

"It seems like she's the only one who knows something."

Lil' A told Wiggins that he knew Keisha, because she lived on the same floor he lived on, in the projects.

"Well they're going to ask her if she knows you and whether you did those murders," Wiggins said.

"What do you think she will say?"

Lil' A exclaimed, "Nothing!"

"Well, okay. Let's go."

The cops took Lil' A to the lineup. They asked Keisha if she knew A.

She confirmed, "Yeah." Then they asked her if he killed Token and his brother. Keisha stood quiet for a minute or two and then she said, "No."

Then Wiggins said, "Okay. We're done here. Let my client go back to Manhattan, so I can fight these other cases."

The cops asked Keisha one more time, "Are you sure?"

"Yes, I'm sure." Then she repeated her previous answer, "No."

Wiggins immediately said, "Well champ, we got by the first two murders. Now let's get ready for the next two, but I could get you out on bail next month when you go back to court, but I'm going to need $50,000 for the whole case."

Lil' A said, "Okay. My mom's will bring it to your office."

Lil' A was on his way to Rikers Island. As he rode the bus, he remembered when he first met Locks and the story

A Father's Burden

Booberlocks told him. He said, *when you hit the Island, you won't be smiling on Rikers Island.* The first stop was the 4 Building. Lil' A was searched, he had to strip down and open his mouth wide. They were checking for weapons and drugs. Then he and other new prisoners had to take a shower with a special soap that is used to fight off ticks and crabs. Lil' A was then given a number, cover, pillow, cups and a towel.

Lil' A's first night was not a restful one. He heard dudes yelling all night long. Booberlocks was not able to get his partner all the things he needed on the first two days. Lil' A called his mother and told her where he had hidden the money, and for her to take $50,000 to his lawyer, Mr. Wiggins.

Yvette asked Lil' A so many questions. He just told her to not worry.
"I'm okay. I'll talk to you later. Okay?"
Yvette said, "Okay baby. I love you. You'd better be careful and protect yourself."
Lil' A tried to assure her. "Don't worry ma. I'm okay. I love you too," he said prior to hanging up.

As a mother, Yvette was worried but knew her son would and could protect himself. So, she went to her old house, found the money and arranged to meet with the lawyer. She paid the lawyer and went back home to wait for her son's call.

Little did Lil' A know that he had been on TV. So, all the convicts just stared. There were two brothers who came to Rikers Island with Lil' A. One was there for a stolen car and the other was there for gun possession. The one with the gun charge was a quiet dude. His name was, E. Lil' A and E were about to become really close. The television news said they had Lil' A in for four murders. Lil' A and E stood for a while and talked. E lit a Newport and passed one to A.

Lil' A started to smoke, now the other guy, Remo comes over. He was locked up for a stolen car. As they all talked, and everyone woke up, it was finally time to go to lunch. They all got in line. So A, E, and Remo were at the back as they walked through the hallway. They passed other houses. Everybody knew this was the intake house. Lil' A had on some uptown Nikes, white on white, and they were all looking at his feet.

As they ate E said, "A, man we going to get into something real big over those sneakers."
Lil' A said, "Well I hope they ready."
'E' said, "Well I'm going all out, but I don't know about Remo."
'E' and Lil' A started laughing.

As the night hours passed ticking away, Lil' A and 'E' got closer, talking about their girls and family, but Lil' A never told 'E' all about himself. They kicked it about dirt bikes, and basketball. 'E' didn't know that Lil' A was the next big thing, but as that night passed, so did the next morning.

During the time Lil' A was in Rikers Island, he grew to know 'E' more. They talked about their girls, and their family more. The next day, they were told they were being moved to another unit. They were going to Pod 9. Now this was one of the wildest places in Rikers. Word was that people would sometimes leave there with 150 or more stitches.

A Father's Burden

The three of them Lil' A, 'E', and Remo walked down the hallway. 'E' told Lil' A, "I hope you're ready because it's about to jump off."

Lil' A said, "I'm ready to die. Ain't nobody doing nothing to me!"

'E' sparked up another Newport. He and Lil' A just smoked as Remo went into the TV room. Two hours passed. Then they heard laughing in the TV room. When they got there, they saw Remo dancing on a table.

'E' looked at Remo and said, "What the fuck you doing, get down?"

As Remo got down, a Spanish dude said, "Did I tell you to get down?"

Remo responded, "Nah!"

Then Lil' A got into the act. He yelled, "I did!"

The kid said, "Who the fuck is you, nigga?"

"I'm Big A... Remo! Come here."

The Spanish kid wasn't a shot-caller, he was just a soldier. So he walked up to Lil' A with a razor in his hand. He put it up to Lil' A's face.

"So, *Big A*, what you want to do for your sneakers?" Lil' A looked at the Spanish dude's hand, saw the razor and said nothing at all.

Then the Spanish dude said, "Take them off."

Lil' A bent down and acted as if he was about to take off his sneakers and swung on the Spanish kid, hitting him with one, two, three punches. Lil' A knocked the kid straight out. Another kid jumped in and E was right there on him, then third guy jumped in as they all began to fight. Someone yelled, *C.O.!*

That meant the police were coming, so they all stopped as the C.O. came in. The one Spanish dude was still on the floor knocked out.

The C.O. pulled Lil' A, E, and two other boys out and asked them what happened. But nobody said anything, so the police sent them back in. 'E' wound up picking up the razor. Remo was crying. Lil' A said, "Nigga, ain't no time for that. Are you ready for war or not?"
Remo said, "Yeah."

Now everybody said, play the bathroom. They all went back in there as Lil' A was fighting. He beat up three dudes that night. Finally, the big man who ran the house had to fight Lil' A. The dude was a bigger heavier size and all, but Lil' A didn't back down. 'E' wound up cutting the dude and a little war broke out. Finally, a squad came in and took them all out. So 'E', Lil' A, and Remo were in the hole. The kid 'E' cut was named Bam. and he had a lot of support on Rikers Island.

Finally, the C.O. that Booberlocks was fucking came back to work, but she couldn't find Lil' A, because he was in the hole. 'E' had to flush the razor down the toilet, and they were about to have major beef behind that cutting. So finally, the C.O. broad that Booberlocks was fucking, Ms. Dot, came around.
Now Ms. Dot was a bad girl, and if you're somebody on the streets, you're somebody in jail, especially if you got the money. Everybody was yelling Ms. Dot or Ms. D as she walked her high yellow ass down the tier fussing.

"Shut up, shut up, before I come through and check all of you. Just give me a second."

A Father's Burden

As she pulled up to cell number 21 and 'E' and Lil' A was in the same cell, she said, "Who's Adrian?"
Lil' A looked up and said, "Me."
Ms. Dot said, "Okay. Are you all right?"
"Yeah."
"Did you use the phone?"
"No not today."
"Okay chill out a second. Let me make my rounds."

Lil' A watched as she stopped by certain cells laughing speaking to everybody. You could tell she was young, but she looked good.
'E' said, "Lil' A who that?"
Lil' A said, "I don't know."

20 minutes later, she came back with the phone. She said, "Lil' A I heard a lot about you. Your man Booberlocks said what's up, and for you to call him."
Right then Lil' A knew who she was. She passed him a brown paper bag. Lil' A passed it to 'E', and then he opened it. There was some weed, about 4 blunts, and a box of razors.
Then Ms. Dot said, "A you know what time it is, but you got to be on point."
Lil' A said, "Okay."
Then 'E' said, "Lil' A who the fuck are you man. You got one of the baddest cops bringing you the phone, razors, and drugs."
Lil' A just smiled, as he dialed Booberlocks.
"Hello."
"Lil' A yo."
"What's up homie?"
"Yo Lil' A what's up. What took you so long to call?"
"I got into a little drama."
"You alright."
"Yeah."
"Yo, did my boo set you out?"

"Yeah."

"Yo now Lil' A she is crazy cool. She's one of us. Remember I told you I was going to go back to Rikers Island and get her?"

"Yeah."

"Well, I've been messing with her ever since you put me on. I always talked about you, but you never got to meet each other."

"Word. That's cool. Booberlocks, I need you to make some calls for me."

"Okay, who?"

"The first one to Angie." Booberlocks, linked them up three way.

"Hello."

"Hey momma, what's up?"

Angie said, "What took you so long to call. I'm about to push out this baby."

He cut her off. He said, "I didn't want to tell you but I'm locked up."

Angie's whole tone changed. "Do you have bail? I'm going to send a lawyer."

Lil' A said, "Don't worry. I've done all of that."

Angie asked, "How long you been locked up?"

Lil' A told her the whole story. He told her everything, how he had two murders thrown out already and the other two he was going to beat, because the victims had guns on them and they were wanted for murder.

She said, "I'm flying up tomorrow." Angie wanted to see Lil' A before she went into labor. He tried to talk her out of it, but she wasn't hearing it, and hung up.

Booberlocks said, "Your Spanish mami is crazy." Then he said, "I know who you want to call now."

Lil' A called Tiffany. She told him how she missed him so much. Tiffany was crying. She said she was flying up to see him too. Lil' A hung up from Tiffany. The next call was to Red. They talked for a while, and then Lil' A hung up. 'E' wanted to use the phone. He only had one girl to call and that call lasted over 20 minutes.

Ms. Dot came back to the gate and said, "Are you finished?"

"Yeah, thank you."

"Don't worry about it, baby."

'E' said, "A you had the phone for three and a half hours."

"Word."

Lil' A said, "Thanks."

Ms. Dot said, "A I'll come check on you tomorrow."

"Okay."

Lil' A and 'E' stayed up in the cell all night, smoking and talking. The more they talked, the closer they got.

Angie finally arrived. She was nine months pregnant, but she looked good. She had driven up in a 600 Benz, a car that cost more than any of the cars in the parking lot. Angie patiently sat waiting for her visit, and finally she heard Lil' A's name being yelled out for a visit.

Angie said, "Baby, I'm going to drop money on your books, bring you some soap, sneakers, T-shirts, everything. I'm going to push out your baby in Miami. I'm not coming back until you come home just in case the Feds are watching me or you. You should get bailed out right?"

"Yeah. Do you have the money close?" Lil' A asked, as they just talked.

He rubbed her stomach before she left. She dropped $10,000 on his books. Then she went and bought Lil' A everything new. He was just waiting for his court date. After the visit, he walked back to get strip searched.

"Are you a superstar?" The C.O. asked him.

Lil' A's response was, "Yeah!" Now the whole Rikers Island was talking about the Spanish girl and her Benz.

Ms. Dot came threw to check on Lil' A again with one of her co-workers. This was a dark-skinned sister that reminded Lil' A of Verwana. She was thick and all.

Lisa looked at Lil' A and told Ms. Dot, "I know him, he was just at that party Red threw and he was messing with Red and those stank ass tramps China and Brandy."

"Oh yeah," Dee said.

Lil' A had to reply, "Ain't none of those girls my woman," as he tried to pinpoint where he knew this girl Lisa from, but couldn't remember.

As Lisa flirted with A, the whole dorm sat back and wondered why all the hoes come by these two cats' cell.

Lil' A told Dot that he needed some more weed, and she said okay.

Another week passed, and Tiffany came up with Yvette and the baby. Tiffany looked bad after her pregnancy. She looked like a thick Jada Pinkett. On the visiting floor, Lisa, just stood there watching. She let Lil' A have extra visiting time.

They were finally going to let Lil' A and 'E' out of the hole. As soon as they did, they didn't last 20 minutes, because A and 'E' had to cut up a whole house of Puerto Ricans. They even cut up the head of the Latin Kings.

A cut at least 5 dudes, and 'E' cut up several himself. This was one of the biggest moves they'd made on Rikers Island. Now 'E' and A were *Red Carded*, meaning there always had to be a lieutenant walking around with them.

A Father's Burden

They were also required to wear mittens because they were always cutting someone.

Suddenly, the niggas who had been hating on A and 'E' unexpectantly had love for them, because they stood up against the Latin Kings. A and 'E' started to form a group known as the Black Mob. A bought the whole house sneakers, and it came up to $1,000. He quickly acquired friends and so-called friends, nearly everyone had loved for Lil' A.

Lisa worked the hole late night shift. She used to crack A and 'E' out and let them use the phone all day. Lisa also made sure the entire hole stood smoking weed.

One night, Lisa had on a skirt. She looked very attractive to Lil' A. He would imagine what it would be like to be with her if circumstances were a little different. Lisa knew A was good with the ladies just from seeing how he had Angie and Tiffany visiting him. Lil' A liked good looking women.

Finally, another time when Lisa was working the 11 p.m. to 8 a.m. shift, she seemed friendlier than usual. This night she was wearing a skirt. She walked up to Lil' A and said, "I don't have any panties on."

That was all he needed to hear. A bent her over the top of the plastic chain and fucked the shit out of her. After that, Lisa would come every day and bring Lil' A weed. She was doing whatever he asked her to. She would even come sometimes just to suck his dick.

One day 'E' was like, "A, man my baby mother don't got her own crib. I need to get money with you."

A told 'E', "From now on you are my man, so I got you. Don't worry, just don't ever steal from me, lie to me, or snitch on me."

'E' responded, "I'll never do that, A, never. You're a good motherfucker, better than my own peeps."

When 'E' went to court and didn't have bail money, Lil' A arranged the $5,000 bail. He even called his car man and his real estate guy to get 'E' and his baby mother their first crib, and bought 'E's baby mother a Honda. A then told 'E' to wait until he came home and he would buy him a better car. 'E' didn't realize it at the time, but he had just locked down a real friendship forever. 'E' would do anything for Lil' A. A found himself calling 'E' every day. 'E' was very loyal, sometimes he just stayed in the house waiting for A's call.

Lil' A just had to show off. He bought Lisa a brand-new Land Rover. Lisa was so in love with Lil' A, but she knew he had a wife and a whole bunch of baby mothers. Finally, his court date came up. His lawyer got him a bail of $250,000. As soon as they let Lil' A go, Lisa was there waiting for him in the truck with, 'E'.

'E' told Lil' A, "Yo A, you took care of me and my son. I'm your soldier forever. I'll die for you."

"We're about to take over the world!" Lil' A boasted to 'E'.

Before A and 'E' parted ways Lil' A finally met 'E's baby mother.

Later, he hooked up with Lisa and stayed with her all night. The next morning Lil' A went to see the lawyer. He also gave his lawyer money to help 'E' beat his case. Then Lil' A jumped on a plane to see Angie and his new baby girl. He stayed with her in Miami until his next court date. When A returned, 'E' was right at the airport to pick him up.

Lil' A's enterprise was really starting to grow. It was picking up more and more. He was hitting half of Harlem

A Father's Burden

and a few dudes in Queens. A was also hitting his crew from out of town, and his name was ringing out there.

But what Lil' A had failed to do earlier, and ultimately what his father Big A failed to do for him, Lil' A was starting the cycle again. A was so caught up in his poisonous life in the streets, that he wasn't spending time with his kids. He didn't mind sending money and helping his children's mothers financially. But A wasn't spending time with the kids he claimed he loved so much.

Tiffany and her mother were doing real estate. Tiffany was finishing school to become a lawyer. Lil' A had just bought Verwana a big hair salon in the Bronx with a flat screen TV and 15 chairs. So, everything seemed alright, or so he thought.

Lil' A was using his father's drug of choice, he was sniffing coke and doing it hard. Angie, however, was still madly in love with him. In fact, she was head over heels in love with him. Their sexual encounters were even wilder. A would put coke in his dick, yeah inside the hole. He even put coke all in Angie's butt hole. He would suck it out, or sniff it out, and then butt fucked her all day.

A was really turning Angie out and she was game for it too. Angie would pour a key of coke on his chest and stomach. Then, she would suck and lick it off. She would even lick it off his dick. Those two were nuts. They were going all out for their own kind of fun. But Lil' A would forbid anyone, except for E in his crew to do it. E was his right-hand man. When you saw Lil' A, you saw E. Yeah, they were like shirt and pants.

A was grooming his crew to be the sixth crime family. Yeah there were five crime families, but they were all Italians. Lil' A had bigger plans. By this time, rap music was what allowed a Black person to become rich and famous, because everybody knew drugs wouldn't last. So A invested one million dollars in a 10 to 20-year plan.

While it looked as if he were just building an empire for himself, A really wanted to leave something in place for all his kids. If that was the best move, he ever made, time would tell, because the old saying was what goes up, must come down. *Yeah Baby, rise and fall.*

Angie was out of control, and nobody could handle her but A. When he wasn't enjoying personal pleasures, A was devoted to his work. He established a closer relationship with Ricco. A was moving tons of coke and dope a month. He would fly out to Ricco's house in San Juan where he had a 62-Room mansion.

Ricco had five daughters. One of them was better looking than Angie. Lil' A wasn't about to push up on her, but he was fascinated by her. So, for her 18th birthday, she broke the news to her father. When everyone gave her gifts, Lil' A flew her out a customized Benz, one that was so special that there were only five of them made. Needless to say, his gift was the nicest. Others had given gifts, but of course Lil' A's made a statement. It was a nice gesture, but this infuriated Ricco. He got up and left the table mad.

Later, the maid came out and whispered in Lil' A's ear. Ricco wanted to see him in his office. Lil' A went to him.
"Hey Ricco, what's wrong man?"
Ricco looked at Lil' A, "You're a good boy. I've watched you grow into a man and into a friend in this game. Those are two things that's hard to say, but this is something I can't prevent, but there's one thing or should I say two things that's stopping this. One is Angie." A stood shock, because he didn't know what was going on. "And two, our further business plans." When Ricco said, *NaNa come here,* A became even more confused. This was Ricco's daughter.

A Father's Burden

"For two and a half years NaNa has had a crush on you. She said she's not happy until I give her permission to date you. But I know your history with Angie, and if my baby girl gets hurt in any shape, form, or fashion, I will send a mini army over to New York for your head."

A cut him off, "Ricco there is no need for that, because I wouldn't disrespect you like that at all."

"A you don't have a choice, because she told me that all she wants is you, or at least my permission to date you."

A said, "So what you saying, Ricco?"

"Well I told her yeah. If that's what she wanted. See A she's my baby, so I must spoil her to the fullest. But A, you must never let Angie find out."

This was an unusual turn of events. Here, this man Ricco, was giving his daughter permission to date his business partner. Ricco was doing so, knowing that he had close ties with other women, and had babies with other women. Would most fathers do that? Probably not, but he thought a lot of Lil' A and he wanted to please his daughter.

Lil' A was really attracted to NaNa. She was very beautiful. Ricco had sort of given Lil' A an ultimatum.

Ricco had NaNa leave the room, then he said, "NaNa is right now a virgin, but you got up to a year or two to make her your wife. Just think now A, you will come closer to me. That means more money, more power, and more respect." He stood up and shook Lil' A's hand. "Let's get back to the party."

The two men walked out of the office. Even NaNa looked happier than she had been when she was opening her gifts. Lil' A and 'E' went to the balcony where they smoked fresh green weed, and pure coke. Lil' A told 'E' what happened and how he was put in a fucked-up position, because if Angie found out, she would flip. He told E why he was happy that Tiffany was far away and would not bump heads with none of the other women. Verwana was the one who was close enough to cause a problem.

E said, "A, do you want the truth from me?"
A said, "Yeah."
E said, "Man Angie scares me, you need to cut her off. NaNa, she's so pure, and it looks like she's never been touched. She also sounds so sexy when she speaks English; *like thank you A Gracias*. Her smile lights up the room, she might be the one for you."
"Yeah E, you might be right, or it might be a bad choice.

A and his partner talked for a while longer before leaving the balcony. He opened the glass door to see NaNa in a night gown.
He asked her, "How long have you been watching me?"
NaNa answered, "I've watched you for a while. He grabbed her hand and asked if they could walk and talk.
NaNa told him, "A, my life is devoted to you."
A asked, "Are you sure?"
She replied, "Yes. I couldn't wait until my 18th birthday. All I did was ask my father if you were coming."
"Stop lying NaNa – For Real?" As A kept walking and talking, he felt like a kid again. It reminded him of being with Verwana, but this was different. He was feeling a different kind of love.
"A how long have you known my father?"
"For about 4 years."
"Do you remember when you first met me?"
"Yeah."
"I was thirteen going on fourteen and Angie was here with you. I was so skinny.
"Yeah a nobody."

"You and Angie were doing it in the room. You were so drunk A, and all I could do was watch you. How old were you then?"

"I was 18."

"Well I've been in love with you ever since the first day you came to my house. I watched you every day you were here. I was there every time you fucked Angie; even when she was sucking your dick on the yacht early in the morning."

A thought to himself, *NaNa you crazy*. But in all reality, she just had a mean crush on him.

A said, "NaNa, how you know what she was doing?"

"A I got older sisters, plus we watch porn flicks," she sassed, as they both laughed. "I swear to God A, nobody in the world was going to fuck me before you." A looked over at her. "Yep, you had to be my first. My sister said daddy wouldn't let that happen, but I'm the baby, so I always get my way."

A said, "Oh, you do?"

NaNa said, "A, I know all about your baby mamas, but I don't care about them. I would love to see all your beautiful kids, but I got plans on giving you a whole soccer team. Shit, I already know you're rich, so you taking care of the kids ain't a problem."

"Plus, I have ten times more money than you.

"Oh, you do?"

NaNa said, "All I want is to be your real side wife."

"Okay NaNa. You think you could handle that?"

"A baby, if I can't I'm ready to learn. I'll do whatever you say. I will leave my father for you now."

From that statement, A knew she was as real as breast cancer.

NaNa said, "A, I've never been to New York, so when I do go that's where I want to lose my virginity, okay. And I want my king of all kings to do it."

A said, "Who is that?"
"You baby," NaNa said, kissing his forehead.

NaNa pushed A and he started to chase her. *This girl is fast*, A thought to himself, as he tackled her on the sandy beach. A pulled her into his body, and they kissed for the first time. To NaNa, it felt like A's first time kissing. As A rubbed NaNAs perfect breast, her long blond hair, and her skin were soft like baby skin, he knew she was something great. NaNa was almost like bronze. Her complexion from sitting in the sun so much had given her a crazy tan.

As NaNa moaned from all of A touches, she couldn't help but beg. "No Papi! A no... A not now," she whined, pushing him away.

She got up and ran again. As A chased her down, he said, "Oh, so you trying to tease me?"

She replied, "So! Shit I waited for five years. I know you can wait until you fly me to New York."

A said, "You're right."

One thing A didn't know was that NaNa was crazier than Angie. She'd been in training with her sisters on how to handle a man. NaNa even thought back to when her sisters were showing her how to suck dick. They wanted to be sure she knew how to be good at it, where she should do it, how to switch positions, when to push it back, when to moan, scream, scratch, everything. They showed NaNa how to be a pro. One told her that black guys had big dicks, so she had to be careful, but NaNa knew what she wanted.

As NaNa snapped back to reality, she wanted to see how much she could control A. You see, A was supposed to leave that Sunday, but NaNa asked him to stay. So A and 'E' stayed for a whole month. That turned out to be a good

A Father's Burden

decision too, because that gave A the chance to get to know her better.

They went surfing, jet skiing, and hunting was the best, because NaNa kept out-shooting A and 'E'. They went mountain climbing and all. One night, A was in the shower. NaNa came in trying to sweet talk him, because she wanted him to stay, but A had to go back to New York to take care of business.

NaNa said, "A when you get back to New York, call me. Baby, do you have a house in L.A.?"

"No," A said.

"That's where I want you to put me at okay."

"NaNa, anything for you."

"Well, if that's the case, buy me one of those cars that have the doors that lift straight up."

"Okay, you mean a Lamborghini."

"Whatever, all I know is that the doors lift up."

"Okay Ma. I got you."

NaNa kissed A and walked out to open the door back.

"Did you tell my father I'm going to New York?"

"No, I thought you did."

"No, I left that one for you. Plus, this pussy is overflowing Papi. A I'm hot, so don't take so long."

The next morning, A and 'E' were ready to leave. As everyone ate breakfast together, they all talked.

A said, "Ricco I'm leaving today."

"Why are you leaving?"

"I got to go take care of a few things. Plus, I'm about to buy a big house in L.A. I want NaNa to pick it out."

Ricco eyes opened wide.

"My baby has never left Puerto Rico; not even with me as a child."

"Ricco, I will guard her with my life. She's getting older now, so let her fill her oats, okay. Plus, she will be in great hands."

Ricco hesitated for a minute or two then he spoke. "You're right A. When will you be ready for her?"

"I'm not really sure. Just give me a week or two and I'll call for her, okay.

Ricco wiped his mouth, as A got up to shake his hand. "I'll call you later."

As A walked away, she winked at him.

"NaNa go give him a kiss before he goes,' Ricco said. "You're not daddy's little girl anymore.

NaNa got up to give A a hug and kiss. Before that, she hugged her father.

"Yes, I am Daddy. I'll always be daddy's little girl, but that's just my baby daddy," she teased running behind A, 'E' and Ricco's bodyguards.

"A!" she called out his name. As A turned around, she hugged him and kissed him. "Call me as soon as you get back to New York. I love you. Bye 'E'."

As A and 'E' got into the Range Rover to go to the airport, 'E' smiled.

"Dawg, that girl really does love you," 'E' said.

"I know, 'E'."

"I would be in trouble, but I'm with you, so I'm good. Plus, A we stayed here a whole month. Damn, we went from one weekend to an extra month."

Lil' A thought to himself, *'E', you're right, but fuck it. I'm young, dumb, rich and full of cum.*

During the flight back, Lil' A was sniffing coke and thinking about the world of trouble he was in. There was something he loved about each one of his baby mothers. Just as well as his freak, he loved them even more, because they knew their positions. Lil' A thought of Brandy for a second, when he used to try and get a quick nutt. Brandy would jump up and tell him that she was a hoe and to make love to his wife, not her. Lil' A would snap, grab her hair and then smash her asshole.

Next, Lil' A thought about Lisa. She was just happy with the fact that she messed with a gangster and her specialty was sucking a good dick. She would make Lil' A cum in seconds. Lil' A sat for a second reminiscing about the time they were on the island and she sucked his dick over and over as soon as he made bail.

A couple of hours later, they landed in New York. Lil' A had his Benz at the parking lot waiting. In order to get the car out, Lil' A had to pay $2000.00 but money wasn't a problem. Lil' A jumped on the phone and called all his troops to check on his business. He didn't touch the drugs anymore, he let Booberlocks do it all. Lil' A just smoked weed all day, sniffed coke, and drank his ass off.

Later, A stopped by to see Red, He had been ducking her for so long, it seemed like every time they hooked up, something happened.

Boy did she want to give A some pussy. A bought her a new house and another salon. He was always calling her, so she became more of his home girl on some mentor type shit. Red always did have the answer for him, so A pulled up at her shop. As A walked in, all the girls said, *Hi A!* A was rich, but never dressed like he was. He wore a pinky ring that was worth $500,000 and that's it. That one ring shined so bright; it was crazy.

"What up girls," A greeted. He entered the shop with 'E' right behind him. 'E,' was packing an Uzi on his waste, A had a Nine on his. Red was on the phone, so A just sat in a chair talking to Red's sister. All she kept asking about was Booberlocks.

A said, "I just got off the plane. I'm tired, and don't want to talk about no Booberlocks. Red's sister just stood there shocked. Finally, Red got off the phone.

"Hey, what up, Soldier. How was your trip?"
"Shit! Red that shit was hella alright."
"What happened, Baby?" As Red grabbed his hand, they walked to the back to the little office. 'E' sat right in front of the door while A talked to Red.
Red just looked into his eyes. She could tell, something was really messing with him.
"Baby wait; I know what you need," she said and pulled out a bottle of Hennessey. She poured them both a cup, then A spoke.
"Red, I just came back from P.R. and the craziest shit in the world happened to me."
"What?"
"My connect's youngest daughter pushed up on me."
Red stood shocked. "Finish."
"Come on Red, this motherfucker is a Billionaire. He only got one young daughter. And he never lets his baby mess with people he does business with."
"Okay and," Red said.
"And she just chose me."
Red, I saw her about five-years ago, she was all boney and shit, now she all thick and fine."
"Okay A," Red said, as she cut Lil' A off from jealousy. "How old is she…"
"She's eighteen-years-old…"
"Oh my God, she's still a baby… What are you going to do about your crazy baby mother Angie?"
"I don't know…"
"You and these Spanish bitches, why can't you just stick with your own kind… Well A, this is a tough one because if you hurt her in any type of way, you could mess up your relationship with her father and that's your connect…"

A Father's Burden

Red and Lil' A talked some more and sipped some wine and sparked up a blunt.

"Well you know what to do," Red continued, "either you're going to fuck with her and keep getting money or stop fucking with everything. I know you got enough money saved..."

"But Red, I'm not turning my back on all this shit I've built..."

"Okay, well snatch her up and just keep her away from everything... She already knows what she wants, and she won't stop until she gets it, so to me, this girl had this planned for years and now her wish is coming true. She might be two years ahead of you. A, to me that bitch is about to become whatever she wants to become, and she knew that she needed you by her side."

Lil' A just listened to Red as he kept pulling on the blunt. Finally, Lil' A got up and hugged Red tight as Red fell in a little trance from the hug because she really loved this little motherfucker. Red stood frozen as Lil' A kissed her on the forehead and asked her if she was hanging out.

Red said, she would love too, but she would pass.

A said, "Why?"

"Because I don't want to be like your little 18-year-old."

They both laughed. He knew she was being smart, so he changed the subject.

"So are you okay? Do you need anything?"

"No, I'm fine. I got you. Plus, your back home safe, so I don't have to worry about you."

As Red smiled, A smiled back, and then headed for the door.

As A said bye to the girls up front, he and 'E' walked out. Red watched them through the front glass. *Umm A's smooth ass*, she thought as he walked off. Suddenly, a tear ran down her face. Red's sister, feeling sorry for her, hugged her.

She said, "You still didn't tell that boy you love him?"

Red shook her head no.

"Well, it seems like you're not made for that. He treats you like you one of his home girls. He buys you cars, houses, new shops, sends you gifts, but has never had time for you," she smirked. "Damn girl, how long were you back there talking?"

"Not long why?"

"Shit, I thought y'all tried to sneak in a quickie on me."

Red wiped the tears off her face and laughed.

"Shit, if I would have gotten his little ass back there, we wouldn't have ever come out."

The two sisters walked back to their chairs, and all the girls in the shop started talking about A.

Red said, "Y'all act like he is a movie star or something."

One of the girls said, "He is a ghetto superstar." She smiled, thinking out loud she said, "Every woman in all five boroughs wants him or somebody in his crew. Shit the word is a car, a house, and $10,000 is straight out the gate. That is, if you're lucky enough to be one of their girls. Oh, I forgot you also got to have some fire ass head and pussy."

All the girls laughed, even Red. But the thought just stood out in her mind, because she knew it was true. That's how A and his whole crew got down.

Red looked at her sister for fucking with Booberlocks, and then to herself for messing with the boss. She could get anything she wanted, but A never got the pussy or head. Red zoned out

Finally, A drove to his old hood to go check on his pops. Big A was so happy to see his little man.

A Father's Burden

"What's up, Baby Boy?"
"Ain't nothing."
"I see you got your other half with you."
"E, yeah I can't leave home without him."
They all laugh.
"Pops, who's that young dude with you?"
"Oh! That's my little man. I got him in training."
"O' yeah. What's his name?"
"Doug. We call him God. He's a hustla.
"Are you sure?"
"Yeah, I'll call him over."
Big A said, "Dougy come here. My baby boy is here."
As Doug came over, Big A said, "Doug this is my oldest son Lil' A."
Doug said, "Yeah I hear about you every day, all day."
Lil' A said, "Oh you do. Well what you doing, Little Solider."
"I'm trying to get this money you know. I'm trying to come up big, but your pops make more than me."
Lil' A laughed, because he knew how his pops was.
"Well, how much money you got saved?"
"I got $2,500."
"Oh yeah! How much work you got?"
"I got 28 grams now, because all these suckers be selling garbage."
"Oh, they do?"
"Yo' Doug, you smoke weed?"
"Yeah."
"Well come hang out with me."
Doug said, "Okay," jumping in the Benz.
Lil' A said, Doug you got work on you?"
Doug said, "Yeah."
Lil' A said, "Doug give it to my pops."
Doug said, "I just gave him some."
Lil' A said, "Doug look, do you want to become a baller or do you want to stay a crawler."

Doug called Big A, "Here A this is for you."
Big A said, "Doug my son is about to put you on."
Doug was in shock.
Lil' A said, "That's all of it?"
"Yeah."
"Okay Pop Dukes, I'm out of here.
"Later son, send me back something, okay?"
"Okay," Lil' A responded.

Lil' A gave Doug a bag of green and then told him to roll it. Then Lil' A let Doug give him the run down on his life. Doug was the same sign as Lil' A, Doug's birthday was August 10 and Lil' A's birthday was July 31, they were both Leos.

Next, Lil' A went to Manhattan to see one of the twins. China answered the door. Lil' A mentioned to 'E' that he could tell Brandy and China apart because of their titties, China's was bigger. Brandy's son came out and Lil' A picked him up and asked him was he doing well in school. Brandy's son let him know that he was getting his report card the next day and that it would be a good report card. Lil' A told him that he would have a surprise for him when he got home from school.
When he finished talking to Brandy's son Lil' A asked 'E' to get Booberlocks on the phone. Tell him to come to Brandy house.

Brandy came in and saw Doug. Lil' A saw Brandy's expression, and explained to her that in two months he would be big shit and would be picking her up in a Benz. Brandy told Lil' A that she would drain Doug and turn him out. Lil' A asked Doug if he wanted something to eat and Doug agreed. Lil' A told Brandy to cook something for Doug.
Doug liked how the twins looked and told Lil' A as much. Lil' A schooled Doug that the two twins were money-

A Father's Burden

hungry hoes that would sell water to a whale. 'E' came back and told A that Booberlocks would be there in less than an hour. Lil' A informed Doug that he was going to give him a chance that only comes once in a lifetime.

"I'm going to give you 500 grams and you got one week to finish it."

"How am I going to do that with all those people on the block?"

"I can't do it all for you because if that was the case, I would be out there with you... Look, just make your bags bigger than everybody else's. The work is booming so just put in the work and it will come..."

Doug just sat and listened.

"Also, I'm going to give you 125 grams extra for my pops. I usually give it all to him, but you give him half of it and when he runs out, you just bless him."

"Okay... Who do I call, when I'm finish?"

Brandy came out of the kitchen and interrupted with a plate of rice, beans, and steak.

"Do you want something to drink?" Brandy asked, Doug as she handed him his plate.

"Yes," Doug replied.

Ten minutes later, Booberlocks popped up and Brandy let him in. Lil' A and Booberlocks greeted each other and then got right to business.

"Booberlocks, this is my pops soldier so we about to bring him up..."

'Do you think he's ready?" Booberlocks responded.

"I think he's ready, I like his style."

Booberlocks told Doug the key to the crew.

"Doug, it don't matter what age you are, you could still die, so if you with us then you better not snitch, never steal from us, and don't lie. If you follow these rules, you'll be alright kid..."

"Okay," Doug replied.

Next, Lil' A told Booberlocks to give Doug 625 grams and then told him to take what he owes and start serving Doug.

"I got Doug going to the top," Lil' A said, to Booberlocks.

"Yeah, whoever fucks with us goes to the top."

"No doubt... Did you talk to Tiff?"

"Yeah, she needs a call from you. She hips to me lying for you, she not going for it anymore. Plus, she said she got some big exams coming up..."

"I'll give her a call," Lil' A was ready to move on to the next subject. "What's up with the streets?"

"I'm about $3,000,000 short of what I'm supposed to give you."

"Okay, I'm still going to load you up, we'll figure out the difference later."

"That's cool...oh yeah; I'm throwing a big party. I spent $500,000 on liquor; drinks are free all night..."

"Word? I'll be there then...." Lil' A said, he loved doing it big.

"Hope so... I got to make some runs, I'll get at you later."

"Okay... take Doug with you and drop him back off for me," Lil' A said, as he walked out the door.

"I got him..." Booberlocks replied, just as Doug appeared coming from the kitchen.

"Where did A go?" Doug asked, confused.

"A's doing what big dogs do... do you want to reach that level? If so, come on, he'll catch-up to you later."

Booberlocks walked out the back door and drove away in his Benz. Meanwhile, in the front of the house, E told

A Father's Burden

Lil' A that he was going home to spend a couple of days with his kids. Lil' A explained to 'E' that he wanted to hideout from everyone for a while, so he asked 'E' was he taking the Benz. 'E' told Lil' A he had called a driver to come get him, so he would not need the Benz. He also told Lil' A that he wanted him to call him when he was ready to come out.

'E' felt safe leaving Lil' A because he knew Lil' A was going to stay indoors, which meant he didn't have to worry about him. Lil' A only chilled with Brandy when he didn't want to be bothered because as long as Brandy could suck his dick and go shopping, she loved Lil' A to death. Brandy even stopped fucking with other niggas, she just wanted to claim the richest dude in New York and have all the hoes and dudes mad at her.

A little while later, Lil' A fell asleep, so Brandy and China jumped in his 600 Benz and drove around Harlem, just so everyone knew she was fucking with Lil' A. Therefore, Brandy felt it was necessary to drive by Red's shop just as it was closing. The two twins double parked, jumped out, and walked into the shop. China set up an appointment, and Brandy used the payphone as her and Red gave each other two deadly stares. If looks could kill, one of them, or both would have been dead as Brandy hung up the phone.

"Come on, are you ready?" Brandy said to China out loud. "A wants me to bring him some Louie the 13th, so we got to run up to 145th street... Come on girl, I can't leave my man waiting..."

The expression on Red's face let Brandy know that her job was done, so she walked back to the Benz while China stood there talking to Red's sister.

"Why you don't call me no more?" China said to Red's sister. "Call me later, we might swing by the Tunnel."

Now that's a club in lower Manhattan. China walked out as Brandy hit the horn in the Benz and turned the music system up, causing the shop windows to shake as she played, *Real Love,* by Mary J Blige.

"That bitch just had to pull up over here..." Red's sister said.

"I know, wait until I see A, I'm going to curse his ass out. I keep telling his ass about those tramps, but he just doesn't learn."

"He just dicking that bitch, but he got feelings for you, so don't compare the two..."

Red tried to call Lil' A, but his phone was off, so she knew he was sleep. If you ever watched soap operas, this was just like that, but a *hood opera* instead.

Next, Booberlocks took Doug to one of his stash cribs. He told Doug to give Big A another 125 grams from him. Doug explained to Booberlocks the instructions that Lil' A gave him, but Booberlocks told him to give him the 125 grams from him. Booberlocks gave Doug 750 grams all together, his phone number, and a reminder that he would see him in a week. Doug replied, "I'll give it 110%," and then Booberlocks's phone rang. It was the driver informing Booberlocks that he was ready to take Doug home safe. About an hour later, Booberlocks phone rang, it was Big A.

"Why haven't you come to see me?" Big A asked, Booberlocks.

"I've been really busy, very busy..."

"Okay, but come check on me Boo-Boo," (Boo-Boo is what Big A called Booberlocks.)

"No doubt, I will. And make sure you lookout for Doug..."

"Shit, he looks out for me... shit he's the next one..."

Next, after Big A hung-up the phone with Booberlocks, Doug and Big A began to talk as they stood on the block.

A Father's Burden

"Damn, Big A, you get more grams to smoke than I ever have to sale. Why you didn't stop and get back rich?"

"Look Doug, I really don't want to get into that, but as long as you get right, I'm good. I just had to plug you into my son so you won't have to fuck with these ducks, you feel me?"

"Yeah, I feel you…"

Even though it took a month before Doug finally met Lil' A, it was worth the wait. Now, Doug finally believed all the stories he heard about Big A. Before, he really couldn't believe a crackhead used to be so powerful, but now he could see.

Doug got the work cooked up by a dude named Monster Ron, the best cook in the Bronx. The work was so powerful; it all came back to 850 grams. Last time Monster Ron saw coke like that was in the days when he was rolling. Big A and Monster Ron were both legends in the game, but fell victim to the drug they pushed.

Doug gave Monster Ron 50 grams and $200.00, and he was good. Next, Doug gave Big A 125 grams and then 62 more grams, and held the rest; Big A was happy. Doug took the rest of the work to his house and kept 50 grams on. Everybody was using bottles, so Doug decided to be the first one to use bags. He started with 12/12 size bags packed with crack. The whole project was running around looking for those bags; Doug was about to blow.

Lil' A woke up around 4:00 A.M., everyone was gone, so Lil' A jumped in the shower, and then rolled a blunt. Next, he began to play PlayStation, and about an hour later, Brandy and China came walking in drunk. Lil' A wasn't mad, but when Brandy tried to rub up on him, A pushed her away. Brandy felt like shit after that. She knew that he must not have wanted to be messed with, so she jumped in the shower.

China and Lil' A started talking. China began to run her mouth about who was in the Tunnel that night.

"Your man Kay was in the Tunnel too..." China said, trying to catch a reaction from Lil' A.

"Word?"

"Yeah, you know... doing his usual, popping bottles."

"Word?"

"Yeah, and earlier, I had to make a hair appointment... Why this bitch had to show off, Brandy came in there yelling your name with the music all loud just to make Red sick. You know Brandy swears you be fucking Red..."

"Yo, your sister is crazy..." Lil' A said, as he laughed. He loved the attention.

Lil' A smoked another blunt with China and then decided to go back to sleep. He went into the room with Brandy, who was lying on the bed butt naked.

"I know you're mad at me daddy," Brandy said, in a seductive way. "But I just want to suck your big dick..."

Lil' A let her suck his dick; she did it for one hour straight. The way Brandy sucked a dick; it was just like fucking her, that's how good she was at it. Lil' A passed out, which made Brandy happy she was able to give her baby what she wanted.

The next morning Lil' A woke up and called back to Puerto Rico. It was a call that he was ready to make. A Spanish woman answered the phone, it was the maid. She ran as fast as she could to give NaNa the phone.

"Baby, why haven't you called me, I was worried..." NaNa said into the phone. "Are you okay?"

"Yes, I'm fine..."

"Great, now I can stop worrying about you... Baby, when you sending for me?"

A Father's Burden

"Next week I'll fly to L.A. and you'll fly out the same day..."

"Okay... And you get to bust this cherry. It's nice and tight. I'm just waiting for you, baby."

"Okay, I'll call you later and tell you when to go to the airport...okay baby?"

"Yes baby, I love you."

"I love you too..."

Lil' A got off the phone with NaNa just as Brandy walked in the room. She heard him say, *I love you too*. Brandy almost spilled Lil' A's orange juice on him out of spite, but he told her, "Bitch, play around if you want to... if you would've dropped that juice on me, I would've had to fuck you up... You better stay in line hoe, or I'm out!"

Brandy smiled and then shook her head in agreement. Next, Lil' A called his car man.

"Look, I want you to order me something special..."

"Hey, A, what's up, what do you need?"

"I need a Lamborghini and a Ferrari, but I need it sent to L.A., I'll give you the address later, okay?"

"Of course, oh, they just came out with the B.M.W. drop tops and a new c230 Benz, it's smaller..."

"Okay, get me two of each; white and black in the drop top B.M.W. and a black one... wait, a second," pausing Lil' A focused his attention to Brandy. "What color you want the Benz I'm about to get you Brandy? You not going to be fronting around in my shit anymore."

"Gold," Brandy answered, with a huge smile on her face.

"Make the Benz gold, I'll come out there to pick that one up later. But, the other one, send it to 127th and 7th

Ave..." Brandy was infuriated. She couldn't believe he was buying Red a car too. "Put a red bow on it and a card that reads, *From A, to a good friend.* And make that one white, and the black one, send it to Rikers Island for officer, Lisa Brown. Just put on that card, *Surprise from your secret admire, I'm out of town and I'll see you in two months.* I'll be there around closing time. I'll get the money to you tomorrow."

"Okay," the car dealer said, with a big commission on his mind.

After he hung up, Lil' A noticed that Brandy had a stupid look on her face.

"Look, you my little boo, I never hate on you when you do your thing..."

"But I don't want to do my thing, I just want you."

"Well, you can't have me, so do you want me to stop coming over?"

"No," there was no way that Brandy was going to mess up getting a new car.

"Okay then, so just make sure you make a nigga bag up with them condoms. I want to be the only one to hit raw."

"You are the only one hitting me raw..."

"So keep it that way, and maybe we'll move pass just being friends. But you'll run me off when it comes to Red. How many times have I told you to stay out of Red face? I'm not fucking her, but you're going to make a nigga fuck her ass..."

"So, why you buying that bitch a car then?"

"At least you the only one getting the dick," Lil' A began to laugh. "You not sharing me like you and her husband did."

"He used to chase me..."

"Shit, whoever chased who, just be glad you the only one fucking me. And if you don't like it then this can be the

A Father's Burden

last time you see me..." Brandy looked at Lil' A, but didn't say a word. "So, hurry up and get dressed so you can pick up that car, I got to go do a few things."

Lil' A got back on the phone and called Tiffany. She cried the whole time they were on the phone. He continued trying to comfort her by explaining that she had to stay strong and finish school. Tiffany just wanted Lil' A, so what he said went in one ear and out of the other.

"Look, I got to make a run, I'll call you later..."

Tiffany didn't want to hang up, so Lil' A stayed on the phone a few minutes longer. Brandy came into the room and could sense that Lil' A was on the phone with another woman.

"I'm ready A, come on..." Brandy said, to make her presence known.

"What bitch you with?" Tiffany screamed in the phone.

"Well, if I tell you a friend, you won't believe me... I'm about to send her out of town so I'm taking her to pick up the car..."

"Yeah right! A, you're lying... Booberlocks do everything now! Who is the bitch?"

"Hold on..." Lil' A handed Brandy the phone.

"Hello..."

"Who the fuck is this?" Tiffany yelled into the phone.

"Oh, my name is China, I fuck with Papi. We just about to take care of something..."

"I know Papi, so I'm going to call and find out if you're full of shit!"

"Okay, I'll talk to you later..." Brandy responded, handing the phone to Lil' A.

"Okay, are you satisfied, because you think I'm lying and I'm not..."

"You ain't slick, you got those bitches trained now!"
"Look, I'll call you as soon as I'm done, okay?"
"Don't hang-up, I think your son wants to talk…"

Lil' A talked to his son and told him that he would be there in two days. Next, he told him to put his mother back on the phone.

"What you tell him because he seems happy, talking about his daddy coming."
"Yeah, I told him I'll be there in two days…"
"So, you're going to lie to your son, too?"
"Look Tiffany, I don't want to beef. I'll be there, okay?"
"We'll be waiting. So you can go back and entertain your bitch for now."
"I would respond, but I'm going to let that slide… Later…"
"Later? You can't say, *I love you baby*?'"
"I love you, and tell my little man I love him too."
"Okay, I'll see you in two days."

Lil' A gave Brandy the keys and told her to drive.

"I see what got your gangster ass in check, your baby mother…"
"You say another word and I'm out."

Brandy didn't say another word as they drove off. Next, Lil' A told Brandy to drive to the big liquor store on 145th street so he could buy a bottle. Then, Lil' A decided to drive past Kay's block first, since it was nice outside.

"So, don't go to 145th street first?"
"Do you have money on you?"
"Yeah…"
"How much?"

"Like $1000..."

"Look stupid, that shit can't even buy me a bottle right now. Go to Kay's block..."

Brandy drove to where Kay conducted business. Kay and his crew were out as usual when they saw the Benz pull up. They knew who it was even though Brandy had to front. She rolled the window down so everyone could see it was her.

"Woo, I saw your joint yesterday at the Tunnel," Kay said, to Lil' A. "I knew it was your joint... so you let Ms. Harlem drive it?"

"Yeah... Yo, Kay, I don't have any money on me..."

"What do you need?"

"Some spending money."

"Okay, tell her to pull around the corner..." Brandy pulled around the corner and about ten minutes later, Kay came with a black nap bag.

"That's $75,000, that's all I got."

"Don't worry, that's good...What up, what you doing tonight? I'm going to this club called Mirage. It be lit in there."

"Word, let me know because a party ain't a party if you don't come... don't matter how I try to do it, I can't ever top you..."

All Lil' A could do was laugh because he knew it was true. Next, Lil' A told Brandy to drive to the liquor store.

"Damn, you sure you got enough money?"

Brandy asked Lil' A in a sarcastic manner.

"Yeah, this should hold me for a few hours..."

"Let me find out Kay is getting money like that."

"Yeah, you might try to get with him because you getting on my nerves."

"I move forward, not backward! What the fuck I look like fucking with Kay and he give my man almost $100,000 just to spend. I'm not no silly hoe..."

Lil' A just leaned back and sparked up a blunt, taking few hits of coke. Finally, they reached the liquor store, he gave Brandy $4,800 and told her to buy two bottles of Louis the 13th. Next, they drove to E's house to pick him up. However, E was mad at Lil' A because he didn't call him when he left out. Security was first before anything.

They drove to the car dealer which was an hour and a half away. All the cars were ready, so Brandy jumped in her new Benz. Brandy felt so grateful that she sucked Lil' A's dick in front of the car dealer and 'E'. The two men watched as Lil' A came in her mouth.

"I had to suck my daddy's dick first in my car, now I can go style on these bitches."
"You're crazy ma... you need some money?"
"Yeah..."

Lil' A gave her $2500, and then told her when he was free, he would call her. She said, "Okay," and drove off.

Lil' A and 'E' went on about their business. Next, the phone rang, it was, Wiggins, Lil' A's lawyer.

"You must be at the next court date. It's in two months from this date. Plus, I'm getting this shit thrown out, that case is so weak."
"Okay... Wiggins, you're a very good man, I'll see you later."
"Okay," Wiggins said, as Lil' A hung up the phone.

A Father's Burden

Afterward, Lil' A decided to shoot out to Verwana's crib. For some reason, Verwana never asked Lil' A any questions at all, but if she ever got horny, she'd just call and Lil' A would pop up. Out of all his baby mothers, Verwana had him on lock, she didn't even know it.

About four hours went by, Red called Lil' A, but 'E' told her that he was not around. Red told 'E' to tell Lil' A she was thankful for the new car. Lisa, also called all day trying to tell Lil' A that she was so happy about the car he gave her. Red's sister was happy too because Red and her sister had the first two drop-top BMW's on the street. Brandy had the first c230 Benz, but those drops were hot, so that night they all met up at the Mirage. Brandy and her twin sister were in the c230 Benz, but Red and her sister came through in the drop-top BMW's and they shut it down. Knowing she was the shit that night, Red felt total satisfaction in getting a little revenge when they all met in the parking lot.

"Sis look, I get new cars and don't even have to suck dick for it," Red said, loud enough for Brandy to hear her. "So, you could call me the pimp, or co-pimp, she sucks and I still get half and could get A whenever I want too…"

"I'll see you later girl," China responded, as Brandy stood quietly.

She was sick as they made their way in the club.

Lil' A never showed up. He chilled with Verwana for two days, then he made his way down south to spend time with Tiffany. Angie was still away so Lil' A was able to play. Next, Lil' A called Papi.

"Hey, what's up, Papi?"
"Long time no, hear from you my friend."

"Yeah, I know. I've been running around like a mad man."
"You better take a break, A, don't burn yourself out."
"Yeah, Papi, I know... Yo, when was the last time you seen China?"
"Man, I had to stay away from her for a while. She will fuck up a happy home."
"Yeah, I know."
"Well, she thinks I'm in Puerto Rico..."

Lil' A and Papi finished making small talk and then told each other to be careful and then hung up. Lil' A went back to bonding out with Verwana. She was able to see a side of him that nobody else could see. They talked about old times, and where they were currently at.

Two lovely days went by, so Lil' A flew down south to see Tiffany and his son. The first day was a little slow. Tiff and Lil' A had one little argument, but Lil' A told her if she kept it up, he would leave, so Tiffany shut her mouth.

Lil' A took Tiff and his son to the park and Chucky Cheese to play video games with his little man as Tiff just cried. Finally, while the baby was sleep, Tiffany was able to talk to Lil' A with his full attention on her.

"I'm not beefing, but don't you have enough money, A?"
"Yeah..."
"So, why don't you retire and stay with me and your son. Don't you see how much he loves you?"
"Yeah, I do."
"Well, when are you going to stop?"
"Tiff, to tell you the truth, *I don't know...*"

The week went fast, Lil' A was ready to see NaNa. He was tired of everybody, so he gave his word he was leaving everyone except NaNa and Verwana. Lil' A felt that

A Father's Burden

everybody else was starting to want too much of his time, so he changed his cell phone, got new numbers, and told Booberlocks not to give his number to anyone. Lil' A told everyone that he was going to Puerto Rico for an indefinite stay and he didn't want to be bothered. He informed them that if anybody needed any money, Booberlocks would take care of it.

Lil' A was the first one to get to L.A. NaNa made it there later that day. The cars were ready; the Lamborghini and Ferrari, but Lil' A only took the Ferrari out. NaNa got off the plane with a smile so big it lit up the airport. She jumped in Lil' A's arms and tongue kissed him.

"Finally, I get to see you," Lil' A said, happy to see her. "I got your car…"

"Let's pick it up later after we find a house to purchase," NaNa responded.

NaNa used her father's company for purchases. Her father's company sold oil and fruits. It was worth billions, so they spent a lot of money. They stayed in a hotel that night; it was the biggest one in L.A. They reserved a $5000.00 a night room. Amazed at everything Lil' A had planned the eighteen-year-old was excited.

When they went to dinner, Lil' A got word that Death Row was throwing a party that night, so he decided to take NaNa.

Lil' A paid the bouncer $1000.00 so he and NaNa could get in. NaNa had on a Gucci dress with no bra or panties on. She looked like a model. Lil' A had on an Armani suit. He was low key as Snoop Dogg and the whole Death Row performed. Later, Lil' A and NaNa had the opportunity to interact with Snoop Dogg and whole Death Row.

"Snoop, I know you got some of that fire on you?" Lil' A asked Snoop Dogg.

At first, Snoop Dogg hesitated, but then he looked in Lil' A's eyes and knew he was all good.

"Yeah Cuz, who are you?" Snoop asked.

"My name is, A, I'm about to buy a house out here, I'm from New York though…"

"Oh yeah… Man, are you sure you can handle this fire?"

"Snoop, I can handle anything that comes my way…"

Snoop lit up a blunt and passed it to Lil' A, the first two pulls, Lil' A was choking.

"Yeah, that shit is raw…" Snoop laughed.

"Bartender, let me get some drinks over here…"

"Naw Snoop, I got you player, it's on me," Lil' A said, to Snoop.

When the bartender came over, Lil' A pulled out $30,000, all in hundred-dollar bills.

"Give us the most expensive bottle you got…"

"Man, what you do, you gotta be a hustler?" Snoop Dogg asked.

"Naw dawg, I'm a business…"

"Yeah right…" NaNa came off the dance floor and made Snoop Dogg lose his train of thought. "Damn man, where she from?"

"Naw Snoop, that's mine, you can't have that man."

"You the man, A…"

"NaNa, this is Snoop Dogg, he's down with Death Row records…"

"Oh yeah, nice to meet you," NaNa said to Snoop Dogg as she hugged on Lil' A.

As the night started to pop off, Snoop Dogg and Lil' A got closer.

"I'm going to come pass your hotel room and smoke something with you later on," Snoop Dogg said, to Lil' A.

"That's what's up… Snoop, let me buy the rest of that fire off of you."

A Father's Burden

"Naw Cuz, you don't have to buy nothing, here go 28 grams of it... I'll come check you out later."

When Lil' A and NaNa left the club, the Ferrari pulled up. They drove off with 30-day tags. Finally, they made their way back to their hotel room. NaNa was so happy. She jumped in the shower as Lil' A walked around in his boxers. NaNa came out of the shower butt naked. Lil' A couldn't help but to kiss her perfect body. He kissed her neck, and then pulled her hair as she let out a slight moan. Next, A made his way down to her bellybutton. Then, he picked her up and carried her over to the bed. Lying her down gently Lil' A sucked on her pretty feet, toe by toe. Kissing his way back up to her ass, he licked and played with her butthole, until she began to shake.

"Papi, don't stop...," NaNa pleaded. "Ooo..."

Lil' A finally got to her young virgin pussy and began to lick it. He ate her pussy for over an hour straight. NaNa was climaxing over and over, making all kinds of sounds. She'd even tried to scoot away when the sensations became too much, but Lil' A wasn't having it. He only took a break just to sip some liquor and smoke a blunt.

NaNa was just lying there in awe not moving; as she sensed the feelings of her pussy contracting and pulsating. Lil' A started laughing at her because her legs were shaking from the orgasms. I mean they were really shaking. NaNa tried to stand, but she fell back on the bed, her legs were too weak. Lil' A made his way back to her. Her juices were all over the sheets.

Lil' A tried to put his dick inside her, but NaNa was tight, and I mean *tight*. However, after a few minutes, Lil' A slipped in and NaNa held him tight as he penetrated her deeper. A went slowly, and then he went faster and faster as NaNa yelled out his name in Spanish. She scratched and whined the first ten minutes, leaving marks all over his upper body. Her screams became louder and louder causing Lil' A to nut back to back. Finally, he stopped and blood was all over him and her. The sheets were even bloody, it looked as if someone had been stabbed on the bed.

Next, Lil' A took NaNa to the shower and washed her off. NaNa began to wash his back and private parts as they continued to make love. A was like a mad man that night from the shower, to the bed, the couch, floor, Jacuzzi, and balcony. NaNa drained him and she loved every minute of it, they fucked for four hours straight, but finally fell asleep.

Chapter Fifteen

The next day, NaNa was more in love and hooked. When Lil' A woke up, she was on the phone with a big smile on her face.

"Who is that?"
"My sister…"
"What are y'all talking about?" Lil' A asked, knowing he had her hooked.
"About how you fucked the shit out of me…"

Next, NaNa told her sister that she would call her later. She started kissing A and then told him that she wanted more. A couldn't wait to jump back in it, but this time, NaNa was fucking him back, making the sex more sensuous. Then, the phone rang. It was the front desk informing Lil' A that Snoop Dog was there to see him. Lil' A let the front desk know that it was okay to let Snoop come to the room. Rushing, he jumped in the shower and threw on some clothes before their guest arrived.

"Yo Cuz, what's up with you?" Snoop said as he entered.
"Ain't nothing Snoop… waiting on these real-estate people to call me so I can go buy her the house she wants…"

Lil' A rolled a blunt as NaNa got out of the shower. She walked by with a long shirt on. She was still wet and they could see her curly hair. Her nipples were firm; their firmness being revealed through her shirt.
"Hi Snoop," NaNa said, as she walked to the back.
"Hi…" Snoop responded, and then brought his attention to Lil' A. "She's a bad motherfucker…"
"Yeah, I know, she wants to marry me."
"Shit, you better," Snoop said, with a smile.

About thirty minutes later, NaNa was dressed and ready to pick up her car. Snoop offered to take them to dealer and they both agreed. Snoop drove them there in a 63 Impala. It was a smooth ride that Lil' A and NaNa loved. When they arrived at the car dealer and Snoop saw that she was picking up a Lamborghini, he knew that Lil' A was a major player.

Next, Lil' A asked Snoop to call his girl so she could show NaNa around while the two men did their thing. Snoop had a better idea; he called his baby sister. The real-estate people came to pick NaNa up and showed her different houses. Lil' A gave NaNa $150,000 and told her to go shopping in Beverly Hills, as Snoop and Lil' A rolled around the different hoods. Lil' A parked his Ferrari and drove around in the Impala with Snoop.

"Look Snoop, I just need a direct line for that fire green while I'm here because I'm thinking about making this my second home."
"Look Cuz, I got you… That's all I fuck with."
"Okay, so I want more than enough for me."
"Yo Cuz, why don't you get into the music business?"

A Father's Burden

"I don't know, I never thought about it, but I might. Snoop, to tell you the truth, I don't need nothing, I'm good for life."

"Okay Cuz..."

Lil' A and Snoop Dogg got closer, so much so, Lil' A and NaNa met Snoop's whole family. NaNa even took pictures with Snoop, Dr. Dre, Suge Knight, and the Dogg Pound. NaNa loved it all. She brought a camcorder and was recording the whole L.A. experience. NaNa even taped her and Lil' A fucking.

NaNa finally found the house she wanted; it was a five bedroom, two and a half bathrooms for $2,000,000. The shit was hot, so 'Lil' A bought it for her. Also, Lil' A bought another condo on the other side of Beverly Hills, where all the rappers stayed. This was going to be his fuck house for when he wanted to get away.

Two months went by. Angie had been flipping out on everybody looking for Lil' A. Also, everyone was worried about him, but Lil' A was happy as hell. Lil' A had a court date, Booberlocks and 'E' were there, and the murder charges were thrown out for lack of evidence. As a result, Lil' A told 'E' to go get Red and bring her and his baby mother to L.A... So a week later, 'E', Red, and 'E's baby mother reached L.A.

Red was so happy to see A. She thought she would finally get Lil' A to herself, but Red was in for a surprise when she got to Lil' A's house. When Red saw Lil' A, she was so happy, but when NaNa came out, Red's smile turned into a frown. Lil' A introduced everybody then he began to talk to 'E' and Red. At first Red had an attitude. Lil' A told her to cut it out and be strong.

"Red, I'm going to start a music label for you and 'E'... Red, you'll run it. Get some talented artist and blow up. Do you want in Red?"

Red stood quite for a few seconds and then spoke.

"Yeah A, you know I'm with you until the end."

"Okay, all I want from all of you is to get ready, we are going to a party tonight..."

Red walked out of the room and 'E's baby mother followed her. They both stood outside as Red began to cry.

"Girl, what's wrong?" 'E' baby mother asked.

"Nothing..."

"Girl, I see the look in your eyes. I know you love A."

"Yeah, I do."

"And he loves you too. He knows the life he's living doesn't last long. That's why he's setting you up with the music company. Remember, stay strong, and hold on, A will be more than happy if you move on..."

'E' walked into the hallway and could sense the two women were in a serious conversation, but decided to interrupt their moment anyway.

"We got front row seats to the Lakers game and then we're going to the after party, so get ready..."

Later that night, they all made it to the game. The Lakers were playing the Bulls in front of a sold-out crowd. The women looked great, however 'E's baby mother and Red were jealous of NaNa because she was so perfect. Plus, NaNa and Lil' A hugged up all night. It was obvious they were feeling each other. However, it was something special about Red too. She stood out during the first two quarters of the game. Someone off the Lakers team, a point guard, just kept looking at Red, but he was missing shots. Red is from Harlem, so she knows when somebody is watching her. Halftime came, and Red had to speak out.

A Father's Burden

"Come on baby," Red yelled at the Lakers point guard. "Keep your eyes on the ball these last two quarters instead of me and you'll win. I'm not going anywhere…"

The Lakers guard walked over. "What up, A," the guard said, to Lil' A.

"What up… You making me look bad in front of my little sister."

"Don't worry, I got you because she finally spoke…" The basketball star directs his attention to Red. "Okay sexy, I'm going to play my game."

"Okay," Red responded, as she blushed and then winked her eye at the Laker star.

Next, the horn blew, and it was time to start the third quarter. The Lakers were down 10 points. After the brief conversation with Red, the Lakers guard scored 35 points. He was dunking, hitting 3 pointers, and doing nice passes. At the end of the game, he looked back to the side, but Lil' A and his crew were gone. They left a little early so they could beat the crowd as they all went to eat. They went to one of the biggest seafood spots in L.A. and drank and laughed.

"Red, you trying to snatch up a N.B.A. player?" Lil' A asked, Red.

"Please, they just like a hustler, always on the move."

"You need a good man like that in your life, someone that's going to really be there for you to the end."

That thought ran through Red's head as 'E's baby mother winked her eye at Red. They both laughed and then got ready for the party.

They all made it to the party and went straight to the V.I.P. section. The Lakers guard was looking all over for Lil' A. It was his party, and they just signed him to an 80-million-dollar deal. Lil' A and his crew were chilling. The Lakers guard had so many girls surrounding him, but as soon as he made eye contact with Lil' A, he walked off quickly to the V.I.P. section and greeted everyone.

"Hi sexy," The Lakers star said to Red as he pulled up a chair. "I've been watching you all night."
"Oh, you have?" Red responded.
"Yeah, you know you made me step my game up…"
"And that you did because you were letting them shine on you…" Red said, with a smile.
"Why you don't take my little sister somewhere quiet to talk?" Lil' A said, to the Lakers star. "Because it's too many hawks on you."

Red rolled her eyes, but agreed to go to the DJ booth. Red didn't know it, but it hurt Lil' A to send her into another man's arms, however, he had to do it. Also, it hurt Red to slide in front of Lil' A, but it was a start of a new beginning as Red and the Laker guard got extremely close. They talked all night about everything. Red was older than the Laker guard, and he instantly fell in love with her because she didn't want for nothing and she was determined.

"Look boy, what you heading for?" Red said, to the Laker star wanting to get straight to the point. "What you trying to do here because you got all these fine girls after you… If you want to go get a nut, go get one of them because I'm not the one…"

"Hold up," The Laker star responded. "I know A, he's a good friend of mine and I wouldn't disrespect him, but I must say it was love at first sight… Your walk, the way you stand, the way you move… I must have you…"

A Father's Burden

"Baby, I'm from the streets, going legit is something new, so I know how to play and the game ain't fair... Plus, my last street husband got triple life in jail and left me with a child. But now I own two houses and two salons and it's rough so I don't want to play..."

"You must slow down..."

"Why?"

"Because, I'm falling more in love with you by the second."

"Are you sure you could handle that?"

"Yeah..."

"I don't think so... Look what happened the first two quarters..." They both laughed.

"How long are you here in L.A.?" The Laker guard asked.

"For just a couple more days."

"Okay, we gotta go eat dinner and lunch tomorrow."

"I don't know..."

"Baby please," the young basketball star begged.

"Okay silly, stop... Let's go back and join the others..."

Red and the Lakers star made their way to the V.I.P. section.

"Hey, y'all were gone for a long time..." Lil' A greeted Red and the Laker player. "Come on, drinks are on me..." Lil' A ordered another 20 bottles while 'E's baby mother and Red began to talk.

"Girl, he's the next Michael Jordan." 'E' baby mother said.

"Yeah, that's what they say."

"Well, what did he say to you?"

"He wants to go eat lunch and dinner tomorrow."

"What did you say, no?"

"Naw, girl..."

"Okay, now what?"

"It's on if he acts right... I might give the young boy some..."

They gave each other five.

Meanwhile, Lil' A, 'E' and the Laker guard went on the deck to smoke some weed. Next, Lil' A put the old press on the basketball star.

"Look Fam, she's a very good girl... She hasn't been dating in a while, in fact, she's crazy stubborn and she might need some dick, it's been like years..."

Lil' A was drunk.

The night ended well; everyone went to their resting place safe. Red and the basketball star later talked on the phone. 'E' and his baby's mother finally got to spend some time together. Lil' A and NaNa were fucking like wild rabbits all night.

The next day, Red and the basketball player went out to eat lunch and got even closer. They also went to dinner that night as well, and the Laker player hit Red with a shot. The Laker star proposed to Red with an 8-caret ring. Red's eyes opened wide from surprise as she almost lost her breath. Red hesitated at first, but then said, "Yes...!"

Are you sure you're ready for this?" Red asked.

"I'm more than ready... Look, go to New York and get your son and come back and pick out our house..."

Red started to cry from extreme joy. That night they made passionate love. The young Harlem Vet put it on the young star. Red didn't even go back to Lil' A's house, she stayed with her man. The next day, E and his baby mother went to hang out with Red and the basketball star, Lil' A felt lonely.

A few more days went by, Red and E took care of the record label, it was called, "Ghetto Records." Red called her

A Father's Burden

sister and her sister told her that the news of her marriage was all over the TV, everything seemed to be going right.

One year later, Lil' A came back to New York. Angie hears the news of his return. She leaves the baby with Lil' A's mother, Yvette as she starts her stakeout. Angie finds Verwana and pulls up on her.

"Bitch, where is he at!" Angie demanded.
"I don't know..." Verwana responded.

Angie was furious, she instantly gunned Verwana down. She shot Verwana 16 times and watched her die on the spot. Next, Angie took Verwana's kids and took them to Lil' A's mother.

"If you find your son before me, let him know that I'm going to kill him..." Scared for her son, Yvette finally tracked him down.
"Baby, I got three of your kids here, that bitch Angie killed Verwana..."
"What...?"

Lil' A drove to Verwana's house and found her dead body lying on the floor. Lil' A began to cry; it was like his whole world ended. Lil' A was enraged, he had to find Angie. Meanwhile, Angie was at her house, she was high as hell, having sniffed at least 2 ounces of coke. Angie called Papi and told him what she had done. Papi rushed to Angie's house, but Lil' A got there first.

Lil' A stormed in Angie's house gun in hand. All the lights were out, he checked every room, but no Angie. He was so out of control that he started to sniff some coke that was left on the dresser and laid his gun down. Angie popped out from behind the blinds, firing three shots.

Bang! Bang! Bang!

She hit Lil' A in the arm, chest, and leg. Then, she fired three more shots, hitting him in various places on his body.

"Kill me bitch..." Lil' A cried out. "Kill me because I don't want you..."

"Why A, what did I do? I made you... You moved with NaNa, why A? If I can't have you, nobody can..."

Meanwhile, Papi reached Angie's house and heard the last three shots. He ran upstairs and saw Lil' A lying on the floor. Papi was shocked and couldn't move. He had a flash back of when he was younger and Angie killed their stepmother. Papi also thought about how he first met Lil' A. So many thoughts were going through his mind.

Angie walked over and kissed Lil' A in the mouth as he was bleeding out. Her next action was to finish him off. She shot Lil' A two more times in the head. **Lil' A's life was gone.**

The sound of the last two shots caused Papi to return to his senses.

"Angie, what the fuck are you doing!" Papi yelled, as he watched Angie crying over Lil' A's dead body.

"Baby, come back!" Angie cried. "Come back A, I'm sorry baby, please..."

Papi looked on the dresser and saw Lil' A's gun and picked it up.

"Angie, you're dead wrong! You hear me, dead wrong!" Papi screamed as a tear rolled down his face.

Angie was still crying; she was distraught and totally out of her mind.

"Shut up punk, fuck it!" Angie screamed at Papi. "What's done is done, let's move the body..."

A Father's Burden

"No Bitch!" Papi objected.

As soon as Angie turned around, Papi shot her ten times, all in her face. She died on the spot.

"That's for you kid." Papi directed his attention to his friend's dead body. "I'm on your side, I love you."

Papi cleaned the house out, all the money and drugs. Next, he drove Lil' A's car to Big A's projects. Papi clothes were covered with blood. Big A knew something was wrong. Big A got into the car and sat quietly for the news he knew he was about to hear.

"Look, it's over a million dollars in the stash box and over 1,000 keys. This doesn't amount to your son's life, but he got kids. So you can smoke it all for all I care, but I'm gone…"

Papi got out of the car and shot himself in the head as Big A stood there shocked.

That was the last day Big A got high. In fact, he changed his lifestyle, got back with Yvette and ultimately married her.

Tiffany finished school and got her Ph.D. She's now one of the top lawyers in the country. Tiffany also invested millions of Lil' A's money. All his kids will be set for life.

Furthermore, Red married the basketball player and gave him four more kids. Red and E's music company *Ghetto Records* sold over 500 million records. E and his baby mother got married and had more kids.

Yvette raised all 3 of her son's kids. Lil' A never made it back to NaNa, but she was pregnant with twin girls, Raven and Quanesha. Also, NaNa and Red remained friends. In fact, Red introduced NaNa to another NBA basketball player and they got married.

Years later, Ricco got caught by the Feds, and so did Kay, Booberlocks, B.C., Sleepy, and Big A. They all went to jail for life, but nobody snitched. Moreover, Doug became the man, but was murdered a few years later by a kick in; door robbery.

Each of Lil' A's kids were doing well in school. Two of his sons are going to top Ivy League schools, and the twin girls are getting offers for modeling jobs and movies. Yvette stays in the house now. She's been through a lot. She and Tiffany are exceptionally close. In fact, Yvette is writing a novel called, "A Mother's Burden" and starting a program for kids whose parents are in jail, or got killed. She helps them get through school and adjust to life without their parents.

Brandy had a baby boy, and so did Lisa. They both named their son's, *Lil' A*, in honor of their father's memory. Now, all they could do was sit and pray that they didn't follow in the same footsteps as their father.

About The Author

Kevin Aller, "aka" Bemo was born and raised in The Bronx, NY. He grew up in Sound View Projects, by way of Castle Hill Projects -139th and Lennox Avenue.

He wrote this novel, which was based around true events, while fighting charges under the *"Sex, Money, Murder, Rico Act*, which is still an on going process. He is currently locked up in the USP Terre Haute facility in Terre Haute, Indiana. If you'd like to write him, please contact him at, Underground Novels, PO Box 360587, Decatur, GA 30036.

Also, please be on the look out for Sex, Money, Murder... Gambling Spot ... and "Twice" novels, plus movies!

Please contact him at:
Kevin Aller 45021-054
MDC/ P.O. BOX 329002
BROOKLYN, NY 11232

We Help You Self-Publish Your Book
You're The Publisher And We're Your Legs.
We Offer Editing For An Extra Fee, and Highly Suggest It, If Waved, We Print What You Submit!

Crystell Publications is not your publisher, but we will help you self-publish your own novel.

Don't have all your money? .... No Problem!
Ask About our Payment Plans
Crystal Perkins-Stell, MHR
Essence Magazine Bestseller
We Give You Books!
PO BOX 8044 / Edmond – OK 73083
www.crystalstell.com
(405) 414-3991

Plan 1-A 190 - 250 pgs $719.00   **Plan 1-B 150 -180 pgs $674.00**
Plan 1-C 70 - 145pgs $625.00

2 (Publisher/Printer) Proofs, Correspondence, 3 books, Manuscript Scan and Conversion, Typeset, Masters, Custom Cover, ISBN, Promo in Mink, 2 issues of Mink Magazine, Consultation, POD uploads. 1 Week of E-blast to a reading population of over 5000 readers, book clubs, and bookstores, The Authors Guide to Understanding The POD, and writing Tips, and a review snippet along with a professional query letter will be sent to our top 4 distributors in an attempt to have your book shelved in their bookstores or distributed to potential book vendors. After the query is sent, if interested in your book, distributors will contact you or your outside rep to discuss shipment of books, and fees.

Plan 2-A 190 - 250 pgs $645.00   Plan 2-B 150 -180 pgs $600.00
Plan 2-C 70 - 145pgs $550.00

1 Printer Proof, Correspondence, 3 books, Manuscript Scan and Conversion, Typeset, Masters, Custom Cover, ISBN, Promo in Mink, 1 issue of Mink Magazine, Consultation, POD upload.

We're Changing The Game.
No more paying Vanity Presses $8 to $10 per book!

Made in the USA
Middletown, DE
12 October 2024